Letters from Sara

MICHAEL R. LEITZ

ISBN: 978-1-5356-0999-9

Contents

Chapter One

"I want a divorce," Sara Bennington said to her husband, staring out of the rainsoaked passenger window of their black Lexus.

Scott stole a quick glance at Sara from the driver seat. "What?" he asked.

"We're both miserable, Scott."

"What do you mean we're both miserable? Don't you mean you're miserable?" Scott asked in a quiet tone.

"You're not happy either. I know it," Sara said.

They both sat in silence for a few moments, listening to the windshield wipers swish back and forth. Scott stole another glance at his wife of sixteen years. Her looks were exquisite. A few signs of age had begun to creep in around the edges, but she still caused him to take a deep breath when she entered a room. Scott knew he loved her, but he worried about the changes that he had seen in her in the last few years. He knew when they met that she was focused and driven, but she also had a soft, lovable side. He had to admit that now she seemed driven almost to the point of insanity and her soft side was fading.

What was driving her? They lived in a nice neighborhood; they had an oversized home that was paid for. They had money in the bank earning interest, stocks, bonds, and mutual funds, what more could she want. As much as he tried, he could not figure it out. He knew he was not going to give up without a fight though. Scott was the first to break the silence. "I never see you anymore, Sara. The children never see you. All you do is work. Even when you are home, you're locked in your office."

"Someone's got to pay the bills," Sara said in a huff.

"Money…this isn't about money. We have more money than we could possibly spend in a lifetime. We would like to see you occasionally. I would give up all the money to spend more time with you," Scott said as he glanced over to check for a response. However, he saw no expression whatsoever.

Sara sat quietly; she had thought long and hard about the consequences of asking for a divorce. In her mind, a divorce would be easier than trying to fix the problems at home or admitting that she had failed their marriage. Sara Bennington did not like to fail at anything.

The rain was coming down in sheets now as they drove along the narrow country road. Scott reached up to speed up the wipers a click and let out a long sigh.

A few miles ahead, Eric Phillips was preparing to leave the Harvest Moon Bar and Grill. He was in great spirits after winning thirty dollars shooting pool with some of his old high school friends. He was hot tonight and ran the table all evening. When they were finished, his friends offered to call a cab for him, but he refused. He only drank seven or eight beers, that were over a span of three hours, and besides, Eric considered himself an experienced drinker, never having a problem before. His trusty old car would get him home. It was only seven miles to his house.

"Damn, it's starting to rain," he muttered to himself as he buckled his seat belt and started the engine. He turned on the wipers and yanked the transmission into drive. Pulling out onto the narrow country road, he pushed in the CD that was sticking halfway out of the radio. He couldn't remember what band it was, but it didn't matter; he just needed a little music to stay alert. He was more tired than he thought. He set the cruise at fifty-seven, not too fast and not too slow. After all, he didn't want the local law enforcement pulling him over for something stupid. The speakers came to life with the thunderous drums at the beginning of Metallica's "Enter Sandman." Good, Eric thought to himself as he slapped the steering wheel, trying to keep time with the music. The rain came down harder so he sped the wipers up another click.

"I had an affair," Sara said quietly, looking down at her hands that were folded in her lap.

Scott had suspected she might have had an affair, but was still surprised to hear the words coming from her mouth. There were no obvious, telltale signs, but it was more to do with the general way she had been acting. "Who was it? Do I know him?" he asked, boiling, but keeping his composure.

"Somebody I met in the city."

"Are in you love with him?" Scott asked, speeding up the wipers one more time. He knew he didn't really want to know the answer.

"No… I don't know," Sara said softly.

"What do you mean you don't know?" Scott asked, this time getting a little louder. A brilliant flash of lightning lit up the December sky. Even set on high, the windshield wipers were barely keeping up with the pounding rain.

Eric thought the road seemed a little narrower than usual. I should have eaten something before I left the bar, he thought to himself. Rolling down the window a little to let in some fresh air, he was surprised by a flash of lightning.

"Damn, a thunderstorm in December," he mumbled out loud.

He decided he wanted to listen to a different CD. Turning on the dome light, he opened the compartment between the two front seats and rifled through the unsorted collection of CDs. He couldn't quite focus on the labels, but if he closed one eye, it seemed to help. There was another flash of lightning and he had to shield his eyes to avoid being temporarily blinded. Even over the sound of the music, he could hear the thunder this time.

"Are you still seeing this person?" Scott asked, suppressing his anger.

"No. It's over," she answered weakly, trying to hold back tears. "I just want a divorce," Sara blurted. Breaking out in deep sobs, she buried her head in her hands.

Scott didn't know what to say. She was the one having the affair, but he suddenly felt sorry for her. To quell the pain of the conversation, he tried to remember the last time he'd seen a thunderstorm in December. The windshield wipers whipped back and forth, but with little success at keeping up with the torrents of water falling from the sky. Another brilliant flash of lightning lit up the entire sky and this time Scott could hear the thunder from inside the Lexus.

"Aerosmith," Eric said to himself. He opened the CD case, but couldn't pop the CD out with one hand. He placed his knee on the steering wheel so he could use both hands. Finally releasing the CD from its case, he tried to put it in the slot of the radio. The car must have hit a bump or something because the CD slipped out of his fingers and fell. Swatting at it like a man trying to catch a fly, he succeeded only in knocking it over to the passenger-side floor. He glanced up to check the road, grabbed the wheel with one hand, and then leaned as far to the right as he could. His fingertips could just touch it, but he couldn't manage to pick it up. Frustrated, he unbuckled his seat belt and shifted in the seat to try to reach the CD. He thought he saw another flash of lightning, but he didn't hear any thunder this time. "Shit," he said aloud. Once again he leaned over for the CD.

Scott reached for Sara's hand, but she jerked it away.

"Come on, Sara. It pisses me off that you had an affair, but I know a person wouldn't do it unless something was missing at home." Scott took a deep breath and continued, "Besides, we have more problems than just your affair. We've got to work this out for the kids."

Sara, now sobbing uncontrollably, said, "No, Scott… I want a…a divorce!"

Scott again reached for Sara's hand, and once again she jerked it away. He looked at her, but she just stared straight ahead. He knew by the look on her face she was serious. There was another flash of lightning.

"Gotcha," Eric said as he pulled himself up by the steering wheel. He glanced up and noticed he had crossed the yellow line. He jerked the wheel to correct the vehicle and the car veered sharply to the right. He dropped the CD, grabbed the steering wheel, and, with both hands, jammed the wheel into the other direction. He slammed on the brakes and the car went into a slide. He saw the oncoming lights at the last second.

Scott was still looking at Sara when she screamed. "LOOK OUT!"

Scott saw the flash of headlights. Trying to avoid the oncoming car, he cranked the wheel to the right. It was too late. He heard Sara scream, he heard the crunch of metal and the shattering of glass. Then…nothing.

Chapter Two
Two Months Later

"Pastor Jacob, here's a letter I must have missed when I got the mail earlier. I was putting a letter in the mailbox when I found it," Millie Vanderwall, the church secretary, blurted out as she entered Pastor Jacob Litchfield's office in a rush.

"Thank you, Millie. Just put it on my desk and I'll take a look at it later. I'm almost done with my notes for the Sunday service, and then I've got to get home. Cathy told me to be home by five o'clock sharp or I'd have to check the dog dish to see what we had for supper," Jacob said with a chuckle.

They both knew that Cathy, Jacob's wife of six years, would never really do anything of the sort, but she did get perturbed at him for losing track of time and constantly being late for supper.

Millie, on her way out of the office, smiled knowingly and said, "Well, you better finish up and get home. You've got two children to look after now and some things can just wait until tomorrow.

"Yes, yes...I know. I'll be done in a little bit. Have a good night, Millie. I'll see you Sunday morning."

"You too, Jacob. Say hello to everyone for me." Millie gave him a concerned look, then left the office in her ever-hurried pace.

Pastor Jacob Litchfield, thirty-eight years old, was a wonderful minister for their central Illinois community. Standing at five foot six inches with a full head of dark hair, he had penetrating brown eyes that could bring a stubborn soul to its knees. He had the early onset of a middle-age spread, but was not considered fat. Jacob's complexion was pale due to many hours spent in his office; he found reading much more pleasurable than spending time outside. Having suffered from acne in his youth, his jaw line was shadowed with pock marks. He liked to dress in a black shirt and slacks that he wore like a soldier's uniform. Jacob's idea of casual was removing his clerical collar and undoing the top button of his shirt.

Unlike others in the ministry, he had a humility that kept him in touch with the people in the congregation. Jacob had accepted his calling in his late twenties and was ordained at thirty-two. He was fond of telling people that he didn't choose faith, but faith had chosen him.

Millie worried about Jacob and Cathy constantly. They had just taken in Michael and Mara, his twin sister's children. Two months earlier, his sister Sara and her husband, Scott Bennington, had been killed in an auto accident with a drunk driver. Not only did he have the death of his sister to contend with, but he and his wife now had the responsibility of raising two children. Even for a

Lutheran minister that was a huge task, but if anyone could do it, Cathy and Jacob could. Millie still prayed though. That always helped.

Jacob finished the sermon notes and set them to the side. He removed his black-rimmed reading glasses and gently set them on the desk. Leaning forward to turn off the desk lamp, he noticed the letter Millie had brought in a few minutes earlier. Strange, he thought as he looked at the letter. It was addressed to Jacob Litchfield, but there was no return address, or stamp. It was gnarled and dirty; it also had a strange smell to it, but the odor was so mild that he couldn't place it. The lack of a return address was troubling; the post office had sent out notices after 9/11 with a warning not to open envelopes without a return address. A letter without one would be destroyed if found in the screening process at the post office. They wouldn't deliver it without a stamp anyway. Jacob turned the letter over and inspected the backside, but didn't see anything that would give him a clue as to where it might have come from. He reached for his letter opener and slid the shiny blade behind the tab to slit open the top of the envelope. Pulling out its contents, he noticed the paper inside was in even worse condition than the envelope. The odor was a little stronger than before, but he was still unable to place the smell. Unfolding the dirty piece of paper, he saw that it was a hand-written letter from someone with very good penmanship. He reached for his glasses and carefully placed them on the lower end of his nose, then began to read.

To whom it may concern, Letter One

I am in hell. I have been told that I was damned for my sins. I'm writing this letter for my own sanity and for any peace of mind it might give me.

I remember the car accident. My husband, Scott, and I were traveling together at the time of the accident; we entered the afterlife together. I would have to say the way I died was very painless and quick. I remember seeing the other car's headlights, a sudden jerk, and then Scott and I were standing together some distance from the scene of the accident. We watched the paramedics take us and the other driver out of the cars. Scott's body was put right into a body bag and mine was taken to the hospital in an ambulance. I don't know what happened to the other driver. Scott and I ended up in the ICU ward with my body. We watched people coming and going. He told me that one visitor was my brother and the two little ones with him were my children. I did not know them. It was then that Scott said he was going home and left me. I stayed there and watched my body lying on the gurney until a nurse pulled a sheet up over my head. I knew then that I had died. Someone took my hand and told me it was time to go home. It was an angel. That's when I realized what Scott meant when he said he was going home. I will always remember the unbelievable peace I felt when I was with the angel, even though it didn't last very long. One thing I do remember is that the moment you die is the moment you are judged for your sins. Evidently on earth, each of us dies at our own appointed time, but in heaven that time seems to be the same moment for everyone. Therefore, from heaven's point of view, we all die at the same time.

Suddenly, there I stood with all of humankind to be judged and in a blink of an eye the faithful were allowed to enter into heaven, and the unfaithful were sent to hell. We were told by a grand voice that we were the unknown and were not allowed into the kingdom. Like I said, in the time it takes to blink, I found myself along with many others, crowded into a huge and dimly lit compound surrounded by a tall stone wall. It appeared that this wall encircled an inner wall that, in turn, encircled three towers, all of different heights. The towers were glowing from within with an eerie light. I'm guessing the light to be firelight. I had a human body again and I was still female. We all appeared to be physically in our twenties, naked and covered in filth. I didn't see any children.

The guards were hideous creatures that stalked the compound like dogs. Dressed in crude armor, they walked through the crowds and called out names. The people whose names were called were then taken to the towers. I could hear screaming and crying coming from within the towers. No one that went in ever came out.

Thinking it was safer to stay away from the towers; I stayed near the outer wall and tried to hide. I talked to no one, but I listened for any useable information. I don't know how long I was in this compound, because there is no such thing as time here. Time is only necessary when you have something to look forward to. It was always dark and it was either unbearably hot or unbearably cold. I could never get comfortable. The smell that permeated that place was so sickening that it was hard to catch my breath. The wind blew constantly and the shrill sound it made was maddening. Covering my ears did nothing to stop the painful assault. The only comfort I found in the prison compound was the garbage that littered the ground everywhere, because it was much softer to sit on than was the rocky ground. I have not tried to sleep yet and I doubt if it is even possible.

The brutality I witnessed was sickening. The guards that patrolled the yard would attack anybody that might catch their attention. There are winged creatures that fly above us like skyward watchdogs. They are horrid beasts that I can only describe as some kind of dragons. The vision of their leathery wings and razor sharp claws still haunt me. Their piercing cries still echo in my mind. I have seen them swoop down and take people away numerous times.

Terrible things take place inside those walls. I've seen people set on fire, stabbed, and maimed, making me want to vomit. Rape was a favorite pastime of the guards and even some of the humans. I saw a woman who was huddled not too far from me dragged off by two of the guards. They pinned her down and raped her in ways that I did not know were possible. She was quiet at first; then, as the realization of what was happening to her set in, she screamed and begged. She tried to get away, but they just kept taking turns raping her over and over. Some of the human men and women gathered; they laughed and cheered while they did this to the poor woman. When the guards were finished, they just left her there; six or seven humans then took turns raping her. I should have tried to help her, but I didn't want to be the next victim.

I managed to escape, not too long after witnessing the rape, when part of the outside wall exploded close to where I was standing. Once the smoke cleared, I saw the hole and I ran as fast as I could. Others tried to escape with me, but the slower ones were caught quickly. Before I got to the cliffs that surround the prison, I heard their screams. I don't know how many others escaped in the explosion, but I knew I had to run.

As I made my way farther down the cliffs, I came across numerous butchered bodies. It was dark and I couldn't avoid tripping over the corpses. I went through their pockets, and found weapons and the materials needed to write this letter. I also found the materials needed to make fire.

Back in the prison I had heard the guards talking about some kind of rebellion. I'm not sure, but the explosion at the wall must be part of it. I'm going to try to find these rebels, because my only hope now is that if the rebellion is successful these rebels may be more bearable. I'm ending this letter now because I don't want to use up all my fire supplies.

Sara Bennington

P. S. This place will not beat me.

"Why would someone put a letter like this in my mailbox?" Pastor Jacob whispered out loud. "Sara Bennington's my sister's name!"

He sat there transfixed, hypnotized by the letter. He reread it to make sure he understood everything this person had written. Was someone playing a cruel hoax? He couldn't think of anything more deviant than implying a deceased family member went to hell. The more he thought about it, the more upset he got. After a few minutes of contemplation, he stood up and muttered a short prayer for peace of mind. Then, after a few more moments, he took a deep breath and decided he felt a little better.

"I'll figure it out tomorrow," he said to himself, thinking he'd better get home. Cathy and he were getting along well this week. Taking in his sister's children had not been easy and it put a definite strain on their marriage. He put the letter in his desk and turned out the lights. As he walked from the church to the parsonage, the letter still troubled him. The sick smell from the dirty paper was still stuck in his sinuses. It was like rotten eggs or something to that effect… "That's it!" he muttered to himself. "It's the smell of sulfur."

Proud of himself for figuring out what the mysterious odor was, he almost forgot about the letter. But the sense of dread soon crept back into his mind. Who would play a sick joke like that anyway? If it was a dirty prank, someone went through a lot of trouble with the details. He hadn't made any enemies that he could think of. "I'm a minister, for goodness sake," Jacob muttered.

He knew the post office did not deliver it. He decided not to say anything to Cathy or Millie, maybe it was just a one-time prank by some demented person.

He opened the back door, and, before entering, he listened to see what the mood in the house was. It sounded calm, and after letting out a deep breath, he called out that he was home.

"I'm in the kitchen," his wife Cathy yelled.

Jacob could picture Cathy standing at the sink in her blue sweatpants, one of his old T-shirts, and her blue slippers. The idea made him smile. She would be cutting or dicing up something for the evening meal. She was an excellent cook, but with the busy schedule of work at the hospital, and the added responsibility of the two children, Hamburger Helper was now a mainstay on the menu.

"Hi, honey. How was your day?" Jacob asked as he hung his coat up on the hook she had designated for that purpose. Cathy liked to have everything in its proper place.

"It was okay. I got a call from the school today." Cathy moved across the kitchen to give Jacob a kiss and a hug. "The counselor wants to talk to us about Michael. It seems he has some anger issues."

"Well, I guess that's to be expected. It's only been two months since the funeral. What happened today?"

"He got into a fight with another boy. He's angry, and Mara just accepts it without question," Cathy said as she walked over to the kitchen cupboard and took plates out to set the table. "I've heard Mara try to talk to him about it, but I don't think she's having any better luck then we are."

"Whenever I try to get him to open up, he just clams up and won't say a word."

"I know, dear." Cathy began placing the plates neatly around the kitchen table. She then walked over to the stairway and yelled for the twins. "Michael...Mara, time for supper!"

In a few seconds, Mara exploded into the room. At age ten, Mara was the mirror image of her mother. She had long dark hair. With the face of an angel, she was bright and exuberant; nothing seemed to get her down. Her only fault, as far as Jacob could see, was that Mara hated to lose. If they were playing a game of checkers and it appeared that she might lose, she would make up an excuse to end the game. Sometimes she would get mad and run out of the room, screaming "I quit!" This also reminded him of his sister Sara. During childhood, he could remember Mom and Dad always trying to talk Sara out of a bad mood because she had come in second in a track meet, or her softball team had lost. Sara always took losing badly, and it bothered Jacob to see Mara showing the same characteristics.

"What are we having for supper?" Mara asked while jumping up and down in a circle like a bunny rabbit.

Jacob, always delighted by the little girl's upbeat attitude, laughed and said, "We're having lima beans and whale patties."

"Yuck! I hope we're having something good for dessert then."

"Jacob Litchfield, quit pulling that young girl's leg!" Cathy chided with a smile as she poured milk into the glasses that were perfectly set around the table.

"He's not pulling my leg, Aunt Cathy," Mara said, sliding into the kitchen chair that marked her place at the table. "Uncle Jacob is just being silly."

"I know. Uncle Jacob is always being silly, isn't he? Uncle Jacob, go find Michael."

"Yes, dear," Jacob replied as he left the room to go find Michael.

As Jacob climbed the stairs, then walked down the hallway to Michael's room, he tried to imagine what Michael was going through with the loss of his parents. He knew that Michael was feeling hopelessly abandoned. He also knew that only time would heal the mental wounds inflicted by the loss of his parents.

Jacob knocked on Michael's door, but there was no reply. He put his ear up to the door and he could hear the boy crying. Having only been a parent for two months, he felt unsure of what to do. He gently opened the door and peeked inside. What he saw broke his heart. Michael was curled up on his bed trying to wipe away his tears. Michael resembled his father, with blonde curly hair and very light features. It was hard to believe that the two children were twins. He was a very thoughtful child, almost too thoughtful, and the death of his parents was something he was having trouble grasping. Jacob hoped that the death of his parents would not turn into anger, making him bitter for the rest of his life.

"Michael, supper's ready," Jacob whispered.

"Okay, Uncle Jacob, I'll be down in a second," replied Michael as he wiped away the last of the tears that were streaming down his face.

"That's okay, Michael. Take your time. Do you…want to talk? We can talk now, if you want to," Jacob said, with the feeling that he was in over his head and not about to climb out anytime soon. The thought that bothered him was that he was a minister; he'd dealt with grieving families numerous times, and had done much better with those situations than he was doing right now.

"Michael, I know what you are feeling, I..."

"I don't want to talk about it, Uncle Jacob. I'm okay," Michael interrupted before Jacob could get anymore out.

"I understand, Michael, but you need to talk about it sometime," Jacob said. He did not want to force the issue, and before he could say anymore, Michael scurried out of the room, down to the kitchen.

When they were all seated at the table, Jacob led them in prayer and they began to eat. Everyone was busy eating and the table was quiet. The letter crept back into Jacob's thoughts again. He could almost hear the desperation in the voice of the author. Sara's description of hell was terrifying. He could remember the lectures at seminary. He tried to remember all the accounts of hell in all the modern literature he has read over time.

"What are you daydreaming about, Uncle Jacob?" Mara asked abruptly from the right side of the table.

"Yes, Jacob, what are you so deep in thought about?" Cathy asked.

She was always accusing him of being in the room, but only in body. Jacob could never understand why she didn't leave him alone if he appeared to be so deep in thought. He did understand that she only saw him for a couple of hours a day, and maybe he was being too selfish with his time.

"Nothing, dear. I was just thinking about something that happened at church."

"What happened at church, Uncle Jacob?" Michael asked, surprising both adults at the table with his abrupt question.

Jacob felt that he should give the boy an answer. He couldn't just cut him off without an answer. "Uh…I got something in the mail today and I was just thinking about it, that's all."

"What was it, Uncle Jacob?" Mara asked with an excited look on her face. "Was it a present or something neat like a…"

"Now children, let your Uncle Jacob be. It is probably something that he needs to keep private," Cathy said, noticing the pained look on Jacob's face.

"Okay, Aunt Cathy," they both droned in unison with looks of disappointment.

After supper, Jacob helped Cathy clear the table and wash the dishes. He wished they could afford a dishwasher, but it just wasn't in the budget. He liked doing dishes with her. Since the children's arrival it was one of the few moments of togetherness they shared. The evening schedule of homework, baths, and bedtime prayers usually filled the remaining hours of the evening. With the last-minute drinks of water, or the reading of one more story, bedtime was a struggle, and, after all that, there just was not much energy left for each other.

Jacob enjoyed watching Cathy with the kids; it was as if she were a natural at motherhood. He wondered if she felt the same lack of confidence that he did when it came to raising children. Sometimes he had to admit, the responsibility God had given them scared him.

Cathy had always been a curiosity to him. When he had first started preaching at St. John's, he would see her sitting with her mother on Sunday mornings. He would wonder why such a beautiful woman was not married yet, or why she didn't have a boyfriend. Jacob, with the help of Mrs. Millie, did a little detective work and found out that she was single. Thank God for Mrs. Millie. Jacob had tried for many weeks to work up the courage to talk to Cathy, but he could never find the right words. He would try to say something to her as she filed out with the congregation at the end of the Sunday service. The thought of shaking her hand would send him into a panic, and he would always become tongue-tied. Cathy was five foot four inches tall. She had long brown hair, hazel eyes, and a light complexion. She had a beautiful smile. She was petite, but had everything in the right place. When she entered the church, it amused him to watch the single men try not to be obvious in their lustful looks or the sharp elbows the married men received from their all-knowing wives. Cathy had grown up in the town of Evansville, Wisconsin along with her parents and two older siblings. They lived on a small dairy farm. Her mother and father were hard working people who always attended Sunday services at Evansville Methodist Church. Upon graduating high school, she attended Wesleyan College in Bloomington, Illinois. After receiving her nursing degree, she was offered a job at Covenant Hospital in Champaign, Illinois and then moved to the Cissna Park area. When her father died a few years later, she moved her mother down to live with her.

As a registered nurse at the local hospital, she moved with a certain confidence that Jacob envied at times. At first, she appeared to be shy, but it was Cathy who finally broke the ice and asked him out. Three months later they were married. He managed to propose to her without stuttering or stammering. He did however, have to practice with Mrs. Millie to make sure he had the words right. Once after they were married, he asked her why such a beautiful woman was still single at the age of thirty. Cathy simply replied that she was just waiting for the right man.

She entered the room after taking a shower and noticed him sitting at the table, daydreaming. "What are you thinking about now?"

"Oh…just about how we met, and how wonderful you are." Cathy was wrapped in a loose-fitting towel and his mind began to wonder about the possibility of making love to her later that evening.

"Quit being silly and go take your shower," she quipped with a little grin as she padded off to their bedroom in her blue slippers.

After his shower, he carefully slipped into bed, thinking that if she was already asleep, he didn't want to disturb her. He thought he'd been successful until she rolled over and gave him a kiss and said, "Good night, Jacob."

"Good night," he replied as they wrapped their arms around each other. The earlier thoughts of sex came back to him, but the thought of the letter leaped back into his mind.

The last thing he pictured in his mind before he fell asleep was the way Sara Bennington was signed at the bottom of the letter.

Chapter Three

Jacob slept terribly that night; his mind was racked with nightmares about the world described in the letter. He tossed and turned all night, and Cathy had to move to the couch. Jacob awoke the next morning feeling more tired than he did before he went to bed.

"You kept me awake half the night. What were you dreaming about?" Cathy asked with a concerned look. She was busy primping in the mirror, trying to get a lock of hair to stay in the right place before finally giving up with a sigh. Cathy had to be at work earlier than Jacob, so he got the children ready for school.

"I don't know. I just had a bad night, I guess," Jacob replied, not really wanting to talk.

"Well, I hope you don't have too many of those, or we'll have to build on another bedroom."

"I hope I don't have many nights like that either. I feel like crap!"

"Watch your language, young man. I don't want the children to hear that kind of talk," Cathy said with a mock-disapproving look. Cathy enjoyed giving him the little scolding as she put on her coat. She moved toward him and gave him a kiss and a hug.

Backing away quickly, she waved her hand in front of her face and exclaimed, "You need a shower, dear! You stink!"

"What?" he said as he pulled the front of his T-shirt up to his face. "Ugh, you aren't kidding. I'll jump in the shower quick before I wake the children for school."

"It almost smells like sulfur or something," she said with a chuckle. "I'll wash the sheets when I get home. I love you, Jacob Litchfield," Cathy said giving him a warm smile.

"I love you, too, Cathy Litchfield," Jacob said. The memories of the nightmares flooded into Jacob's mind at the mention of the smell of sulfur. Trying to keep the dreadful thoughts out of his mind, he kissed her on the forehead and asked her, "What if I find a sitter this weekend, so we can go out?"

"That sounds good to me. Who's going to watch the children?"

"Millie will. She is always asking if there's anything she can do."

"Where do you want to go?" Cathy asked with a coy look on her face, as if she already knew the answer.

Jacob, knowing where this conversation was going, answered quickly, "I think maybe…you should decide this time."

"You mean to tell me that you don't want pizza?"

"Now dear, I don't even like the stuff."

"You lie like a rug," Cathy said with a laugh. "I'll see you later."

"Goodbye, dear. I hope you have a good day at work."

Jacob loved it when she laughed, and was glad when it happened. Since the funeral and the arrival of the children, there hadn't been much to laugh at. Cathy headed out the door in her tennis shoes and light-blue scrubs. Jacob went upstairs to take a shower and then wake the children.

It was a normal morning at the Litchfield home. Mara was up and running the minute she awoke. Michael had to be told twice to get out of bed and to get ready for school. After breakfast, Jacob walked them out to the bus to watch them leave for another day at school, and then he walked over to his church office. It was a beautiful day for February. It was about fifty degrees and the sun was bright. The sky was that deep blue, the kind that only happens occasionally during Illinois winters. He always thought if more people would stop to notice the good days, the bad ones wouldn't seem so bad. It's too bad that our human nature seems to focus on the bad things. He opened the back door to the church, deciding he would call Millie to see if she would come in to have a look at the letter. He then decided to read the letter one more time. After the long spell of nightmares last night, he wondered if maybe this was all just a bad dream. He opened the drawer where he had left the letter, and a wave of nausea rolled through his stomach. He wished he'd never received it. The nightmare he had last night seemed to mean more than the mind's trivial playback of the day before. He sat back in his chair and the images washed over him like a flood of icy water.

Jacob stood on the stonewall of the prison, looking down at the hordes of people huddled together. The sheer number of filth-covered and naked humans was astonishing. He was looking for his sister, Sara, but couldn't find her. He could see the prison guards patrolling the compound. They appeared to be large humans, wearing crude armor and carrying various weapons. The smells that emanated from this place, even in the memory of his dream, made him nauseous. He could see the three towers, and even over the roar of the wind, he could hear screams coming from inside the structures. From his vantage point on the wall he could see screaming and begging people being dragged off by the guards. Fights were breaking out among the clusters of humans, and guards would dive in breaking up the mêlée with large clubs and sticks. Dragon-like creatures soared in the space above the castle. Swooping down, the winged creatures snatched anyone that was pointed out by the guards, and then carried them off to the castle. He remembered moving away from the prison's structure, looking for his sister. Jacob walked away from the outside wall and made his way down the cliffs. He carefully climbed down and found something of a walkway that led to a series of caverns. Going in and out of the caves that made Swiss cheese of the mountain, he started calling out Sara's name again and again. For hours, it seemed he looked for her while traveling in and out of the different caverns.

He leaned forward in his chair and told himself that it was just his subconscious trying to make better sense of the letter. He also knew a wise man should listen to his inner feelings.

He picked up the phone and dialed Millie's number. He explained the situation and without any extra chitchat, she agreed to come right over. Jacob arose from the chair, pacing back and forth in the church office. He was trying to get the pictures of last night's dream out of his head when an idea hit him like a punch in the gut. What if there was another letter? Without putting his coat on, he hurried outside. He had just arrived at the mailbox when Millie pulled up. She got out of the car and walked over.

"Jacob, are you all right? I haven't heard that tone in your voice since the night of your sister's accident."

"I'm fine," he said with a sigh.

"I can tell," Millie said in a half-mocking tone. "You look like you've seen a ghost. What's going on?" Millie asked, while trying to get a read on Jacob's actions. He did look a little tattered around the edges this morning. Another question dawned on Millie. What was he doing out at the mailbox? He didn't have any letters in his hands to mail and he knew the mail didn't come for another two hours. "Jacob, are you thinking there might be another letter?"

Surprised by her deductive reasoning, he answered her. "…Yes."

Without a second's hesitation, Millie flung open the door on the mailbox and peered inside. "Nothing… see!" she exclaimed. Turning on a dime toward the direction of the church, she exclaimed, "Let's go inside and take a look at that letter."

They walked back to the church, neither one saying a word. After entering the office, Jacob opened the drawer and handed her the letter. Millie took the letter and sat down across from Jacob. She opened the envelope and carefully pulled the letter out, beginning to read. It seemed like an hour had passed before she finally folded the paper back to its original shape and placed it back in the envelope.

"Well, what do you think?" Jacob asked intently.

Millie sat deep in thought, staring at the wall behind Jacob and then after a few seconds handed the letter back to Jacob and said, "Wow!"

There was another long pause, until Millie asked softly, "What if this is really a letter from your sister?"

"You can't be serious…can you?" Jacob asked with a look of disbelief.

"Pastor, I'm seventy years old and I've seen some strange things. When my husband was dying of cancer, he talked to his deceased brother for three days. I finally started to believe he was actually there… I don't think we're as cut off from the other world as people would like to think."

"But Millie, how many folks receive letters from their deceased sister in hell?" Jacob asked incredulously.

"I'm sure there is a perfectly good explanation for all this," Millie said, shaking her head.

"I still think it someone's idea of a sick joke."

"Well, I don't know. If it is a plan of God's, there will be something else coming down the pipe. Then we'll know for sure. Just relax and try not to worry so much. There is nothing you can do about it. Go home and try to get some sleep tonight… Have you said anything to Cathy yet?"

"No, I don't want to worry her," Jacob said, looking out the window of his office. "She probably knows something's going on anyway."

"What do you mean?" Millie asked.

"I tossed and turned all night with nightmares about the letter. I made so much noise that she ended up on the couch. I'm pretty sure she knows something is bothering me."

"Maybe you should tell her. Wives don't like being the last to find out. Trust me."

"You know me, Millie. I like to learn things the hard way," Pastor said with a sheepish grin.

"Well, I'm going to head back home. If you need anything, give me a call, okay?"

"Oh, Millie, would you mind watching the children Saturday night? I would like to take Cathy out for supper."

"Sure, Jacob. I would be glad to. What time?" Millie asked.

"Could you come over around six?"

"Sure. Don't worry about supper. I'll whip something up when I get there."

Jacob nodded with a smile as Millie put on her coat to head out the door. He hoped he would have that kind of energy when he was her age.

Jacob had some shut-ins to visit in the afternoon and decided to try to forget about the letter and go about his business. Maybe this was the extent of the joke and this ordeal would fade away with time.

Chapter Four

Jacob returned that afternoon before anyone else got home. While walking through the living room, he noticed the photo albums Cathy kept under the coffee table. He grabbed the one from his childhood and sat down. As he flipped through the pages of yellow, faded photographs, memories of his parents and Sara filled his mind. They had grown up in a little town north of Champaign, Illinois. Their father worked in Champaign at a hospital as a boiler operator and their mother worked for the post office. Sara was his twin, and during their early years, she had been the whole world to him. She was so independent, that by the age of six she was giving their parents fits. The memories of childhood were warm ones for Jacob, but high school was a different story. High school was the time frame when their personalities really diverged. The chasm in their relationship widened even farther during their senior year in high school. He was shy, and for a while he had been ashamed of his lack of popularity; but as he grew older, he found strength in it. He was going to Luther League cookouts at church, while she was going to keg parties in town. Sara always seemed to be scheduled for work on Sunday mornings and rarely went to church with the family. She never complained about going to church, but she usually found a way to miss it. Sara graduated from high school as valedictorian and went to college at the University of Illinois. Jacob went to a junior college the first two years and then transferred to the University of Illinois. She completed her bachelor's in business and he completed his in psychology. She also took many psychology classes. One time when they were home on break together, she bragged to him about taking the psychology classes because it would help her fleece the weak-minded. That was how Sara thought, the world was hers, and it was there for the taking.

She met Scott Bennington during the last year of college. Since he was her exact opposite, Jacob could never understand how they got together. Maybe she needed a polar opposite to complete her world. Scott had grown up in southern Wisconsin on a dairy farm. He had been raised in a Methodist home, and Jacob always told him that God had a sense of humor and would probably allow him to enter heaven anyway. He was a huge blond man, and Jacob liked to tease him about being the king of the cheddar-head Vikings. A very polite man, Scott always called their parents Mr. and Mrs. Litchfield. Scott and Sara were married after college, then moved to a Chicago suburb where Sara started her own real-estate business and Scott worked for a construction company. Early in their marriage, they would come home to visit quite often, but as the years progressed and the children came along, those visits tapered off to just a visit at Christmas. It finally got to the point that only Scott and the children would make the trip home for the holidays because

Sara was just too busy to take time out of her schedule. She always had a deal cooking or she had to meet with an important client. Jacob rarely saw her in the last ten years. His parents would ask Scott and the children to join them for the Christmas Eve service and they were always happy to attend. When their mother died, Sara only came for the visitation but didn't stay for the funeral. She said she had to leave that evening because of work obligations. A couple of years later when their father passed away, she didn't even bother to come to the funeral. She sent a note along with Scott telling Jacob how sorry she was that she couldn't make it to the funeral. The letter also said that the deceased would take care of themselves, but the living had shit to do. This really angered Jacob, and for the first time he gave her a piece of his mind. She just laughed at him and told him that when he had a real job, he would understand. Looking back, he realized that was the last time they spoke to one another.

In the years that followed, Jacob worked as a counselor in the Champaign county juvenile detention center. During that time Jacob noticed that nothing could change a young life except the realization that God existed. His hands were tied as to how far he could push religion on the young men and women he counseled, so it was at that point he decided to enter the Lutheran seminary. His sister sent him a letter while he was in the seminary telling him he should get a real job where he could make some money. He still had both letters somewhere. Back then he just wrote it off because that's how Sara was, but now it made him wonder what state her soul was in at the time of her death. After finishing seminary and relocating to St. John's, he met Cathy and they decided to get married. They sent an invitation to Sara and her family, but Scott called Jacob a week before the wedding to tell him that they wouldn't be able to make it. Jacob couldn't even remember what reason Scott gave at the time. Looking back at her adult life, he realized she was so entangled in the world that nothing but her career seemed to matter. He knew early on that their marriage was in trouble. Scott would never come out and say it, but Jacob could tell by the uncomfortable looks he made when he was asked how things were going. Giving up his construction job, Scott stayed home and took care of the kids. He told Jacob on one of their last visits that Sara did nothing but work and that he and the kids rarely saw her for more than a few minutes each day. They lived in a posh neighborhood with a large, fancy house. They drove the latest version of luxury car that was out on the market. She was very successful. It all ended with a drunk driver trying to overcorrect a small driving mistake. They were hit head on, and Scott was killed instantly. Sara held on for a couple of days, but the internal damage was too severe. Sara was still beautiful even in the casket. Jacob, though he knew it was inappropriate at the time, was entertained by the types of people that came to the funeral to pay last respects to his sister. Fancy suits and shimmering dresses, all lined up like a fashion show, there to pay respect to one of their own. Scott's family was so overshadowed by Sara's crowd, that Jacob wished the families would have chosen to have separate visitations. Although it was probably good, for Michael and Mara, that the two visitations were held together because it was one of the few times Sara and Scott were together in the same room. Scott's family thought it would be better if Jacob and Cathy kept the kids. Scott was an only child and his parents were in their seventies. The decision was made, and the children moved in with Jacob and Cathy. Within a month, the adoption was legal, but there was still work to be done with the rest of Scott and Sara's estate. Jacob wondered what that would entail, but he'd let someone else worry about that.

"Honey, I'm home," Cathy yelled.

The flood of memories that covered Jacob like a cold, wet blanket suddenly melted away. "I'm in the living room dear," Jacob answered, trying to fake the exuberance he wanted his wife Cathy to feel.

Cathy walked into the room, picking through the mail. "There's so much junk mail anymore."

The word *mail* brought Jacob out of his self-imposed trance. He rose from his chair and walked over Cathy.

"Here are a couple of letters with your name, dear," Cathy said, passing a pile to Jacob.

Jacob took his letters over to the kitchen table and sat down. He fingered through the mail, relieved to see nothing that resembled yesterday's letter from Sara. Laughing to himself, he realized that he just referred to the first letter as coming from his sister. Starting to feel human again, he was ready for a good night's sleep. Cathy came into the kitchen and started supper.

Hearing the bus pull up, he stood up to watch the children run up to the house. He saw Michael stop and pick something up as he ran through the yard and wondered what it could be. Mara was the first to run into the house with Michael right behind her. Mara ran straight upstairs, telling everyone she was going to do her homework.

"Uncle Jacob, I found this out in the yard," Michael said as he walked into the kitchen. Michael set the letter on the table, then headed toward the stairs to his room.

"Get started on your homework, Michael," Cathy said as she was taking plates out of the cupboard.

"But it's Friday!"

"You know the rules. No television until your homework is finished," Cathy said putting her hands on her hips.

"Wow, we have a whole four channels," Michael said in a matter-of-fact tone.

"Don't give me any sass, young man."

"Okay, Aunt Cathy," Michael replied as he began to trudge up the stairs.

Jacob, missing everything that just transpired, looked up from the envelope he was holding. He was sweating. Once again there was no stamp or return address. It was somewhat different in color, but it was again dirty and tattered. Jacob just sat there staring at it, afraid to pick it up. Cathy, still shaking her head over the little argument with Michael, noticed the expression on Jacob's face.

"Are you feeling okay, dear?"

"Did you drop this when you got the mail earlier?" Jacob asked, picking up the dirty envelope and holding it up for Cathy to see.

"I don't think so. Why?" Cathy asked, walking over to the table and taking the letter from her husband. "I don't think the post office would deliver a letter without a stamp anyway," Cathy said in a nonchalant manner.

"You're right. I don't think so either. I'm going to go to my office. I'll be back in a little bit," Jacob said, grabbing the letter from Cathy. He put on his coat and headed for the door.

"What's going on, Jacob?" Cathy asked with a look of concern. "Supper will be ready in a little while. Can't it wait?"

"No. I'll tell you when I get back!" Jacob snapped.

Cathy just stood there with a look of surprise on her face, but didn't say a word. Jacob left the house, walking hurriedly to the church. He thought to himself he shouldn't have snapped at Cathy, but told himself he would apologize to her later. He didn't want to read the letter around Cathy and the children, and besides, he felt better when he was in the church.

Chapter Five

He flipped the lights on in his office and sat down at his desk. Leaning forward, he twisted the switch on the desk lamp. Picking up the letter opener, he slit open the dirty envelope. Not thinking for a moment that it might not be another letter from Sara. He leaned back in the chair, put on his reading glasses and began to read.

To whom it may concern, Letter Two

I am writing this letter from a different cave than I told you about in the last letter. I can only write inside the caves because I'm afraid that the firelight would give away my location. I have managed to move farther down the mountain. I know they are out looking for me. I've heard the beating wings of the flying creatures close by and I cannot be too careful. The farther down I get, the more convinced I am that this is some form of earth. Humanity must have laid this place to waste. It is very slow going without light. Like I said before, there are bodies everywhere. There was either a major war or a devastating disease that wiped everyone out here. I'm going to guess it was a war because of the lack of sunlight. Maybe nuclear fallout covered the earth, blocking out the sun. The one thing I don't understand is the temperature changes, one minute it's sweltering hot and the next it's freezing. I've managed to find a few more useable tools, a knife, and some kind of pistol. I believe that I'm living many years in the future because the knife and pistol are like nothing I've ever seen before. I haven't figured out the pistol yet and I don't know if it even works, but I will try to figure it out after I'm finished with this letter.

I thought I heard someone calling my name sometime back, and the voice sounded familiar. There's no way, in this place, I was going to look for whoever or whatever it was. The guards knew our names back in the prison and I'm not too crazy about going back there. I'm starting to remember a few more details from my mortal life. Not many though. I can now remember the faces of my children. I also remember having an argument with my husband right before the car accident, but I don't remember why we were fighting. I still plan on finding the rebels that blew up the wall. I will not let this place beat me. I have to stop now.

Sara Bennington

Jacob took a deep breath and leaned forward in his chair. He thought to himself that this definitely sounded like his sister. Only Sara would think she could win in hell. Jacob decided to give his mentor, Pastor Jonathon Bailey, a call before he went back to the house. Jacob had served as an intern under Pastor Bailey in Indianapolis during his seminary vicarage. Jonathon, a confirmed bachelor, was a kind, wise, white-haired man of sixty-six. Jonathon always had an interest in the bizarre. He especially liked to talk about the afterlife. He was always telling Jacob about something he'd read about a person dying for a couple of minutes and then being brought back to life. The things these people said they saw mesmerized him. If anyone could help him, Pastor Bailey could.

As he was looking up Jonathon's number in the rolodex, he wondered why Sara couldn't remember anything from her mortal life. Are all the memories forgotten when we die? Interesting, he thought to himself as he dialed the number and heard an old familiar voice boom over the handset.

"Pastor Bailey, this is Jacob Litchfield. How are you?"

"Jacob, how good to hear your voice! How are you doing?"

"I'm fine."

"And how are Cathy and the children?"

"They're fine."

"How's the congregation?"

"They're fine too," Jacob said, starting to get agitated with all the small talk. He knew he hadn't talked to Jonathon for a long time and he was just a lonely old gentleman who probably needed someone to talk to. With a strained voice Jacob asked, "Jonathon, I need your help with something."

"Well, what do you need, my friend?" Jonathon said, sounding concerned.

Jacob told him about the letters while Pastor Bailey listened intently.

"Jacob, I'm not doing much these days. Do you want me to drive out? I would love…I mean, I would like to see those letters."

"That would be great, if it's not too much trouble?" Jacob said almost laughing at Jonathon's Freudian slip. He did feel better that his old mentor would be here tomorrow to help him sort out this mess.

They said their goodbyes and Jacob hung up the phone. He turned the lights off in the office and was about to head back home when he decided he better come clean with Cathy about the letters. This wasn't a church matter that needed to be kept secret. He flipped the lights back on, and grabbed the first letter out of the drawer and the second one off of his desk. He walked briskly back home, sensing he was in trouble for snapping at Cathy earlier. He said a quick prayer asking for forgiveness for his outburst as he entered the house. Cathy and the children were seated around the table, already eating. He quickly glanced at his watch and realized he had been gone longer than he planned. He wished he had a hat to throw into the kitchen and see if anything attacked it, but he decided he'd better just get it over with. It's amazing what trouble a man could get himself into when he's not thinking rationally. He entered the kitchen and the children both said hello, but Cathy continued to eat her supper without looking at him.

"Cathy, I'm sorry," Jacob said pleadingly.

Cathy didn't say a word. She got up and scraped her half-full plate into the garbage. She then went to the sink, rinsed it off, and headed for the living room.

"Your supper is on the stove," she said as she left the kitchen.

Jacob followed her into the living room and sat down next to her on the couch. The living room was sparse compared to many houses he had visited during his ministry. A couch, recliner, coffee table, and a thirty-two-inch television pretty much summed up the living room inventory. A few knickknacks and pictures carefully placed by Cathy helped give it a homey look.

"Dear, I am so sorry for snapping at you…something is going on that I haven't told you about and I want you to read something, if you would."

Cathy looked at him seeing that something was really bothering him. "What's going on, Jacob? You're scaring me," she asked.

Jacob passed her the first letter. She took it out of the envelope and unfolded it.

"Is this the letter that Michael brought in this afternoon?" she asked.

Jacob shook his head and urged her to read. Cathy sat back on the couch and began to read. He could tell by the faces she was making while she read that she was having the same reaction he did. She finished the letter and passed the whole thing to Jacob almost as if she couldn't bear to be in contact with it any longer.

"Where did you get that thing?" she asked.

"I got it yesterday afternoon," he said.

"I don't understand. Who would write a letter like that?"

"That's just it, I don't know. Is it just someone's idea of a sick joke?" Jacob asked. He was starting to get worked up again. "I let Millie read it and she doesn't think we should dismiss it so quickly as a prank."

"Millie's read it already!" Cathy said quietly.

Jacob knew as soon as he said it, he was in trouble all over again, but he was going to try to explain anyway.

"Honey, I didn't want to get you all worked up over this."

"What in the hell do you think I am now!" she yelled. She got up and started to leave the room.

"Cathy, the letter Michael brought in is the second."

Cathy stopped in her tracks, turned around, and looked at Jacob with disbelief.

"When I got the second one, I knew I had to tell you," Jacob said as he rose to give Cathy the second letter. "Like I said, I didn't want to worry you over this if it was just a onetime prank."

"Just give me the letter," Cathy said, a little calmer than before. Jacob gave her the second letter and she sat back down on the edge of the couch and began to read. After a few minutes when she finished she put it back in the envelope, handed it back to Jacob, who then put both letters into his front pocket and stood up. He looked down at her and could tell that her temper was now completely defused.

Jacob, not having much of an appetite, helped Cathy clear the table while the children finished their homework. The children were bathed and tucked into bed before they got a chance to relax. Sitting together in the living room, watching the ten o'clock news, Jacob sat up in his recliner and looked at Cathy.

"I called Pastor Bailey and told him about the letters," Jacob said, not knowing what Cathy's reaction was going to be.

"What'd he think?"

Jacob, seeing no reaction to the news that he'd told somebody else before her, said, "He wants to see the letters… He's coming here tomorrow afternoon." Jacob, waiting for a reaction but not getting one, finally added, "He should be here around three o'clock."

"Will he be staying the night?" Cathy asked, still staring at the television.

"I don't know," Jacob said, tired from the lack of sleep from the night before; he got up and walked over to where Cathy was sitting. He leaned down, kissed her on the forehead, and said, "I love you dear… I'm going to bed. Goodnight."

Cathy replied coolly. "Love you too. Goodnight." She still didn't look at him, but he was too tired to push the issue. Not saying another word, he headed up to bed.

Taking only a few minutes to fall asleep, Jacob was soon snoring when Cathy came to bed a few minutes later. Not wanting to wake him, she carefully crawled into bed, kissing him lightly on the cheek. She didn't like seeing him upset and hoped he would sleep soundly tonight. She tried to calm her troubled mind, but the events of the day would not let her drift off to sleep. She worried about her husband. She worried about living up to the task of raising two children. Since Michael and Mara had arrived, she continually questioned her abilities as a mother. It was like a dark shadow that always lurked in the corner of her mind. She wondered if Jacob shared the same feelings. Cathy knew one thing though, she loved her husband and she would do whatever it took to give Michael and Mara a loving home. With that thought, she took a deep breath and cuddled up to her husband, finally drifting off to sleep.

Chapter Six

Jacob was walking in the place described in the letters. It was dark, windy, and extremely hot. Deciding to move down the mountain, he climbed carefully from cliff to cliff. It was like moving down a giant stairway, but the steps were sharp and dangerous. The castle was the only light source, so the farther he moved away the darker it became. He tried to stay out of the shadows and in the brighter areas, but sometimes he was forced to travel through the dark. Because of the lack of light, he sometimes had to inch his way step by step. He couldn't see how tall the mountain was; he could only imagine in this kind of light. Coming to a large flat area on a step, he peered out into the darkness but his vision was snuffed out at ten or twelve feet. Something caught his eye off to the left. Moving toward it, he went down on all fours. He twisted around to see what tripped him, but he couldn't make out anything. It didn't feel like stone or dirt, it felt like cloth. He gave it a tug and it moved. Then, grabbing it with both hands, he pulled into a lit area so he could examine it. Gasping, he fell backward. The glow of the firelight fell across the face of a mutilated human body. He couldn't remove his gaze from the lifeless stare of the corpse. It was dressed in a military uniform and had started to decompose.

Facial bones were already starting to show through what was left of the rotting skin. He picked himself up off the ground and slowly backed away from the body. Remembering what the second letter said about human bodies being everywhere, he knew where the terrible smell came from. It was a horrific odor. Looking back to the direction of what caught his attention, he saw it again. The tiniest flicker of light came from behind an outcropping of rock. Carefully moving toward the light, he peered around the rock into a small opening that led back into the cave. Getting down on his hands and knees, he crawled in. The farther he traveled in, the brighter it got. The ceiling of the cave eventually rose to a height that allowed him to stand. Then he came to a turn in the tunnel, allowing him to see an opening that led into a large cavern. He moved along the wall of the cave until he could peek around into the opening. He could see the back of what appeared to be a slender woman with long dark hair, rocking back and forth while gazing into a small fire. He moved around her to the left and sat down, facing her from across the fire. She reminded him of a nervous little squirrel, every move she made was jerky and quick. It was Sara.

Even in her filth, she was still a beautiful woman. Her age appeared to be a lot younger than she had been at the time of her death. Jacob wondered why she appeared to be so much younger, but it was a mystery he knew he wouldn't understand until he passed to the next world. She was dressed in a ratty T-shirt, with some kind of leggings, and combat boots she had taken off one of the bodies from outside finished the ensemble. Around her narrow waist she wore a belt with a gun holster attached to it. The weapon looked like something out of *Star Wars*. He noticed a small hobo pack sitting within her reach and figured she kept it close in case she had to move quickly. Lying on the other side of her was a stack of disheveled papers of different shapes and sizes. He said her name softly. Her head jerked up, looking quickly left and right. Jacob could tell she heard something but he didn't know if she understood what he said.

"Sara, it's your brother Jacob. Can you hear me?"

Her head popped up again, she looked around. "Who's there?" Sara said.

"It's Jacob, your brother," he said.

"What do you want? Why are you here?" she said. Her eyes darted back and forth scared and confused.

"I don't know why I'm here. I think it's a dream." He paused for a moment, then continued, "Sara, I'm sorry I didn't try to help you when you were still alive."

She ignored what he said. "I remember you. You were at the hospital when I died."

"Yes, I was there," Jacob said.

"Scott told me you were my brother. Scott was my husband."

"I remember him. He was a good man."

Sara didn't respond to the comment. She sat there for a little while and finally asked, "Why can't I see you?"

"I don't know. I need to go back home," Jacob said, with a sudden sense of urgency coming over him.

"What do you mean, get back home? Are you dead?"

Jacob ignored the question and started moving toward the mouth of the cave. He could hear Sara still asking about home, but something or someone was compelling him to leave. He was about to exit the cave when he heard something move outside the opening. He quickly crawled back into the cave to go back to where Sara was sitting.

"Sara, put out the fire! Someone's coming!" Jacob said in a loud whisper.

Sara scooped handfuls of dirt onto the flames, extinguishing the fire. She crawled to the backside of the cave and huddled down like a mouse hiding from a cat. Jacob's vision was getting blurry. He closed his eyes, trying to clear his vision, but when he opened them again he saw a smooth white ceiling and was lying flat on his back in bed. He slowly turned his head and saw Cathy watching him intently.

"Are you okay, Jacob?" she asked.

He sat up and swung his feet to the floor. "I'm going down to get a drink of water."

"Jacob, I can smell that same smell from yesterday! Can you smell it?" Cathy said, sniffing in the air around her.

Jacob stopped and lifted his shirt to his nose. It smelled of sulfur and wood smoke. Somehow he had carried that smell back from his dream. He gave Cathy a strange look and said, "I'll take a shower. I'm sorry… I don't know what is going on."

He showered and headed downstairs.

Cathy was already sitting at the kitchen table when he got there. Jacob got a glass of water and wearily sat down at the kitchen table.

"Jacob, did you have another nightmare?"

"I just had the most incredible dream," Jacob said, still mystified. He proceeded to tell Cathy about the dream in detail. Cathy sat, taking small sips of her water as she listened, entranced by the story. When Jacob finished, he smiled weakly at his wife, asking her, "Am I losing it?"

"That's probably a fair question," she replied with a smile, but then she became serious again. "Jacob, is the odor that was on you the same one that you smelled in the dream?"

"Yes," Jacob answered.

"I don't know who's sending you these letters, but I think the dreams are tied directly to them. I've learned over time to trust God with the details. I know this is like preaching to the choir, but all we can ask for is the patience to let this all unfold."

"Sometimes I wonder how I managed to marry such a wise woman," Jacob said smiling.

"I wonder the same thing," she said coyly. She looked up to the kitchen clock and said, "It's three in the morning. I'm going back to bed."

"I'm sorry about the sheets."

"That's okay. I'll put on some fresh ones." Cathy stood up and walked over to Jacob. She wrapped her arms around him, moved her lips up to his left ear and whispered, "Why don't you come upstairs with me and I'll try to help you forget about the dream."

"Are you propositioning me, dear?" he said.

"Who me?" she said, trying to feign innocence.

Contemplating the offer, Jacob stood silent for a moment. Then he asked her sincerely, "Would it hurt your feelings if I said I don't think I would be a very good lover right now?"

"No it wouldn't, dear." Then suddenly her eyes shone. "Besides, what makes you think you're a good lover any other time?" She laughed loudly, and it took a second for Jacob to catch on, and then he too laughed.

They kissed, and then she went upstairs to bed. He sat back down at the table to replay the dream he had just experienced. Unlike his normal dreams, this one was all too real. Like the difference between the bits and pieces of a music video and the detail and clarity of a motion picture. Sara looked and acted like a caged animal. It bothered him that she could not remember anything about him from her earthly life except for the visit in the ICU right before she passed away. Didn't she write in her first letter that Scott had to tell her that he was her brother? When he mentioned that he knew Scott and that he was a good man, she ignored that statement. He thought back to what he knew about hell. Hell is the total isolation from God. Jacob always wondered if people really understood how much God has to do with everyday life. He didn't mean food or water, those are a given, but what if God was totally removed from the equation? What parts of nature, if any, would exist without God? Scientists are always trying to prove that the world is just a series of events set into motion. If life was just a roll of the dice, how many throws would it take to come up with the genetic codes that make up every living thing? How does a planet end up the perfect distance from a burning star? Close enough to stay warm, but not close enough to burn up. Not to mention the fact that it rotates at just the right speed.

What if there wasn't any temperance of evil? No white to offset the black. If humans are the mix of God and animal and God is removed, what would just the animal half be like? Wouldn't the human simply be an animal at the mercy of its own basic desires? What would keep a human, if given the opportunity, from stealing the car it wanted? What would stop a stronger man from taking a weaker man's wife? The strongest, unchecked by compassion for the weak, would control society. Jacob didn't think the world would be a very nice place without God.

Jacob looked up at the clock, realized he had been daydreaming for quite some time. It was almost four A.M., and tomorrow was Saturday so he didn't have any reason to get up early. Although he didn't know if he could go back to sleep, he decided to go back to bed just to snuggle with his wife.

Chapter Seven

Morning came quickly for both Jacob and Cathy. They would have slept for a couple of more hours, but the children had other ideas. Cathy got out of bed and padded downstairs to start breakfast. Jacob came down a few minutes later to find Cathy and the children all in the kitchen. Michael was sitting at the table reading a book. Mara was helping Cathy make pancakes. Bacon was starting to fry on the stove and Jacob thought to himself that had to be what heaven smelled like.

"Good morning, Uncle Jacob," Mara chimed from the chair she was standing on next to the kitchen counter. She was busy stirring pancake batter, managing to keep a little of it in the bowl.

"Good morning, Mara. Good morning, Michael," Jacob said. He went to the cupboard and took out a coffee cup. "Good morning, Michael," Jacob said, this time a little louder.

"Good morning, Uncle Jacob," Michael replied quietly as he peeked over the book he was reading.

They finished breakfast together and the kids ran off to play. Cathy washed the breakfast dishes while Jacob wiped the table off and took out the garbage.

"What time do you have to go to work?" Jacob asked.

"Noon," Cathy answered, as she put the last of the clean dishes away. "What are your plans for the morning?"

"I'm going to the office to finish getting ready for tomorrow's service. I'll be back by eleven. If I'm not, just send the children over to the church when you're ready to leave."

"Okay," Cathy said as she gave Jacob a kiss. Jacob put on his coat and headed out the door. It was a gray, damp morning in Illinois, usual for this time of year. His morning was spent typing out the sermon notes he had hand written earlier in the week, finalizing his thoughts by putting them down on paper. Even as a kid, he kept a journal of his daily activities and thoughts. He learned that by putting his thoughts and feelings on paper he could keep his emotions on an even keel. Sometimes reading one's own description of a bad situation was the best way to accept the outcome and to move ahead without overanalyzing something you can't control. Like an actor stepping out of a movie to watch the ending from the theater. Jacob's mother had taught him to do this when she realized that he was such an introverted child. When he had started college, he stopped writing in his journal. College was a lot different from the small high school he had attended. He was finally in the midst of people that were like him. They thought like him and shared the same beliefs. He finally made his first friends. Sara always made fun of him for writing in a journal. She always said that only sissies kept diaries. A thought hit Jacob; maybe that's what Sara was doing now. Some part of her mind remembered this and it was her way of trying to deal with her fear. Jacob also wondered about the dreams he was having. Would God really allow him to talk to his sister in hell, or was this the way his mind was trying to deal with the stressful situation? He also thought about the supposed connection that some twins share. Up to this point, he never believed it might be possible for any connection to exist between his sister and him. He would ask Pastor Bailey about this when he arrived. He checked the time and it was getting close to when Cathy needed to leave for work. He printed out his sermon for tomorrow's service and headed back to the parsonage. Cathy was putting on her coat when he arrived. She gave him a quick kiss, then left. The children were watching cartoons in the living room so he sat down and watched with them for a few minutes. He loved the Road Runner and Wile E. Coyote. After lunch the children went upstairs to play and Jacob decided to take a short nap. The last two sleepless nights had taken their toll.

He awoke two hours later to someone knocking on the front door. Surprised by the amount of time he had slept, he hurried to answer the door. Looking through the window, he saw his friend Jonathon standing on the porch with a suitcase. Jacob swung open the door to greet his guest.

"Jonathon, I'm so glad to see you," Jacob said.

"It is good to see you," Jonathon replied with a huge smile.

They shared some small talk about Jonathon's trip from Indianapolis and the Midwestern weather. Jacob offered Jonathon some coffee, which he accepted graciously.

They settled in at the kitchen table and Jonathon, never one to beat around the bush, asked if he could see the letters. Jacob passed him the two letters. The old man put on his glasses, then moved his arms back and forth as if to bring the words into focus. Jacob smirked to himself, wondering what he himself would be like when he got to be Jonathon's age. He read both letters while Jacob patiently sipped on his coffee. When Jonathon finished reading, he had an expression that looked like the cat that had just swallowed the canary. He passed the letters back to Jacob.

"Well, what do you think? Could these really be from hell?" Jacob asked.

"Do you realize, if these letters are for real, what impact they would have on the world?" Jonathon asked, lifting the letters to his nose and inhaling deeply.

"I guess I never thought any farther..."

"Do you smell the sulfur?" Jonathon interrupted.

"Yes," Jacob said.

"If someone is playing a practical joke, they went to a lot of trouble," Jonathon said looking again at the letter he was holding.

"I agree. Why would someone do it anyway? What would anyone have to gain?"

"Those are all good questions. What does your wife think?"

"She read them last night, but we haven't discussed them much," Jacob said in a way that Jonathon knew there was some buried issue in the statement. "Millie Vanderwall, my secretary, read the first one and I planned on letting her read the second one this evening when she arrived to watch the kids."

Jacob told Jonathon about the two dreams he had. Jacob could see the excitement in his mentor's eyes as he related the tale.

"You carried the odor from your dreams back with you?" Jonathon asked in amazement.

"Yes. It was unmistakable," Jacob said in reply.

"That is incredible!" Jonathon exclaimed.

The two friends talked away the afternoon, and before long, Cathy was home from work. She greeted Jonathon and joined them at the table.

"What do you think about the letters, Cathy dear?" Jonathon asked, surprising both Cathy and Jacob with the direct question.

"I…I don't know. I'm always looking for present-day miracles. I mean, it's one thing for someone to write a letter in hell, but it's quite amazing to think that someone is sending them here," Cathy said.

Jonathon agreed with a nod of his head, then said, "I think anything is possible when God is involved. There is nothing written in the Bible that says He would not communicate with us after the time of its original authors. As long as it does not contradict the original words, I might add. Just think about the reaffirming power these letters would have on people."

"We're having trouble believing they're real. How would anyone else believe them?" Jacob asked.

Jonathon stood up, took a step away from the table, then stopped. He turned and said. "Jacob, the people that already believe still need confirmation. The ones on the fence are always looking for something to convince them one way or another. Of course, some of the unbelievers wouldn't come around if God slapped them on the face, and believe it or not, sometimes he does just that."

Jacob thought about Jonathon's reasoning for a minute before finally saying, "You might be right, but I'm not sure that I want the fact that my sister is in hell made public."

"I understand what you are saying, but that seems a little selfish don't you think?" Jonathon asked.

Cathy, noticing the pained look on her husband's face, said quickly, "Gentleman, don't we have to prove they're really from Sara first?"

That idea stopped the two ministers in their tracks. Everyone took a deep breath and settled down. Jacob was the first to speak. "How do we do that?"

"Well, do you have anything that Sara wrote when she was still alive?" Jonathon asked.

"Yes, I have two letters she sent to me some years back," Jacob said as he got up from the table to run upstairs.

Waiting until Jacob was out of earshot, Jonathon said, "Jacob, looks exhausted."

"He hasn't slept very well the last couple of nights."

"I think the letters have him rattled." Jonathon stated.

"I think they have too, but he's keeping it all inside."

Jonathon thought for a second, then asked, "How was he after the death of his sister?"

"I don't really think that it has all sunk in yet. We've been so busy with the children that I don't think he had much time to think about it."

They heard Jacob coming back down the stairs. They were both sitting in silence when Jacob returned to the kitchen.

"You two weren't talking about me by any chance, were you?" Jacob asked, when he noticed the awkward silence.

Cathy, the first to speak, said, "We're just concerned about you."

"I'm fine," Jacob said with a dismissive look. "Here are the two letters from Sara," he said, handing them to Cathy, who then spread all four letters out across the table.

"Do you folks own a magnifying glass?" Jonathon asked.

"Yes, we do. Hang on, I'll get it," Cathy said. She jumped up from the table and rummaged through a kitchen drawer. The sound of utensils jingling in a wooden drawer filled the room. "Got it!"

She handed the magnifying glass to Jonathon. He leaned over to inspect the letters. He moved the lens back and forth, looking at one, then another. After a few minutes, Jonathon pointed out a couple of items for Cathy and Jacob to look at. They all took turns inspecting the letters. Jacob picked up the two dirty envelopes that contained the newest letters and peered at them through the lens.

"I believe the writing on all the letters is the same," Jacob said. "But the writing on the envelopes is different from the writing on the letters they contained." Jacob passed the two envelopes to Cathy so she could compare the letters to the envelopes.

"They are different," she said as she passed everything to Jonathon.

Jonathon compared the two and after a few minutes he said, "I would have to say that all four letters are written by the same person, but you are right, Jacob. The writing on the envelopes does not match the writing on the letters. Why would that be, I wonder?"

"Maybe the miracle part is not the letters, but who is sending them," Cathy concluded.

"Jacob, when you were there in your dreams, did you ever see anyone with her or around her?" Jonathon asked.

"No, I never saw anyone else, but I did hear someone or something close by at the end of the second dream. Remember when I went back in to the cave to warn her?"

Jonathon nodded, and said, "Let's assume that…"

He was interrupted by a knock on the back door. Cathy got up and opened the door to a smiling Millie Vanderwall.

"Hello, Millie. Come on in," Cathy said as she moved to the side to let Millie enter. "Millie, I want you to meet Pastor Jonathon Bailey." Then, turning to Jonathon, she said, "Jonathon, I would like to introduce Ms. Millie Vanderwall."

"I'm glad to meet you, Mrs. Vanderwall," he said as he reached for her hand.Millie, reaching for his hand, said, "It's Ms., my husband passed away a few years back, and I'm happy to meet you too."

"Millie, if you don't mind, we're all going to stay in tonight. Jonathon and I are going to run to get pizza, and while we're gone, Cathy will show you the letter I got yesterday afternoon along with some other information. I hope you don't mind?" Jacob asked, while flipping through the phone book for the number to the restaurant.

Cathy, Millie, and Jonathon talked quietly in the living room as Jacob ordered the food. Jacob walked back into the room. "Are you ready to go, Jonathon?"

The men put on their coats and left. Cathy picked up the newest letter, then handed it to Millie as they went into the living room. Millie sat down and began to read. When she finished, she handed it back to Cathy.

"My goodness, I guess I never thought there would be another one," Millie said, shifting in her seat.

Chapter Eight

Jacob and Jonathon rode in silence for the first two or three miles. They were both deep in thought about the recent events. Finally, Jonathon was the first to speak. "Tell me about Ms. Vanderwall," he said.

Jacob thought about Millie for a second before answering his friend's question. Millie had been with him since he arrived at St. John's. Always wearing a smile, her attitude seemed to rub off on everyone around her. She reminded him of his own wife Cathy in a way. No more than five foot tall, her vibrant spirit more than made up for her small stature. Jacob couldn't remember a time when she wasn't dressed to the hilt or her hair wasn't done up perfectly. Jacob thought back to another time when he happened to follow a woman out of the church. He was maybe, ten or fifteen feet behind her. By the shape of her body and the way the woman walked, he assumed that the woman ahead of him was in her late twenties or early thirties. She suddenly stopped and turned around; he was surprised to see that it was Millie. He tried to suppress his look of surprise, but he had just mistaken a seventy-year-old woman for a thirty-year-old. Of course, he never told anyone about the incident, but it made him laugh when it came to mind. He also wondered why some of the old bachelors in the church hadn't shown an interest in her. Millie Vanderwall had become an important part of Jacob's life and he didn't like thinking about not having her around someday.

The lights from a passing car broke his train of thought and he answered Jonathon's question. "Oh, so you want to know about Millie Vanderwall? Well, I believe she is close to seventy years old. Her husband passed away right after I started as minister here, six years ago. They lived on a farm three miles west of the church, but now she lives in town by herself. Her husband died of cancer. He was my first church member to pass away. I'd never watched anyone die of cancer before, and in one month he went from a healthy-looking man to a wasted human shell. The thing I found most interesting was that he never lost his sense of humor and neither did Millie. Both of them were so strong in their Christian faith that death seemed like an adventure. The funeral was almost what I would call a joyous event. She has been my secretary ever since. Is there anything else you would like to know?" Jacob asked with a grin.

"Yes, there is. What do you suppose makes her blue eyes sparkle so much?"

They were still laughing when they pulled into the restaurant parking lot. Jacob ran in to pick up the pizza. When he came out, he noticed Jonathon was talking to someone parked next to them.

"Jacob, this man's name is Andrew and he has never eaten at a *Monical's Pizza* before. He's traveling through and stopped to get something to eat," Jonathon said.

Jacob laughed to himself at how easily Jonathon could make friends. "Hello. It's nice to meet you. Where are you traveling from?"

"I'm coming down to visit a friend."

Jacob knew better than to judge a book by its cover, but Andrew looked like a good person. He was probably in his early twenties, six foot tall with curly black hair. It appeared to Jacob that he was, or used to be, some type of athlete. He was driving a four- or five-year-old car that had been well maintained. The thing Jacob noticed the most were his eyes. They looked like they could burn through steel. Looking at the stranger, Jacob felt there was something about this young man that disturbed him, not in a bad way, but there was something that he just couldn't put his finger on. Maybe it was just the fact that everything that had happened in the last couple of days had put his nerves on edge. He dismissed the thought as he listened to Jonathon and Andrew say their farewells. Waving goodbye to their new acquaintance, they drove out of the parking lot.

"He's a nice young man, don't you think?" Jonathon asked.

"Yeah, he did seem nice. Where did he say he was going?"

"Well, I guess he never really said. He just said he was heading south to visit a friend."

"Actually, he said he was coming down to visit a friend," Jacob said, correcting what his friend said.

"Well, if you want to get technical," Jonathon replied to Jacobs's correction.

"What does he do for a living?" Jacob asked while they waited for the last of the traffic to pass before he pulled out onto the street.

"We didn't talk about that either."

"What did you talk about?" Jacob finally asked with a laugh.

"Pizza and…the weather," Jonathon replied with a chuckle.

They both laughed as the last of the traffic passed and Jacob could finally pull out onto the street.

Chapter Nine

When Jacob and Jonathon arrived back at the parsonage, they found Cathy and Millie sitting in the living room chatting away. The children were already bathed and in their pajamas watching television. Then, after a nice meal together, Cathy and Millie cleaned up the kitchen while Jacob and Jonathon played with the children in the living room.

Later, Cathy told the children to get ready for bed, and after losing the argument to stay up longer, they ran up the stairs ahead of Cathy, who went up to tuck them in. Upon her return, all four grown-ups were seated in the living room, ready to resume their discussion about the letters.

"I think we all agree that it's Sara's handwriting in all four letters," Jonathon said. Everyone nodded in agreement. "I also think we all agree that somebody else addressed the envelopes." Once again everyone nodded in agreement. "Does anyone here think that this could still be a prank?"

Millie was the first to answer. "I don't. What would there be to gain from such a prank?"

"I don't know what there would be to gain. It's not like someone is being held hostage and these are ransom letters. These are letters from my deceased sister who is in hell. I can't

65

think of anyone who would get enjoyment from this," Jacob said as he massaged his temples.

Both Cathy and Jonathon nodded in agreement.

"So we can rule out enemies?" Jonathon said.

Jacob answered, "Yes, I don't have any enemies that I can think of."

Millie broke in and asked, "Do you think Sara could be in hell?"

There was a long pause. Jacob started softly. "Of course no one can know for sure, and it's not our place to judge, but she was wrapped so tight in the world of money and finances. There are many things about my sister that I've never told any of you. All that mattered to Sara was money and success. Did anybody read the letter that she sent me when our father died?" Jacob said in a tone that was walking along the edge of anger. "She didn't even bother to show up at his funeral." Jacob's eyes started to glisten with emotion. "I watched Sara grow up to become a self-absorbed workaholic. The last few years that Mom and Dad were alive, she didn't even bother to come home to visit them for the holidays. Scott and the children would come alone."

Jonathon could see that this was something Jacob had held inside for a long time. He was surprised by the information that Jacob was sharing. Millie and Cathy also looked surprised.

Jacob, figuring Cathy could be upset that she had never been told about his relationship with his sister, explained further. "I'm sorry, dear, that I never told you this before. The one thing that I've never been able to forgive my sister for was the way she treated out parents. I don't know how a person who was raised the way she was, ended up like she did." All three people listening noticed the volume in Jacob's voice had raised a few decibels. "My sister changed sometime during high school. Why, I don't know. She went from being a loving and caring person to a calculating, money-hungry little bitch!" Jacob was now speaking loudly. "If anyone deserved to go to hell, she did!"

Cathy had never seen her husband this upset in the six years they'd been married. Jacob sat there red faced and out of breath. He looked around at the group, realizing they could tell he was embarrassed by his outburst.

Jacob looked at Cathy, then Millie, and finally Jonathon, then once again back at Cathy. "I'm sorry, Cathy. I must apologize to Jonathon and Millie too. I've never told anyone the truth about my sister. Whenever any of you asked about her, I just evaded the questions. I figured Cathy knew something was wrong, because twins don't usually go ten years without talking unless there is a problem."

"Well, I hope not too many," Cathy said. "Your sister and her family didn't even come to our wedding. I had a pretty good idea there was a problem. I knew that whatever it was, it happened years ago. But whenever I asked you about it, you acted like it was no big deal. You would always just say that she's busy, or gave some other excuse for her. I guess I figured you would tell me when it was time."

Jacob looked at Jonathon and said, "My friend, I'm sorry I never told you about any of this when I worked with you in Indy. I think it was something I was running from, and until tonight I never thought it would catch me."

"Everyone has secrets, and that's fine, but you really need to forgive Sara, Jacob. Anger like that can really weaken a soul. Anger is the devil's foothold."

"You're right, Jonathon. I've got to admit that until I received these letters I never felt anything but anger for my sister, but now I feel sorry for her. I wish I could have done something before she died," Jacob said, rubbing his forehead, trying to ease some of the tension he was feeling.

"You are not responsible for Sara's choices," Jonathon added.

Jacob looked in Millie's direction, and before he could say a word, she pointed her finger at him and said, "Don't apologize to me. You have nothing to be sorry about. It's none of my business."

Jacob smiled at Millie for letting him off the hook. Jacob continued, "Let me tell you the whole story. When we were young, Sara was everything to me. She could do anything she put her mind to. She was fearless. I, on the other hand, well, let's just say that I was scared of my own shadow. We got along well when we were young. When we got to junior high, she started playing sports. Mom and Dad took me to every one of her sporting events. I would sit in the bleachers, watching and cheering for her. I remember people asking why I didn't play. Sara being so good, well surely I had to be also. I never had any athletic skill, so I never tried.

"It was hard to compete with a sister that did everything perfectly and I'm not kidding about perfect either. If she lost a soft ball game or a track event, there was hell to pay. Mom and Dad would get so upset with her temperamental outbursts after a loss. No matter why her team lost, she always pouted for two or three days. Track ended up being her favorite sport and one time she told me why. She didn't have to depend on anyone else to win." Jacob took a deep breath and finally said, "I guess that pretty much sums up Sara's life up to high school."

"You said she changed in high school. How?" Cathy asked.

After a few moments of thought, Jacob continued. "Well, the first two years she concentrated on running track and getting good grades. She still talked to us during those years, but the summer between our sophomore and junior year, she blossomed into a beautiful woman, and she knew it. Within a month of starting our junior year she had made a completely new group of friends. I believe you would call them "the IN crowd." The people that were her friends up to that point were no longer good enough. I can remember thinking the new crowd was like a pack of wolves just hunting for their idea of weakness in the people around them. They lived to make people feel terrible. I know they teased her about what a geek I was. I also know she was teased about the little house we lived in. She would come home and ask me why I couldn't act normal. Nothing was ever good enough: the house, the car, and especially my clothes. She took a job at the grocery store in town, and every penny she made went to buying the proper clothing for whatever fad was popular at the time. Don't get me wrong, even with the new friends, she kept perfect grades. By the time we were in our senior year I had accepted my place of being a geek. I found solace with my church friends. She would make fun of us and call us losers, but by that time, I didn't care anymore. What I did care about was the way she treated Mom and Dad. She always told them how embarrassing they were. She stopped giving them her track schedules because she didn't want them at the track meets. I'll give Mom and Dad credit though; they never complained, at least not around me. She would come home, if she didn't have to work or have a track meet, and go straight to her room. Most of the time, she wouldn't come out of her bedroom unless it was to use the bathroom or it was time to leave for school.

When we graduated, Mom and Dad wanted to have a party for us. When they told her she just laughed and said no thank you, she had made other plans. I felt sorry for our parents, but as I said, they never showed any emotion toward her attitude. A small number of friends and I had a small party at our house. We had a good time. Dad let us build a small bonfire in the backyard and they came out to join us. We laughed and joked around until late that evening and I remember thinking how much I would miss them when I moved away from home. I know you never met my parents; they were old school, so kind and gentle. They were both in their late thirties when Sara and I were born. They had tried for years to have children. Mom always told us that we were her little miracles. During high school, the other parents were in their late thirties, while our parents were almost in their sixties. I think that bothered Sara a lot. They worked hard, but had enough to live comfortably. They had their faith, each other, and their children. That's all they needed and I think that drove my sister nuts. We both started college in Champaign; Sara went to the U of I, and I went to junior college. I lived at home for the first two years, and then I too moved to Champaign. I came home anytime I could, but Sara would make any excuse to stay in Champaign for a weekend or holiday. Sara met Scott her last year of college. He was such a nice person, her total opposite. She would bring him home a lot in the beginning, and it was like old times at first. Then they got married, moved up north, and had the children. Over the next few years, their visits became sporadic. Finally, it ended up that Scott would bring the children without Sara. I asked Scott once why Sara didn't want to see Mom and Dad and he would just shrug and say she was busy. A few years later, when Mom died from a heart attack, Sara came to the visitation, but left that night, not staying for the funeral. A couple of years later when Dad died, Scott brought the letter from her telling me that she was sorry she couldn't make it. That was the first time I got mad at her. I tried to call her, but it didn't do any good, she just blew me off. I told her I never wanted to see or talk to her again, and until I took her children to see her after the accident, I didn't. I know what I did was wrong, and until the last couple of days, I never felt any remorse. I felt justified in my actions for the way she had treated our parents. It's strange how blinded one can become by anger. I wish I had said something to her when we were in high school, but I was too weak back then. I wish I would have tried to figure out why she did what she did. Maybe I could have helped her change before she died. I don't know and I probably never will." Jacob finished talking and took a deep breath. He felt like the weight of the world was lifted from his shoulders. "It was almost as if the devil paid her special attention."

Jonathon, looking thoughtful, replied to Jacob's statement. "I would have to guess that Sara was an easy mark for vanity and materialism. Growing up in a humble home like she did, she didn't have much. That left a vacuum for possessions and I think Satan loves to fill a vacuum." Jonathon looked around the room as if he was sitting in the pulpit during a sermon. "When she blossomed into a beautiful woman, her vanity kicked in and she couldn't be complete without the proper attire. Your parents were older, and I don't think they cared whether you two wore up-to-date fashions. Sara was embarrassed by that fact and overcompensated." When Jonathon finished, all the heads in the room seemed to nod in agreement.

The night ended on that note. Jacob told everyone he was exhausted and excused himself. Cathy invited Millie and Jonathon for Sunday dinner and told them they could continue the discussion tomorrow afternoon. Jonathon told Millie that it was nice to meet her and looked forward to seeing her tomorrow in church. Millie put on her coat, with the help of Jonathon, and left. Cathy showed Jonathon to the room he was going to stay in for the night and told him to have a good night. Cathy, getting ready for bed, walked into the bedroom and found Jacob already in bed.

"Are you okay?" Cathy asked him softly.

"I'm okay," he answered. "I'm just worn out from all the excitement of the last couple of days. I'm sorry I never told you about my sister. I guess I'm also ashamed of the fact that I never said anything to her. I was such a wimp in high school and I let her treat Mom and Dad like crap."

"Who cares what you were like in high school. None of that matters now anyway. We are the sum of our experiences, and you wouldn't be the person you are today if it wasn't for what happened in the past."

"I'm a terrible person, Cathy. These letters have brought back all the anger and hatred I felt for Sara. I buried it deep inside and I thought I'd forgotten it, but I hated her for treating Mom and Dad the way she did."

Cathy climbed into bed and put her arms around him. She snuggled with him, giving him a kiss. "I love you, Jacob."

"I love you too, Cathy," Jacob said. "I'm sorry. I should never have kept all this from you. You're my wife and I should have told you."

"I wish you would have. It bothers me that you didn't, but I think I understand." Cathy rolled over and looked up at the ceiling. "I saw something once between a father and son that just tore me up. The father, near death with cancer, was a patient on the floor I was working on. His son would never come to visit him, even when the other nurses and I would call and beg him to come visit his father. We called him right before his father was going to die, but he just hung up on us. His father died alone. A couple of days later the son came to the hospital to pick up his father's belongings. He looked like a decent young man. I helped him pack his father's clothes and I asked him why he didn't come to say goodbye to his father. He told me it was none of my business, so I left him alone. I did tell him though that his father kept asking for him during his last hours. The young man's face never changed. I never saw any tears. He never said a word—just took his father's things and left. Can you imagine what that poor man has to live with for the rest of his life? I'm still angry with him and I didn't even know him. It took everything I had that day not to kick him square in the pants. I imagine the anger I have for that kid is the same that you feel toward your sister. It's no different and I don't think I'm wrong for feeling that way. No one should be treated like that. But I think Jonathon is right when he said you have to forgive your sister."

Jacob lay there for a moment, then looked at Cathy and smiled. "Kick him square in the pants, huh? I never knew I married such a tiger."

"Oh, hush. Let's go to sleep," Cathy said, knowing her comment on forgiveness had just been sidestepped.

Chapter Ten

Sunday morning was like a whirlwind at the Litchfield residence. Everyone scurried around trying to eat breakfast and get ready in time for Sunday school. Jacob led the adult classes, and Cathy taught the preschool class. Everything was going well that morning at the service, except that the scheduled organist was home sick with the flu. Martha Perkins, a retired music teacher, gladly stepped up to the plate. Except for missing a few cues, she did fine. Jacob was just starting his sermon when he looked out across the congregation and recognized a familiar face. He was sure it was the young man they had met the night before, but it was hard to tell for sure because he was sitting at the back of the church. Maybe Jonathon had invited him to the service? Jacob finished the sermon, the offering was taken, and then he said the benediction. After the last hymn was sung, Jacob took his place at the main exit to shake hands with the congregation as they filed out. Jacob looked for the visitor from the back pew, but when the crowd had tapered off to the last few people he realized that the stranger never came through. Jonathon was the last person to go through so Jacob asked him if he had seen his friend from the restaurant.

"No, I didn't see him," Jonathon said, looking over Jacob's shoulder to see if he could see him in the entryway.

"I'm sure he was here," Jacob said.

"Hurry and change. Your wife is making meatloaf for dinner and I'm hungry."

"All right, I'll meet you over at the house. Tell Cathy I'll be right there." He went to his office to hang up his robe. As he turned from closing the closet door, he heard someone speak.

"Hello, Jacob."

It startled Jacob so badly he let out a yelp. Before he could turn all the way around, he heard the speaker let out a little laugh. Jacob recognized the stranger from their meeting last evening, but he seemed different somehow. "What are you doing here? I didn't see you when I came in."

"Don't be afraid. I told you I was coming down to see a friend and you are that friend. I must apologize for laughing at you when you jumped."

"That's okay. Can I help you with something?" Jacob asked. The room was filled with the fragrance of fir trees, or maybe that wasn't it, maybe it was something else. Jacob couldn't really place the fragrance, but it gave him a warm, peaceful feeling. He had noticed last night how piercing the stranger's eyes were, but this morning he also noticed how perfect this person's face was. It seemed to brighten the room. The more Jacob looked at the man, the more magnificent he seemed to become. Jacob never felt in any danger. Actually, he felt totally calm with this strange man.

"No. I'm here to help you," the stranger said, never blinking, looking into Jacob's eyes.

"You can help me with what?" Jacob asked as he moved around to his chair. He invited the stranger to sit down across from him. Jacob couldn't explain it, but he felt different all of a sudden. He was no longer tired, his mind seemed suddenly clear, and he felt a peace he had never experienced before.

"Jacob, I have been sent to tell you that you are experiencing something extraordinary. Your sister has been sent to hell, and your Creator has allowed you to communicate with her through the letters and dreams. You will receive one more letter and you will have one more dream. I warn you, though; Lucifer will not like a human looking into his kingdom. The one I speak of relies on the worldly belief that he does not exist. It will be known to him that there is communication being sent from inside his kingdom. I also warn you to be careful when you visit your sister, because if your physical body dies on earth, your spirit will remain in hell for eternity. You have been given everything you will need for this. Always remember your Maker loves you."

Jacob, completely awestruck, noticed the stranger was becoming brighter as he spoke. Jacob managed to blurt out, "Why is this happening to me?"

"I do not have the answer to that question, Jacob. I am nothing more than a messenger." The stranger's face became so bright that Jacob could no longer look in his direction.

Jacob thought he saw something move over to his left and glanced in that direction for a split second. When he looked back to the stranger, he was no longer there.

"Wait!" Jacob yelled. "What do I do if I get captured?"

A voice answered from the hallway. "A second of a dream equals that of a lifetime in hell. Remember, you must… wake…up." The voice trailed off into nothingness.

"What the heck?" He shot out of his chair and ran to look out of the office door to see if there was any trace of the stranger. He looked down the hallway in both directions, but he didn't see anyone. He felt as if he had just awakened from a dream. Did the previous conversation actually take place? He turned around to head back into the office, when he saw another letter lying on the chair where the stranger had just been sitting. Jacob picked it up and noticed that it looked like the others he had received, except this time the envelope was a different color. Just like before, there was nothing on the envelope but his name and address. He decided he was going to take it home where everyone could read it with him. Then he stopped. An angel had just visited him! He said as he left the office, "Wait till they hear this one."

Jacob, practically running, carried the letter over to the parsonage. He was still mentally replaying the last fifteen minutes through his head. Was there any chance he had mistaken what he had seen and heard in his office? Jacob felt like a new man. He had gotten a good night's sleep for the first time in two nights, and the mysterious visitor seemed to have enchanted him with a new spirit. Jacob repeated the words to himself as he hurried to the house. He didn't want to forget what he had just been told. He came up to the back door and could smell the dinner Cathy had prepared. He burst into the house finding everyone sitting around the kitchen table.

"You're not going to believe what just happened!" he blurted out.

Catching everyone by surprise, no one said a word for a second, and Jacob continued in a rant. "I was just visited by a…" Jacob, realizing that everyone might think he was crazy if he continued in this manner, stopped in mid-sentence.

"Who did you see, Uncle Jacob?" Mara asked excitedly.

Jacob stopped for a moment and thought before he said anything else. "I met a new friend this morning, Mara."

"Who was it, Uncle Jacob?" Mara asked again.

"Yes, who was it, Jacob?" Jonathon asked as he took the last bite of food from his plate. Jonathon was giving Jacob a curious look, and everyone at the table had the same look on their faces.

Jacob, starting to calm down, walked over to the table to pick up a plate. He took his seat and started scooping food from one dish and then another. When he had taken what he wanted, he said, "I don't want to say anymore with the children here." Before the children could complain, he continued, "I will tell you the whole story later, but for now you two must be patient. If you're done eating, you may be excused from the table." Both children scooted out of their chairs and headed upstairs. The grownups could hear both children mumbling complaints to one another as they climbed the stairs.

"I was just visited by an angel!" Jacob blurted out like a child with a huge secret.

"What?" Cathy, Jonathon, and Millie all exclaimed at the same instant.

Jacob told the whole story, between mouthfuls of food. He finished eating and telling the story at the same time. He then sat back to enjoy the expressions on everyone's faces. He realized how things were going to change for him now that the little thoughts of doubt were no longer going to creep into his mind. He wished that every Christian could feel what he felt now. Having faith is one thing, but seeing the magnificence in person was another.

"What did he look like?" Millie asked and soon the questions were flying. Jacob answered them the best he could. After thirty minutes of questions, Jacob remembered the third letter he had put in his pocket. He pulled it out and everyone got quiet.

"I'll read this to everyone," Jacob said as he took the letter out of the envelope.

To whom it may concern, Letter Three

I have finally made it to the bottom of the mountain. The destruction I mentioned earlier is still everywhere. The land here turns into what I think is a desert. If I look out across the desert, the sky looks lighter. It makes me wonder about my theory on the ash cloud. It is still dark and I still have to crawl along at a snail's pace. The dead bodies don't seem to be decaying very fast and I hope that I do not have to look at them forever. Maybe it takes time for decomposition and time is something that doesn't exist. When I look back up the mountain, I can still see glimpses of firelight from the castle. Memories from my mortal life started coming back some time ago. I think they started after I talked to my brother in the cave. If this is hell, I can't figure out why he was here. He was always the good one and I could never compete with that. I could feel the goodness in him, anyone who was around him could. I feel bad over the grief I caused him growing up. I remember loving him so much when we were young, but as I got older I wanted to be better than he was. I hated him, and for that, I am truly sorry. If I ever get to talk to him again, I will tell him so.

One of the rebels found me some time ago and I am now traveling with him. I am going with him to meet with the other rebels in his group. His name is Acubus. Actually, it was right after the visit from Jacob that I met him. Jacob warned me that someone was outside the cave before he vanished. I kicked dirt onto the fire, and as the last of the firelight vanished, I hid in the back of the cave. I heard him enter, light a torch, and look around the cave. I watched him for a while and I could see that at one time he was a beautiful creature, tall and muscular, though now he looked beaten down and tired. He carried himself with a sense of pride and I thought he was a great creature. He was built different from what I would call human. He had long black hair that fell to the middle of what I can only describe as wings. He used these wings much like a second pair of arms with small pinchers at the ends. His head was shaped like that of a human, but his eyes were extremely large and showed no color except for black. They were round and came to sharp points on the sides of his face. I wouldn't say he had a normal nose either. It was very narrow and came to a sharp point. His skin was almost white in appearance. His shoulders were very wide and angled down to his waist like the body of a swimmer. His legs, much like his arms, were very muscular, or at least what I could see exposed in the tunic he was wearing. His feet were built more like something you would see out of a prehistoric movie. The heel was sharpened into a claw, and where his toes should have been there were two large appendages with large talons. I noticed his hand had only two large fingers and an opposing thumb, each with long nails or claws.

I tried to be quiet, but he must have heard me. He finally told me to come out. I walked toward him and he told me to start a fire. I did what he commanded. He told me it would have done no good to hide anyway, because the smell of human had already given me away. After the fire was going, he looked at me and asked if I was Sara Bennington. I couldn't believe he knew my name. I told him that I was, and I asked him how he knew my name. He just laughed. I told him that I didn't know why that was funny, but he told me that someone was very upset that I had escaped. The group of rebels had heard about it and he was sent to find me before the horde did.

We sat by the fire for a time and talked. I asked him, "How did you end up here?" "My name is Acubus, I am a fallen angel."

"What do you mean by fallen?"

"After the time of creation, after man was created, there was a great rebellion in heaven. An angel named Lucifer, who had been told by the Creator of his intentions for man, led this

rebellion. Lucifer was of the highest order of angels and was greatly loved by the Creator. But he was jealous of this thing called man, and did not think it was fair for God to love half-breeds more than he loved his own heavenly creation."

Acubus told me later that Lucifer was always comparing (how did we put it on earth?) apples to oranges.

Acubus continued, "Lucifer turned many angels to his side and a war ensued. It did not last long, if you can imagine, trying to fight against the Creator."

"I remembered some of this story from childhood, but I never put much stock in those stories."

Laughing loudly, he told me, "That is how it works."

"How does what work?"

"Humans had the same power that the first fallen had; it is called free will. The free will in heaven is a little different from the free will on earth, but we all had to make the same choice eventually. After our fall from grace, Lucifer made it every fallen angel's mission to cloud man's judgment when it came to the love of the Creator. Lucifer believed if he took enough souls from the Creator, he could eventually win the war against him. Lucifer took down Adam and Eve so quickly, we actually thought he might stand a chance. Lucifer believed that if he took the first of the Creator's creation, then the Creator's plan would be ruined. This idea worked well for thousands of mortal years, until the Creator sent His son to earth to be killed by the same creatures that he loved. Imagine if you would, the spirit of the Creator became man, and with the perfect sacrifice, set all the condemned souls free. Up to that point, except for a few

of the Creator's chosen ones, only a sinless soul could make it to heaven. Lucifer thought he had won. A lot of us supported Lucifer until that time, but when many of the captured souls were set free, some of us knew we had chosen the wrong side. Some still believe that Lucifer stands a chance if he can take enough souls, but those of us who are rebelling know we are doomed to spend eternity in this place."

He compared Lucifer's plight to keeping butterflies in jars. What are the chances of the butterflies ganging up and destroying the jar keeper? When he put it that way, I understood. God was the jar keeper and the rest of us were the butterflies.

I asked him how this place worked and he told me the three rules of hell.

One: No one leaves.

Two: There is only pain.

Three: You are here by choice.

Rule one means you are here forever, you can never leave. The Creator is not going to change his mind. You cannot die to escape. Sleep is not an option for escape because it does not exist.

Rule two means what it says. The only thing in this place is pain. The only thing to look forward to is when the pain ends. The only measurement of time in hell is the time it takes to inflict a wound multiplied by the multiplier.

"What is the multiplier?" I asked.

"Six hundred and sixty six," he replied simply with a smirk. "If you put your hand in the fire for a count of six in hell, (He drew a horizontal line six inches long in the dirt.) "It takes six

counts, (pointing again to the line in the dirt), multiplied by six hundred and sixty-six seconds, to heal." (Next to the line in the dirt, he drew an X, and then he wrote the number, 666.)

It looked like this (---- X 666). "I understood everything, except, if there is no time here, how do you know that it took six seconds to receive a wound?"

He shook his head, because I wasn't getting the point. (Pointing back to the line he drew in the dirt). "The line might be one inch long, or it might be twenty seven inches long. The length of the line depends on the length of time it takes to receive the injury. If you are cut with a knife the injury time is short. If you are thrown into the river of fire and are immersed for a count of thirty, the injury time is longer. Do you understand?"

"Yes, I do." I then asked him, "How is the pain here different from the pain on earth?"

"It's pure."

"What do you mean?"

"During mortal existence the Creator put so many little defenses into the human body that a human only experienced pure pain for seconds. Think back to when you injured yourself on earth. Did you ever burn yourself on something hot?"

"Yes."

"Do you remember the initial pain," he asked? "Do you remember for that split second it was the only thing your human mind could focus on? Then what happened? Soon your human body started putting out chemicals that dulled the pain, or some humans would go into shock or even pass out.

Even with the worst injury, your mortal body had ways to deal with pain. Pain here is like the initial pain you felt at the time of any injury during mortal life, and it does not end until its time is done. You cannot get away from it. Do not be fooled into thinking that because I was once an angel that I can stop pain. Even the Creator's angels cannot stop pain or suffering without his power. Once a human is wounded in hell, the time it takes to heal cannot be changed. However, Lucifer and his legion will tell you that if you do things their way, they will not cause you any pain. What is that worth to a human soul that has nothing to look forward to except an eternity of pain?"

Acubus then explained the third rule, which I did understand. "It was everyone's own choice to be here. Do not blame anyone but yourself. Every single human is designed with the knowledge of the Creator built in. It was your clouded choice to reject the gifts of God." He chuckled when he said the last statement.

I asked him a few other questions. "What powers do the fallen have?"

"We can no longer move as fast as we once did, since we were given a physical body at the time of judgment. We still have strength superior to that of humans. We also have great knowledge gained through years of watching humans, not to mention the spiritual knowledge we have from being angels. We cannot read your thoughts, but you had better believe we know what you are thinking. Think back to when you were a child in the mortal world, and of the things you knew then. Now remember back to the time right before you died, look at the knowledge you gained in that short period of time. Now

multiply that by the number of years since creation. Do you understand what I am talking about?"

"Yes. What exactly is this place?" I asked.

"Lucifer and his minions wanted the earth so badly that the Creator gave it to them at the end of time. At least what was left of it after the last great battle, and there was not much left. Kind of ironic, is it not? When the Creator's influence was removed from the earth there was nothing left that a human would recognize."

"Why is there no light?"

"This kingdom is deep inside the earth. The temperature difference comes from across the desert where the opening to upper earth exists. The barren surface blows icy-cold air into this place and the heat and cold are constantly at war.

"What about the prison compound I saw when I first arrived?"

"That is Lucifer's palace, and all the human souls that enter hell go through there first. Humans enter the castle and Lucifer shows them exactly what he can do to them if they don't pledge their loyalty to their new king. Humans that are sentenced with a certain punishment go to their assigned locations, and the ones that have no specific punishment, either go in the service of the king or choose the alternative. The screaming you heard was his little way of showing what power he has to cause pain and anguish to the ones that choose the alternative.

Lucifer has an affinity for government. It seems to be his only hobby. However, remember Lucifer may rule this kingdom, but the Creator is still the landlord, so there are limits to Lucifer's powers, but I would try to stay as far away from him as possible.

"Why is Lucifer still the ruler here?"

"This place is ruled like the feudal system of mortal earth. Lucifer has all the power for now. It is every man for himself here, or angel in my case. Dog eat dog, is the phrase humans used, I believe."

He went on to tell me that a number of the first fallen have banded together and are planning to wage war against Lucifer. I asked him if they had any humans on their side, and he told me that they didn't. He went on to explain why. "What can you do against a legion of fallen angels?" Answering his own question, he replied, "Nothing."

"I don't agree. You have a physical body, don't you?"

"Yes," he replied.

I asked if he would allow me to show him something, and he nodded. I motioned for him to hold out his hand, and he did. I then pulled out the knife I had found on one of the dead soldiers. Gently at first, then, gradually pressing harder until I was using all my human strength, I ran the blade roughly across his palm. A small slit opened up and he flinched just a little. I have to admit if I would had done this to a human hand I would have easily sliced through it, but I had injured the creature. I thought he was going to rip my head off; I could tell that he was angered. He looked at me for a few moments and then laughed.

"Let me show you something, human."

I figured I owed him that much. "All right."

He asked for my hand and I gave it to him. He lifted his hand and extended what I would call his index finger. A claw seemed to grow out of that finger, and as effortlessly as I could poke my finger through a piece of cake, he quickly ran it through the palm of my hand. I did not scream, but the pain was some of the most intense that I ever felt. If I still had the ability, I would have wet myself, but I refused to make a sound. I looked him in the eye for what seemed like an eternity, when he finally told me to look at my hand. I looked down and the cut had healed, and as quickly as I received the wound, it was gone. "Humans are soft and weak in this world.

I asked him if I could travel with him and he said that I must, because he thought I might be the chosen one. I asked him what he meant by this, but he ignored my question. He warned me that the fallen blamed humans for their misfortune and he did not know how they would react to being in my midst. I told him I didn't care and that I didn't want to stay here alone. I'm glad to find Acubus. I'm going to end this letter now.

Sara Bennington

Jacob finished reading and set the letter down on the table. He looked at the three people sitting around the table and could see they were as hypnotized as he was by the words in the letter.

"That is incredible!" Jonathon said like a child seeing a circus for the first time.

"You are a disturbed old man," Millie said, looking at Jonathon with a mocking disbelief.

"That's not a place I would ever want to visit," Cathy added.

Everyone looked at Jacob, who was still staring at the letter. He was still having trouble believing all this, even with the visit from the stranger.

The four of them spent the rest of the afternoon discussing the contents of the letter. Cathy asked them to stay for supper, but Millie couldn't stay and Jonathon was going to head back to Indianapolis. Millie told everyone goodbye and told Jacob she would see him tomorrow. Cathy noticed the look Millie gave Jonathon as she was walking out the door, but didn't say anything. Jacob helped Jonathon take his bag to the car.

"What should I do now?" Jacob asked, putting Jonathon's bag in the back seat of the car.

"I want to talk to a couple of people first. We will have to figure out the best way to bring these to the world. I'll keep you up to date with everything that is going on," Jonathon said, opening the driver's door of his car. Jonathon became serious, then said, "Remember what the stranger told you. Be careful not to get yourself into trouble when you're dreaming, and if you do, you know who to ask for." Jonathon looked at his watch and said abruptly, "I've got to get going."

"What's your hurry? Aren't you retired?" Jacob asked.

Jonathon smiled and climbed into his car. He started the engine, and began backing out of the drive and then stopped. Jacob, seeing Jonathon roll down the window, walked over to Jonathon's car.

"Something just hit me. Remember what the stranger said about Lucifer not liking the idea of people seeing into his world?"

Jacob replied, "Yeah…your point?"

"Well, just be careful, okay," Jonathon said with a smile, then backed out onto the road. When he had driven out of sight, Jacob went back into the house. Cathy was standing at the stove fixing supper and both of the children were sitting at the kitchen table. Mara was coloring and Michael was reading a book.

Lifting up the picture she was working on to show Jacob, she said. "How do you like my picture, Uncle Jacob?"

"It is very nice, Mara. What are you reading, Michael?" Jacob asked.

"It's a book about dinosaurs," Michael answered.

Jacob realized that watching the children was like turning the clock back to when Sara and he were children. Mara was outgoing and confident, while Michael was quiet and withdrawn. The difference between Jacob and Michael was that Jacob had both parents to support him while growing up. Jacob suddenly wondered how they would end up with the loss of their parents. He also wondered what he would have been like without the love and support of his parents.

"You're in la-la land again, dear," Cathy said, breaking Jacob's train of thought.

"What did you say?" Jacob asked, catching only a little of what Cathy said.

"Never mind, space case. Are you ready to eat?"

"Yeah, I'm always ready for that," Jacob said, pulling a chair out to sit down. They said grace and began to eat.

"Honey, did you notice that Jonathon was in a real hurry to leave?" Jacob asked before taking his first bite.

"Yes, I did. I wonder if he might have made a detour on his way home."

"Yeah, that's what I was thinking. You don't suppose he stopped by Millie's place? When we were on our way to pick up the pizza, he asked me all about her."

They both laughed about the possibility of a budding new romance. They finished supper and the nightly routine ensued. After the children were tucked into bed, Cathy and Jacob both agreed they were tired and that it was time to go to bed. They were both asleep in a matter of minutes.

Chapter Eleven

Jacob was walking in what he thought was some kind of desert, the temperature still fluctuating between hot and cold, but the overall atmosphere was a little more bearable. The wind blew from different directions, making it hard to walk in a straight line. The smell wasn't as bad here as it had been closer to the castle. It was not as dark as it had been before, making it easier to navigate the rough terrain. Bodies could be seen every now and then, but not as abundant as before. He walked for some time before he saw a flicker of light off in the distance. As he got closer to the light, he could see that it was a small square structure made out of dirt and rock, no bigger than a single-car garage. There was firelight reflecting through a hole in the wall, cautiously he walked up to it and peered in. He saw Sara and someone sitting together by a fire. Jacob figured it was the fallen angel from the last letter. She still had the characteristics of a nervous squirrel, moving in quick, jerky little motions, rocking forward and backward. Jacob could hear them talking in a low murmur, but couldn't understand what they were saying. He continued around the building until he found an opening in the wall. Carefully he walked in and sat down by his sister. "Hello." Sara jumped at the sound of his voice, but the creature didn't seem to be startled.

"Jacob, is that you?" Her eyes darted around like that of a caged animal. "Acubus, it's my brother. Can you see him? Acubus, can you see my brother?" Acubus remained silent.

"Yes, it's me. Who's your friend, Sara?" Jacob asked.

"Why can't I see you? I want to see you," Sara said, still looking around trying to find him.

"I don't know why you can't see me, Sara. Who is that sitting next to you?" Jacob asked again, this time a little more loudly.

"His name is Acubus."

Jacob looked at Acubus and to his surprise, Acubus looked right back at him.

"Yes, I can see and hear you. I could smell you long before you entered the building. Sara didn't tell me she had a preacher for a brother. It is not often that you see a preacher in this place. Well, I should say that you do not see a faithful preacher in this place. You do know where you are, Preacher?" Acubus asked, picking up a stick and poking the fire.

"Yes, I know. I know you were with Lucifer when the rebellion took place in heaven," Jacob replied, never breaking eye contact with the creature. There was a look of surprise, if only for a split second, that showed on the creature's face. "How did you know I was a preacher?" Jacob asked the large creature.

"I can smell it on you. You have something that we never see around here. I believe you would call it hope. It has a definite odor."

"Acubus, can you see my brother?" Sara interrupted, never stopping the rocking back and forth.

"Yes, I can see him. Why is he here, Sara?" Turning to look at Jacob, the creature spoke directly to him. "How is it that you are here? I can tell that you are not of this world. You have not died."

"I am here to talk to my sister," Jacob said. He looked closely at the creature and remembered what Sara had written about him in the last letter. He was a magnificent being. Tall and broad, his voice had a reverent tone that echoed in Jacob's ears and mind. Because Jacob wasn't ready to trust this creature yet, he didn't want to give him too much information.

"How is it that you are here, Preacher?" Acubus asked again, this time with a little more authority in his voice.

At first, Jacob couldn't figure out why the creature was so concerned about his presence here, but then it dawned on him that creature might think he was a spy. "I'm not here as a spy. Your rebellion means nothing to me." Jacob saw a second look of surprise on the creature's face with his last statement.

"How do you know about the rebellion?" Acubus asked, standing up abruptly and backing away from the fire. "I want to know why you are here." This time he was demanding an answer with a loud voice.

"Acubus, leave my brother alone," Sara pleaded.

"It's okay, Sara; I'll tell you both what I know." Hoping to maintain a sense of calm, Jacob motioned for Acubus to have a seat. Then the thought of where he was and the idea of keeping this situation under control suddenly caused him to laugh.

Giving him a strange look, Acubus sat down and asked, "What is so funny, Preacher?"

"Nothing is funny," Jacob said, dropping the humor from his voice. Realizing that he shouldn't make the creature any more nervous than he already was, he continued, "I was told by an angel that I would be allowed to visit my sister here. I don't know why and I don't know how…but here I am." Turning to his sister he asked, "How are you, Sara?"

"I'm okay," Sara answered. She looked over to where Acubus was sitting. "Acubus, would you please wait outside for a bit?"

"Yes, I will wait outside, but before I leave, I want to understand something. You are the spirit of a human who is still alive in earth time. You are a preacher of faith and you are this woman's blood relative." Jacob nodded. "Do you share the same day of birth with this woman?"

Jacob nodded again, then asked, "Why are you asking me these questions?"

Not saying a word, Acubus stood up and left through the opening in the wall. Jacob could tell by the look the creature gave Sara that he did not like being asked to leave.

Jacob moved closer to his sister and asked, "Sara, how are you doing here?" Sara didn't reply. Jacob added, "I guess there is no need to ask, is there?"

"No, there is no reason. This is not a place anyone would choose to stay, if they knew the truth," Sara said, still rocking back and forth.

"You're right, Sara. I'm sorry I asked."

"It's okay, Jacob. I don't want you to feel sorry for me. I know this is my own fault, Acubus told me that"

"Sara, what do you remember about our childhood?"

Sara, still rocking, took a deep breath and spoke softly. "I can remember everything now, Jacob… I remember how I treated you when we were growing up."

"Why did you do the things you did? Why did you treat Mom and Dad like you did?" Jacob asked.

"Mom and Dad were always saying how good you were and what a good heart you had. I could never be like you," Sara said, starting to rock a little faster.

"Sara! Mom and Dad were always saying how good you were at sports. I could never have been the athlete you were. We may have been twins, but we were two different people," Jacob said in reply.

Sara, staring into the fire, turned in the direction of Jacob's voice and asked, "Can you ever forgive me? Do you think Mom and Dad forgave me before they died?"

"Mom and Dad loved you so much. I never heard them say one angry word about you when they were alive. I think they understood something I didn't. I don't know what it is, but now that Cathy and I are raising Michael and Mara, I think I'm going to find out."

"How are they? I miss them so much." Sara suddenly started to cry. Jacob was surprised by her show of emotion. He didn't remember her ever showing any emotion except anger when she was alive on earth. Sara, still sobbing, continued loudly, "I never appreciated them when I was alive, but now I would give anything to hug them one more time." Sara, now sobbing uncontrollably, was now rocking back and forth so fast that she reminded him of a psychiatric patient in an asylum. "I was so busy trying to hide in my work that I didn't spend any time with my husband or my children the last few years I was alive. Do you know what I told Scott the night we died?" Not giving Jacob a chance to answer, she continued with her confession. "I told him I wanted a divorce. I told him that I had an affair and that I didn't want to be married to him anymore. That's the last thing I said to him before the car hit us." Sara suddenly got quiet. She stopped crying, and for the first time, she stopped rocking. Then, looking right to where Jacob was sitting she said, "I'm not mad at God because I'm here." She then said in a louder voice, "This is what I deserve. I deserve to be damned for eternity!"

They both sat for a bit without saying a word. Jacob finally broke the silence. "I forgive you, Sara."

"Thank you, Jacob."

A thought suddenly hit Jacob. "There is something you could do for your children!" Jacob said with an air of excitement.

"What could I do from here?" Sara asked, with a confused look.

"Sara, you know the letters you have been writing?"

"Yes?"

"Someone sent them to me! I got all three of them! Write a letter to the children telling them what you just told me. They will need to hear those words from you some day."

For the first time during her existence in hell, Sara smiled.

"Sara, I wish I could help you, but there is nothing I can do," Jacob said.

"I know. Acubus told me that this was my choice, and now that I'm here there is no leaving," Sara replied.

"Did you ever have faith?" Jacob asked her.

"I remember hearing the stories in Sunday school and remember what Mom and Dad used to tell us when we were children."

"But did you ever believe?"

"No," Sara said in a remorseful tone.

"Why not?" Jacob asked. "Didn't you ever question what happened to us when we die?"

"I don't think I wanted to know."

Jacob thought to himself for a bit, then said, "I think that's Lucifer's plan. I think his plan is to keep the human mind so busy with worldly thoughts, cares, and desires, that the questions that matter will never be asked."

"They were always in the back of my mind. I know that now."

"It is written on everyone's soul, but if it's not given the time to grow, it's as useless as a seed planted in dry dirt." Jacob reached out and touched her hand.

"What was that? Did you just touch my hand?" Sara said, moving closer to the where the touch came from.

"It's me, Sara," Jacob said gently. "Stand up, would you?"

Sara did what was asked of her and she stood up.

"Don't be afraid. I want to give you a hug."

"Okay," Sara said timidly.

Jacob moved close to his sister and put his arms around her. Sara moved to hug him in return. While Jacob hugged her, he whispered in her ear.

"Sara, I don't trust this creature you are with, be careful… I love you." After whispering the message in her ear, he let go of her. A feeling of relief washed over Jacob. He had finally forgiven Sara after all these years. Jacob realized that this was not for Sara's sake, but this was meant for him. To help him finally forget the anger and hatred he had felt toward her. "I'm going to go now. I don't think I will see you again." Jacob's eyes started to well up. There was nothing he could do to help her in this place and the thought of that was hard to bear. "Remember to write the letter to Michael and Mara."

"I will. Goodbye, Jacob."

Jacob opened his eyes and was back in his bedroom in Illinois. He looked at Cathy who was sleeping soundly. He looked at the clock. It was four A.M.

Chapter Twelve

Early the next morning, Jacob and Cathy were enjoying coffee together after getting the children on the bus for another day of school. Mondays were Cathy's day off, so Jacob made it his day off also. She had already put the bed sheets in the washer and he had already showered. The odor was not as bad as the previous two dreams, but it was still present when Jacob awoke. Cathy joked with her husband that with all the extra bathing he would probably start to rust.

Jacob told Cathy about his journey from last night's dream. Explaining that it must have been part of God's plan for him to forgive his sister. Cathy agreed. Cathy told Jacob that she was going to start to clean the house and for him to get lost. Jacob gave her a kiss, then headed over to his office. He sat at his desk, thinking about the last few days' events, when the telephone rang. He picked it up before the second ring. "Hello, this is Pastor Jacob Litchfield of St. John's Lutheran Church. How may I help you?"

"Hello, Jacob! You sound so impressive when you answer that way."

Jacob recognized Jonathon's voice instantly. "Hello, you old geezer, did you have a good trip home?"

"Yes, I did."

"What time did you get home?"

"Oh, I don't know, probably around ten."

"You mean it took you six hours for you to get back to Indy. You must have stopped somewhere for a long, long dinner."

"Have you been talking to Millie?" Jonathon asked.

"Well, I guess I don't have to now, do I?" Jacob said laughing.

"I fell right into that, didn't I?"

"Yes, you did. Did you have a nice time?" Jacob asked.

"Yes, we did. I think I might have two reasons to visit the flatlands of Illinois now."

"Well, that's good. So, did you just call to confess about your secret dinner, or is there something else you want?"

"Well, I was wondering if you could send me a copy of Sara's letters. I would like to show them to Pastor Abrams. You remember him; he's the pastor who replaced me when I retired."

"Yeah, I met him at your retirement party. Are you sure you want to involve him in all this?" Jacob asked.

"Jacob, those letters are amazing, and I think you should stop worrying about what everyone will think about them."

"Well, you… You might be right. I'll fax them to you right away," Jacob said. He told Jonathon about the dream from the night before and when he had finished, he told Jonathon he would send the letters right over.

"I'll call you when I get them."

"Okay. Take care, Jonathon," Jacob said and hung up the phone. He laughed to himself about Jonathon and Millie's little rendezvous. He couldn't wait to tease Millie about the fact that he knew. He walked over to the house to get the three letters. He also grabbed the two letters he received earlier from Sara when she was still living, thinking it might be a good comparison for Pastor Abrams. Once back at his office, he placed the five pieces of paper in the fax machine, dialed the number, and pressed the send button. The machine did its job, running each paper through one by one, finally beeping to tell him that the task was accomplished. He went back to work at his desk. The phone rang again. He figured it was Jonathon so it picked it up and answered it with a simple hello. Jonathon told him only two of the letters made it through and that something must have gone wrong with the other ones. Jacob told him he would try it again. After hanging up the phone, Jacob carefully faxed each piece of paper again. Everything seemed to work okay so he went back to work. The phone rang again. It was Jonathon.

"Only two came through again. I don't think your machine is working, Jacob."

"Well, all the letters fed through okay. I don't know." Then a sudden thought struck Jacob and he asked, "Which ones didn't go through?"

"Hang on I'll look." After a few seconds Jonathon was back on the phone. "All I have here are the two old letters from your sister. You know the one from when your parents died and the one from when you decided to enter the seminary."

"That's what I thought. Hang on one minute, I want to try something." Jacob picked up the three newest letters and walked over to the copy machine. He laid the first letter on the glass and shut the lid. He pressed the copy button and the machine came to life, spitting out a clean piece of white paper. He put the next letter on the glass, repeated the previous action, only to get the same result. Then he placed one of the earlier letters on the glass and pressed copy. This time when he picked up the ejected piece of paper, it was a perfect copy of the original. He picked up the phone. "Jonathon, you are not going to believe this, but I can only copy the two letters she sent to you before she died."

"That's amazing. Do you think someone doesn't want those letters to be copied?"

"Who? Who do you think is responsible for this?" Jacob asked.

"Did you mention anything about the letters to the fallen angel?" Jonathon asked.

"No, not while he was in the building, but that doesn't mean he wasn't listening from outside. I forgot where I was and who I was dealing with. Maybe Sara mentioned it to him. I'm afraid Sara trusts him too much and I told her that."

"Remember what I said, Jacob. Lucifer will not appreciate the fact that his kingdom might be exposed. His main objective is to hide. Without belief in him, would anyone need to believe in God?"

"Yes, I remember what you said. I guess I'm having trouble with the idea that Lucifer would think that these letters would make that much of a difference."

"Well, I think he will do anything he can to avoid being exposed," Jonathon said.

"Try one thing for me, would you? Do you have a lighter or some matches in your office?"

"Yes. What do you want me to do with them?" Jacob asked.

"Light a corner of one of the last three letters, but be careful not to let it go up in smoke."

"Okay," Jacob said. He opened his desk drawer and picked up a book of matches. Lighting a match, he held it up to one of the last letters. The flame danced around the corner of the paper, but it was not consumed by the fire. "It didn't burn," Jacob said.

"Well, does that give you the answer you wanted?" Jonathon asked.

"What do you mean? What answer are you looking for?"

"God is protecting the letters," Jonathon said, getting excited.

"Why wouldn't God let me make copies?" Jacob asked.

"I don't know, maybe it's all part of the miracle," Jonathon answered.

"Maybe so, but what if the devil is the one that's not letting it be copied? Sara's third letter pretty much outlines the power that Lucifer holds. But it said nothing about him being able to manipulate earthly objects," Jacob argued. He thought for a minute, and then whispered, "Wait a minute." He jumped up from his chair, grabbed the last letter, and walked over to the mirror in his office. Carefully unfolding it, he held the written side up to the mirror. "Nothing," he murmured to himself. Jacob went back to his desk and picked up the receiver. "The writing does not reflect in the mirror."

"What?" Jonathon said with disbelief. "Why?"

"I don't know why," Jacob answered.

"That's why the copier and the fax machine wouldn't work. Do you think it might be the fact that the letters were written in a different dimension?"

"I don't know. We're dealing with something way beyond our experience."

"Yes, I agree with you on that," Jacob said. "I tell you what. I will type out the letters on my computer, and then fax them to you. At least Pastor Abrams could then read them and give you his opinion."

"That sounds good," Jonathon said.

"Well, take care of yourself old friend, and be careful." They said their goodbyes. Jacob began typing out the first letter. When he had finished, he then printed it out. Well, at least it printed, he thought. He placed the newly printed copy on the copy machine to see if it would copy and it worked fine. He went back to his desk, typed out the last two letters, and printed them. He put the copies in the fax machine and sent all three to Jonathon. He never received a call, so he figured they must have gone through. He sat at his desk wondering about the letters. The only thing that kept running through his mind was that this was an amazing miracle, but why him? Why was he the one that was chosen for all this? With all that had happened in the last two months, he didn't need the distraction. "The Lord works in mysterious ways," he said to himself.

Chapter Thirteen

tevie "Moony" Jenkins was a twenty-one-year-old man, obsessed with his desire for crystal meth. Being a slave to meth had turned him into a picture of human wreckage. At first he was fooled into thinking he had control over his little addiction, but in time it grew into an uncontrollable monster, finally growing to the point where he didn't even try to hide it anymore. Starting with a few harmless drags on a joint one day after high school, his weakness escalated into a full-blown crystal meth addiction. Growing up in a small town south of Champaign, Illinois, the kids had called him "moon face" or "moony" due to his protruding chin. He grew to almost six feet and at one time would have been considered muscular. He grew long brown curly hair in high school to help hide what he considered to be his facial imperfection. This also helped him fit in with the stoner crowd. Four years of drug abuse, coupled with a total lack of hygiene, had made him into what he was today, a six-foot tall, bone-skinny, long-haired grease ball. Stevie's friends, one after another, had turned their backs on him, except for his roommate, Jimmy. To Stevie, the others were judgmental idiots.

Their apartment was riddled with different small appliances left in pieces from bouts of tweaking. The crystal meth had rotted

Stevie's teeth and his face had a splotchy red rash, but in his mind, when high, he thought of himself as handsome. Today he was feeling ugly. He'd been told by a user friend to meet him at one o'clock that afternoon. Stevie had been fired from his bartending job at a little hole-in-the-wall pub a couple of weeks ago and now he was broke. He was counting on his friend spotting him just enough to get by until he could find another job. The guy had better come through with the stuff. He shut the lights off as he was walking out of the door, when he heard a voice. He wasn't sure whether it came from the hallway or from inside his apartment. Looking back into the apartment and then leaning out into the hallway, he said, "If somebody is talking to me, I didn't hear it." He heard it again. Stevie thought he recognized the voice, but he couldn't be sure.

"Moony," the voice said in a reverberating tone.

This time Stevie heard the voice clearly and he answered, "What do you want? Who are you?"

"Moony, I can tell you are not feeling very well, are you?"

Stevie was starting to get nervous and went back into his apartment. Since he'd started using his little treats, fear of the police was always in the back of his mind. "Leave me alone, I'm not doing anything."

"Moony, I just want to be your friend. I do not think you have many of them left, do you?"

"How do you know that?" Stevie asked, walking from room to room, looking for whoever was speaking.

"I can help you, Moony. I can give you what you need. Do you want my help, Moony?"

"What do you think I need? You don't know anything about what I need," Stevie said as he opened the door to the last room in his dumpy little apartment.

"Look at yourself, Moony. You are a quivering mess. You need some treats, don't you, Moony? You see, I do know you."

Stevie licked his lips at the mention of treats. He wouldn't have to take the time to get the meth from his buddy now. Stevie had no money because that asshole at the bar had fired him for being late. No one understood him and he was getting tired of judgmental assholes. "What do you know about treats?" Stevie asked.

"I know everything there is to know about treats, but I need your help first, Moony. Can we come to some kind of agreement?"

"What do you want me to do?" Stevie asked. He wondered to himself if he was starting to lose it, but the voice sounded so kind and soothing, and it had been a couple of days since he talked to anyone.

"I want you to go to Indianapolis. I have something for you to do there. When you accomplish your given tasks, I will give you all the treats you want."

"I don't have enough money to get to Indianapolis. I'm broke."

"Your neighbor is gone, and I know he keeps an envelope of money in the drawer next to his sink."

"Yeah, that's a good idea. He's an asshole anyway." Stevie left the apartment and went down the hall. He stopped at his neighbor's door, looking around to make sure the coast was clear. He tried the door, but it was locked. He put his weight against it, but it didn't give.

"Hit it hard, Moony! It will open," the voice said from behind.

Stevie threw his full weight against the door and it flew open. He went to the kitchen and opened the drawer as described by the voice. In it was an envelope stuffed full of twenty-dollar bills. It must have been around four hundred dollars. Stevie left the apartment thinking that it was going to be nice to have a guardian angel. He went to his car and left the parking lot.

"That was easy, was it not?" the voice asked.

"That was cool. What do you want me to do in Indy?"

They talked all the way to Indianapolis.

Chapter Fourteen

Jonathon, combing his hair in the bathroom, was getting ready to take the letters that Jacob had sent him to the minister of Our Savior Lutheran Church. Pastor Abrams reminded him of the Lutheran ministers from his youth, and Jonathon liked that about him. With steel-blue eyes that could scare the rebelliousness out of any disobedient child, he was a man that nobody messed with. He had a good heart and a strong faith and Jonathon felt he'd left the church in good hands with Pastor Abrams. The morning's events still weighed heavily on Jonathon's mind. He couldn't believe that the letters would not copy or fax. Somebody was busy on the other side working to accomplish something, but *who* was the question. Jonathon put on his coat and headed out to his car. started the engine, and backed out of the garage and out onto the street. He looked at his watch; he had an hour before the time he'd told Pastor Abrams they would meet. Jonathon decided to run to the bank on his way to the church.

Stevie arrived in Indianapolis late Monday afternoon. He was feeling terrible, but the voice kept telling him he would be okay and to just keep driving. The voice was so soothing,

Stevie thought. Zooming in and out of traffic on the bypass that borders Indianapolis, he was glad not to be alone.

"Turn here," the voice said.

"Okay. I'm hungry; I've got to eat something." Stevie never got a reply either way and pulled into a McDonald's. He parked the car and walked in. What is everyone looking at, Stevie thought to himself? People were working hard to get out of his way. He walked up to the counter to order. He tried to read the menu up on the wall, but they put those things so far back he couldn't see it clearly.

"Hurry up and get out of here!" the voice said loudly in his head.

"Why?" Stevie spat.

People in the order line were trying not to stare at the strange man talking to himself, but Stevie was making it difficult. He shuddered with every breath he took. Moving ahead in line, he placed his shaking hands on the counter and ordered his meal.

"I want a hamburger and fries," Stevie said to the lady behind the counter.

"What would you like on your sandwich, sir?" she asked.

Stevie stood without answering the clerk for a few seconds. "I said I want a hamburger and fries!" Stevie barked.

"I know that sir, what do you want on it?" she said, trying to keep her composure.

Stevie, confused at first by the question, finally understood. "Ketchup, mustard and pickle," he said, looking around at the people who were watching him. "What are you fucking people looking at?" he screamed.

Everyone, suddenly minding his or her own business, looked back toward the counter trying not to stare. The girl passed him the food and then he left the restaurant. He climbed into his car, and the voice told him where to go. Stevie drove for about ten minutes, and then pulled up to the curb across from an old church and parked. Eating his sandwich, he asked, "What now?" with part of a French fry hanging from his mouth.

"Just be patient," the voice told him.

"How long are we going to sit here? I feel like shit," Stevie complained.

"Just a little bit longer, he will be here soon," the voice said.

"Who'll be here soon?" Stevie asked, gripping the steering wheel tightly.

"Would you shut up! Soon you will have more treats than you will know what to do with!"

The thought of the euphoria that was soon to come settled Stevie down. He would do anything to procure the feeling. No more pain, no more fear, well at least for a little while. That was the trouble with the treats; they never seemed to last as long as they used to, but for those fifteen to twenty minutes everything is perfect. Stevie thought back to a few years earlier when he was a gangly boy in high school. He never played sports or competed in physical activities. He was always referred to as a loser. Well, not anymore; his new friend was going to make sure of that. Besides the feeling of insects crawling under his skin, he was feeling good about himself today.

Jonathon finished at the bank, then drove to the church. The parking lot ran the whole length of the west side of the church grounds. He pulled in the south end of the lot, just north of the two handicap spots, and parked near some trees. The West Fall Creek Parkway ran along the south end of the church's triangle-shaped parking lot, and Jonathon could hear the cars passing by. Darkness came early this afternoon with the help of the overcast sky.

"There he is. Kill him in the parking lot and get the letters; you will have your treats," the voice said in a caressing tone.

"What do you mean kill him?" Stevie asked, starting to panic. Stevie could see what he thought was an old man in the car.

"Kill him for treats! Get the letters! Kill him for treats! Get the letters! Kill him for treats! Get the letters! Kill him for treats! Get the letters!" The voice repeated the words soothingly over and over in Stevie's mind. He got out of his car that was parked in the street on the west side of the church parking lot. Stevie was saying the words to himself as he walked into the parking lot. How was he going to kill the old man, he thought to himself.

"Check your coat pocket," the voice said in his mind.

He felt around in his coat pockets and found a pocket knife with a four-inch serrated blade. Where did that come from, he wondered. It didn't matter anyway. Now that he had his new friend he would have to get used to all these new surprises.

Jonathon shut off the car and grabbed the letters. He got out of the car; pushing the lock button on his keychain. The car horn chirped to signify that the electronic lock had been activated. He turned around and started walking toward the church. He heard someone behind him.

"Kill him for treats! Get the letters! Kill him for treats! Get the letters!" Stevie was saying the words aloud as he walked toward the old man. He could see the letters the voice had told him to get. He quickened his pace as he neared the old man. In his mind, the words kept playing over and over. "Kill him for treats! Get the letters! Kill him for treats! Get the letters! Kill him for treats! Get the letters! Kill him for treats! Get the letters!"

Jonathon turned around and looked at the dirty man who was now within twenty feet of him and closing fast. He sensed that something bad was about to happen. Then he heard the words the man was chanting like a crazy mantra. Jonathon clutched the letters and ran for the church.

"Kill him for treats! Get the letters! Kill him for treats!" The words were playing so loud in Stevie's mind that they blocked everything else out. He looked down to see that the knife had found its way into his hand and was opened. Looking up again he saw the old man starting to run. He sprinted after him. "Kill him for treats! Get the letters! Kill him for treats!"

Jonathon heard him saying the words from within a few feet behind him and knew he was going to be caught in a matter of seconds. If only he could make it to the door! Jonathon felt a hand grab the back of his collar and felt himself jerk backwards. He saw the letters flying through the air as he fell. Hitting his head hard on the asphalt, he thought he was going to pass out, but then the weight of his attacker brought his mind back into focus. Seeing the knife at the last second, he tried to reach up and catch the man's arm.

"Kill him for treats! Get the letters! Kill him for treats!"

Jonathon managed to deflect the knife from entering his chest the first time, but felt it slice into his left shoulder. He remembered what Sara's last letter had said about the human body's ability to deal with pain. He realized that he didn't feel the first cut. The man drew back for another one; Jonathon tried to lift his left arm but it would hardly move. Trying to bring his right arm around to counter the blow, he missed and the four-inch blade sunk deep into his chest. He heard himself scream, but it was cut short when the blood from his wound filled his airways.

"Good job, Stevie! Don't stop! Finish him and get your treats!" *the voice said.*

Jonathon tried to defend himself, but his arms were so heavy. The man shoved the knife into his chest repeatedly. He was having trouble breathing and started choking. Every time he coughed, crimson specks covered his attacker's distorted face. Jonathon thought he saw something move behind his attacker but darkness was starting to filter into his mind and he could barely make out the man sitting on his legs. He wished the man on top of him would stop repeating those silly words. It dawned on him just as the darkness filled his mind. The attacker was talking about Sara's letters!

Chapter Fifteen

Stevie was pulling the knife out of the old man's chest for the last time when he heard someone yell behind him. He jumped up and scrambled to pick up the five pieces of paper scattered around the parking lot, and then ran as fast as he could to get to his car. He jumped in, started the engine, jammed it into gear, and gunned it. Tires squealing and the roar of the engine drowned out the voice in his head. He pulled out onto the West Fall Creek Parkway and headed south. He realized that the voice no longer was speaking in his mind and he welcomed the silence. He drove two or three blocks, and then merged onto the northbound lane of Interstate 65. What did I just do, he thought to himself. It all played back in his mind like a nightmare. He could see the surprise in the old man's eyes as he buried the knife deep into his chest. Like a slow-moving fog, panic crept into his tattered mind. Then the voice spoke for the first time since the murder of the old man.

"Good job, Stephen. I am going to call you Stephen now; you deserve a better name than Moony, especially with the good work you just accomplished," the voice said. "Now head back into Illinois, I have another job for you."

"But what about the treats?" Stevie asked in a panic.

"You don't have time right now. You need to find a place to clean yourself up.

You do not want anyone seeing the blood you have all over you, do you, Stephen?"

"No, you're right." Stevie continued to drive up I 65. He looked at himself in the rearview mirror and couldn't be certain that the face he saw was his. Blood-streaked and dirty, he hardly recognized himself.

"You look like a warrior who has just done battle with a great enemy. I bet if you were alive back in the time of kings you would have been a great warrior," the voice said, filling Stevie with pride.

"Yeah, a warrior," Stevie said to himself.

"If the worthless pukes that used to pick on you could see you now, they would not be laughing anymore."

"No, they wouldn't be laughing anymore," Stevie said, repeating what the voice was telling him.

After driving for an hour, the voice told him to find a place to park for a while. They had a couple of hours to kill. Doing as he was told, Stevie pulled off the main road and found an abandoned farm lot. There was an old tool shed in the back of the lot and Stevie hid the car behind it. The voice told him to burn the letters while they waited, and clean himself up. Finding a couple of old oil buckets filled with stagnant rain water, he wiped the blood off his face. He spent the rest of the time sitting in the car and fantasizing about the great warrior he had become.

Chapter Sixteen

Jacob and the family were settled in the living room watching television. Baths had been taken and the homework was finished. Cathy was reading the paper with her feet up on a footstool. Jacob was watching a sitcom with Michael and Mara. The phone rang but Jacob pretended not to hear it, causing Cathy to give him a dirty look as she got up to answer it in the kitchen. He couldn't hear what she was saying, but sensed by her tone that it wasn't good news. He got up and went to the kitchen. Cathy eyes were welling up with tears as she listened to the caller. She hung up the receiver and asked Jacob to have the children go upstairs. The children could tell by the tone in Jacob's voice they better not argue and went upstairs. Jacob came back into the kitchen to find Cathy sitting at the table, her head was buried in her hand and she was sobbing softly.

"What happened?" he asked.

"Sit down, Jacob. I have some bad news."

Jacob pulled out a kitchen chair and took a seat. "Tell me what happened," Jacob asked again, starting to get anxious.

Cathy took a deep breath. She looked at him, and then wiped her eyes with a tissue. "Jonathon was attacked in the parking lot at Pastor Abrams's church in Indianapolis."

"What do you mean attacked?"

"He was stabbed in the church parking lot, and Pastor Abrams doesn't think he has long to live. He also said it looked like he was attacked by someone looking for drug money," Cathy said, then started to cry.

"Oh my, God!" Jacob moaned. "Did he say what hospital he's in?"

Taking a moment to blow her nose and wipe away the tears that were streaming down her cheeks, she replied, "Clarion Methodist Hospital."

"That's a good hospital. I remember it from when I interned in Indy with Jonathon. He's in good hands," Jacob said.

"Are you leaving right away?" Cathy asked, already knowing the answer.

"Yes," Jacob said, as he got up from the table to go upstairs to get dressed.

Cathy yelled as he went up the stairs, "I'll make some coffee for the trip."

"What would I do without her?" he thought as he finished dressing. He then went to each child's bedroom and told them he had to leave because Pastor Jonathon had been in an accident. He gave them each a hug and told them goodbye. Cathy handed him a thermos and his coat as he reached the bottom of the stairs. Putting on his coat, he gave her a kiss, then headed out the door. He stopped, turned around and asked, "Where's my cell phone?"

"I put it in your coat pocket."

"Call Millie, tell her what happened, would you?" Jacob asked.

"I will," Cathy said, still wiping her nose. "Please be careful, Jacob."

"Yes, dear," he said. He gave her a weak smile, then left.

Chapter Seventeen

Jacob tried to drive under the speed limit, but his mind was wandering and his foot weighed heavily on the accelerator. He was angry at God for letting this happen to his friend and prayed for forgiveness for his thoughts. Selfishness wasn't a good reason for being angry and he knew better. He wondered if the letters had anything to do with the attack on Jonathon. What limits did Lucifer have when it came to influencing the human mind? Jacob surmised that a feeble mind was easier to manipulate, though he didn't mean feeble by the lack of intelligent thought, but a mind weakened by an outside influence, such as drugs or alcohol. A mind totally obliterated by drugs would be wide open to whatever thought was put into it. Who knew what effect someone's faith would have against the ghastly influence of a tempting devil, but surely a faithful mind would have more strength to stave off an attack from a dark influence than would an unfaithful mind. Jacob's mind filled with many questions during the two-hour trip. He didn't realize he was entering Indianapolis until he saw the sign for the 865 Bypass. There wasn't much traffic at this late hour, so he made it to the hospital without any trouble. He found a place to park, then ran into the hospital, telling the receptionist his name and asking her what room Pastor Jonathon Bailey was in. She looked at Jacob, pushed a button on the phone and waited a few seconds before she mumbled something into the receiver.

"Someone will be here in a second to take you to Rev. Bailey. Please have a seat over there," she said, pointing to a couch behind him.

In a few minutes, Jacob saw a man in his fifties wearing a security uniform walking toward him. "Are you Jacob Litchfield?" the man asked.

"Yes, I am."

"Please follow me."

Jacob followed the officer down a series of hallways until they came to the front desk of the ICU ward. The security officer excused himself and left.

"We have been expecting you, Mr. Litchfield," the nurse at the desk said.

"It's Pastor Litchfield, if you wouldn't mind."

"I'm sorry, Pastor Litchfield. Pastor Bailey has been asking for you," the nurse said. "Please follow me."

Jacob followed her to Jonathon's room. When the door opened, Jacob gasped when he looked into the room to see his friend lying there helpless in the mechanical bed. He could hardly recognize the man that had visited him last weekend.

"What is the prognosis?" Jacob asked the nurse.

"I'll have Dr. Cheever talk to you," The nurse answered, then quickly left the room.

Jacob walked up to the side of Jonathon's bed. An oxygen mask covered his pale face. Jacob could hear a monitor next to the bed amplifying his friend's heartbeat. He reached and took Jonathon's hand in his.

"What have I done to you?" Jacob whispered. Jonathon squeezed Jacob's hand at the sound of his voice. Jonathon's eye fluttered open, but he just stared blankly into space. He tried to say something but Jacob couldn't make it out. Jacob leaned closer to Jonathon to hear what the old man was trying to say.

"Let… letter," Jonathon whispered.

Jacob couldn't believe what he had just heard. Then he said something else.

"Kept saying…get the letters…get the letters." Jonathon closed his eyes again and appeared to have gone back to sleep. Then his grip tightened around Jacob's hand and he pulled him close. Jonathon's vision cleared. He looked directly into Jacob's eyes and said, "Get home…must protect…family." Then he faintly smiled and the monitor next to Jacob's head started to scream. A nurse ran into the room and hit a button on the wall. "*CODE BLUE ROOM TWO TWENTY-SEVEN!*" The intercom system announced throughout the ICU ward. Two more nurses sprinted into the room, one of them telling Jacob to get out. On his way out, he stepped aside to avoid the doctor who was responding to the call. He went into the waiting room, found a chair near a window and sat down. He prayed silently to himself.

Jacob looked up from praying. He could tell by the look on the faces of the medical crew leaving Jonathon's room that it had not gone well. The doctor he almost ran into a few second's ago, walked over to him.

"I'm Dr. Cheever. Are you the Jacob that Pastor Bailey was asking for?"

"Yes, I'm Pastor Jacob Litchfield," Jacob said, standing up.

They shook hands and Dr. Cheever continued, "I regret that I must tell you that Pastor Bailey didn't make it. He put up one heck of a fight, though. He had something he really wanted to tell you. I don't know how he lasted as long as he did. He had severe arterial damage to his chest and arms. We tried to repair it the best we could, but he'd lost too much blood."

"I'm sure you did everything you could, doctor. Thank you," Jacob said. The words the doctor had said about Jonathon really having something important to tell him suddenly sank in. Jacob quickly went to the nurse's desk to grab a piece of paper. He scribbled down his phone number, handed it to the doctor, then took off down the hallway. As he ran, he turned and yelled, "I've got to get home. You have my number!"

He heard the doctor say something about the police wanting to ask him some questions as he ran down the hallway, but at this point Jacob's only thought was to get home. He had a sick feeling that this was only the start of the trouble that was about to come. Jacob ran through the hospital and out to his car. Roaring out of the parking lot, he picked up his cell phone and dialed his home number. Thank God, Cathy answered.

"Hello," Cathy said in a tired voice.

"Cathy, Jonathon's gone."

"What hap…?"

"You've got to listen to me," he said, interrupting her. "I think somebody is after the letters! That's what Jonathon told me before he died. You have to warn Millie. Whoever is doing this is not fooling around and I'm afraid they're heading our way! Get Millie over to our house and lock the place down. I'm on my way right now!"

"Okay!" Cathy said, jumping out of bed. She had never heard her husband so frantic. She woke up the children, telling them to get dressed, then immediately went back into her bedroom to do the same.

Chapter Eighteen

After sitting for two hours and driving for another one, Stevie's body was screaming for a fix, but the words being repeated in his mind were overpowering. "You look like a great warrior. Stephen Jacobs is a great warrior." Except for the occasional driving directions, the voice was quiet on the return trip to Illinois. Stevie knew he was now somewhere north of Champaign, Illinois, but he was not familiar with the area.

"Where are we going?" Stevie asked.

"Just keep driving," the voice commanded.

Stevie followed the voice's directions until they pulled up in front of a little house on the edge of the small town.

"What do you want me to do?" Stevie asked.

"There is a woman in there who doesn't want you to have treats. You know the kind, the 'holier than thou' type."

"Yeah, I know the type, the ones who look at other people in disgust. The ones who like to judge people because they think they're better," Stevie said growing angry.

"You know it, Stephen. Go inside and show that bitch she shouldn't be judging people...and wanting to take their treats away!" The voice started chanting into Stevie's mind. "Kill

the bitch, she wants your treats! Kill the bitch, she wants your treats! Kill the bitch, she wants your treats!"

Stevie got out of the car and ran up to the front door. Without hesitation, he kicked it in. He ran through the house looking for the woman who wanted to take his treats away from him.

"She is in the last room. She is hiding in the closet," the voice said in his head.

He found her hiding in a bedroom closet. "Kill the bitch, she wants your treats! Kill the bitch, she wants your treats! Kill the bitch, she wants your treats!" The words kept repeating again and again in his mind.

Millie Vanderwall heard her front door being kicked in. She calmly picked up the phone next to her bed and dialed 911. After confirming that someone answered, she laid the receiver on the floor and ran to the closet to hide. She heard a voice coming down the hall saying something repeatedly. She heard her bedroom door burst open. Trying to get as far back in the closet as she could, she pushed the hanging clothes in front of her and kneeled down. She heard the footsteps of the intruder coming toward her, holding her breath, trying not to give away her position. She could see his feet through the crack at the bottom of her closet door. She tried not to scream when the door flew open, but she made the littlest of peeps. Hands ripped the clothes off the hangers and then she saw her attacker. His dirty long hair framed a face that was speckled with dry blood. His eyes had a blank expression in them, and his face showed no emotion. He kept repeating the words, kill the bitch, she wants your treats. Then someone touched her left hand and she looked over. There sitting next to her was a kindly looking young man. He smiled at her and told her not to be afraid. She never felt her attacker grab her by the hair, drag her into the center of the room, and plunge a knife repeatedly into her body.

Stevie pulled the knife out of her chest for the last time. The mutilated body he was straddling looked like a package of raw liver. He wiped off the knife using the blood-soaked nightgown of the woman he had just killed. Making sure to get both sides of the knife, he switched from side to side as he wiped.

"Get out! They are coming to get you," the voice screamed in his head.

Stevie ran out of the house, but seeing a police car coming down the street with its red and blue lights flashing, he took off around the backside of the house. The voice told him to run. He went from house to house, working his way to the north end of town. He heard the sirens from a number of emergency vehicles heading to the house he'd just left.

"Served that bitch right," the voice said.

"Yeah, she didn't know what hit her, did she?" Stevie said, breathless from all the running.

"Go to the yellow house; there is a car there with the keys in it. Take it."

"What about my car? They're going to know who I am," Stevie asked between breaths.

"Don't worry about that. I will never let them catch you," the voice said.

Stevie opened the door to the car and found the keys in the ignition. He couldn't believe his good luck and thanked his new friend. With his help, he knew he would never be caught. He started the engine and carefully backed it out of the driveway. He watched for the lights to come on from the house, but nothing happened. Driving carefully out of town, he headed north on Highway 49. He then drove a couple of miles north of town.

"Turn right here," the voice said.

He turned onto a small country road and followed it east, until he came to a large wooded area.

"Turn left here and shut off the head lights," the voice commanded.

Stevie did what he was told, following a grassy lane back into the trees. He stopped, shut off the engine, then asked, "Now what?"

"We sit here until I say it is time to go," the voice answered.

"I've done everything you wanted; I want my damn treats now," Stevie whined.

"Huh… I thought you were the one, but maybe I was wrong," the voice said with a sad tone.

"I'm the one for what?" Stevie asked.

"The one to carry out all the tasks I need done," the voice answered, then continued in a cajoling voice. "Stephen, you are my chosen one. Only you can accomplish the tasks I need fulfilled. Are you the one, Stephen? Are you my chosen one?"

"Yes, I am the one," Stevie said with pride.

"Rest now. I will tell you when it's time to finish all this."

Stevie laid his head back on the headrest, and the words " you are the one" kept repeating themselves in his head. He really was the one; the pain his body was feeling was not going to stop him, because he was the chosen one. He was not going to let his new friend down.

Chapter Nineteen

athy and the two sleeping children turned onto Millie's street and were greeted by the flashing lights of emergency vehicles parked in front of her house. Cathy rolled down her window as she drove up to Millie's house, and an Iroquois County deputy walked out to meet the slowly approaching car.

"May I help you?" the officer asked.

"What's going on? Has something happened to Millie?" Cathy asked as she shielded her eyes from the flashlight the officer was shining into the car.

"I'm not at liberty to talk about it now, ma'am," the officer said as he tried to get a look into the minivan. "May I ask you what your name is?"

"I'm Cathy Litchfield. Jacob Litchfield is my husband. He's the minister at St. John's Lutheran Church," Cathy said. She could see a stretcher with a body bag being wheeled out of Millie's house. "Oh, my God!" she said with a gasp. "What happened? Is she okay?" Cathy screamed, struggling to remove her seat belt.

"Ma'am, please remain calm and stay in the automobile," The officer said through the van's opened window.

Cathy began to cry. "Please, tell me what happened," she pleaded between sobs. Both children began to wake up from the commotion.

"What's going on, Aunt Cathy?" Michael asked, rubbing the sleep out of his eyes.

The question calmed Cathy down. She didn't want to frighten the children. "Everything is going to be okay, Michael. Just go back to sleep."

"Why are you crying, Aunt Cathy?" Mara asked.

"I'm not crying. Just be quiet for now and I'll tell you everything when we get home, okay." Although, not satisfied with her answer, both children leaned back in their seats and remained quiet. The flashing lights from the emergency vehicles turned the inside of the van into some sort of psychotic disco, making her nauseous.

The officer, seeing her face turn white, asked, "Ma'am, are you okay?"

Cathy took a deep breath. "I'm okay," she stammered.

"Ma'am, what are you doing here?" The officer asked. He wondered why a mother with two small children would be out at this time of night.

Cathy knew the answer she was about to give would make the alarm bells go off in the mind of the officer, but not wanting to lie, she answered, "My husband called me on his way back from Indianapolis, asking me to check on Ms. Vanderwall."

The officer didn't say anything for a few seconds. Then he asked, "Why would your husband wonder about the well-being of Mrs. Vanderwall while driving back from Indianapolis?"

"He said he had a bad feeling that something was going to happen, so he told me to check on her," Cathy said. She wasn't sure about what was going through the officer's mind with her last statement.

He stood there for a minute and said, "Please wait here. Someone will be back in a minute to ask you a few more questions. May I please have your car keys?"

Cathy started to protest and then thought better of it. She pulled the keys out of the ignition and passed them to the officer. He walked over to another man, who was dressed in a long tan coat, and they talked for a bit. The man in the tan coat looked in her direction, then walked over.

"Hello, Mrs. Litchfield, I'm Detective Harms from the Iroquois County Police Department. Would you please step out of the van? I'd like to ask you a few questions."

Cathy turned in the driver's seat to tell the children that she'd be right back. Getting out of the van, she shut the door quietly and walked a few feet to where the detective was standing. He was in his middle thirties and had tired-looking eyes.

"Mrs. Litchfield, I'm having trouble understanding why you showed up to a murder scene. How did you know Millie Vanderwall?"

"She's a member of the church where my husband is the minister," she answered, still wiping the tears out of her eyes.

The detective passed her a handkerchief and asked, "Do you have any idea why your husband wanted you to check on Mrs. Vanderwall?"

"Thank you," she said. Cathy didn't know how to answer the question without making Jacob and herself sound like lunatics. On the other hand, taking too much time to answer would make the officer even more suspicious. "He just called and told me to check on Millie. He said he had a bad feeling."

"Does he have these feelings often?" the detective asked without expression.

Cathy knew this conversation was going nowhere fast. "Listen, Detective, I don't know why he asked me to come over here, but I could tell by the tone in his voice that he was serious. That's all I know." Cathy was starting to get perturbed with all the questions and she figured the detective could tell it, too.

"All right, Mrs. Litchfield, give me your address and phone number and then you may leave." The detective passed her back her keys, took down her information, then motioned for her to leave.

"Can't you tell me what happened to Millie?" Cathy pleaded with the detective.

He started to walk away, then after a second thought, he stopped and turned. "She was murdered tonight. Someone stabbed her to death in her bedroom." He turned around and walked back to where the other officers were gathered.

Cathy got back in the van and drove off. She reached for her cell phone to call Jacob. The shock of the situation was starting to hit her again as she listened to the digital ring of the cell phone. Her hands started to shake and her stomach knotted, feeling like it could turn inside out. She took deep breaths trying to calm herself. Finally, Jacob answered.

"Cathy, what's going on?" Jacob asked.

"She's dead, Jacob! Someone murdered her in her bedroom! What's going on?" Cathy asked, finally reaching panic.

"What do you mean someone murdered her."

"I just left her house. There were police cars everywhere. They took her out in a body bag, Jacob. What the hell is going on, tell me!" Cathy screamed into the cell phone.

"I don't know, but I think it has something to do with the letters. Get home, lock the doors and windows and do not let anyone into the house. I'll be home as soon as possible… Cathy?"

"What?" she asked, in a weary voice.

"I love you," Jacob said, almost in a whisper.

"I love you, too," Cathy replied. The words from her husband brought everything back into focus. Cathy drove home and did what Jacob had told her to do. The children were nestled with her on the couch, one on each side. They sat in the darkness and waited for Jacob to get home. Cathy could not stop crying.

Chapter Twenty

"Stephen, wake up! It is time!" the voice said, causing Stevie to jump to life.

"Okay, okay. I'm awake," Stevie grumbled. "Where are we going now?" Stevie asked. He was feeling terrible. His hands were shaking so badly it took him two tries to turn on the ignition.

"Go back to the main road you came in on."

Stevie did what he was told. The voice told him to turn right. He drove about three miles north before the voice spoke again.

"When you get to the church, turn left and go west for about a mile. You will find another church on the right. When you get there, pull into the parking lot and drive around to the back. I want you to enter the house and find the woman. Tell her you want the letters. Do not hurt her or the children until you have the letters.

"I got it." Stevie turned left at the old church and headed west.

"She is a preacher's wife. She pities pathetic men like you. You know what kind of woman I'm talking about?"

"Yeah, she's the type that always wants to help because she pities you."

"She feels nothing but fucking pity for you, Stephen. She thinks you are a worthless human. Do you hear what I am saying, Stephen?" the voice asked.

"She thinks I'm worthless!" Stevie growled, gripping the steering wheel so tight that Millie's dried blood fell off his hands like crimson snowflakes.

"You are not worthless, Stephen, not to me. You are a great man! No one messes with you, do they?" the voice said, bringing Stephen's temper to a boil.

"I am a great man! No one messes with me!" Stevie said pounding the steering wheel as he drove.

"Turn here. This is it. Drive to the back of the lot. Remember you are my chosen one, Stephen. You are my chosen one," the voice said.

Stevie pulled into the church parking lot and drove to the back as instructed. He looked at the house but didn't see any lights. He liked that idea; it was going to be easier if he caught them by surprise.

Jacob didn't care about observing the speed limit any longer. Something in his mind told him to get home fast. Something was causing his mind to panic and he couldn't fight it any longer. He figured he was twenty minute or so from home, smashing the accelerator to the floor, he decided he was going to make it in ten.

Stevie, crouching low, ran west, from the church parking lot that filled the space between the house and the church to the north edge of the backyard. Except for the security light that glowed in the parking lot, it was pitch black.

"Go around and come in from the west side of the house," the voice said.

Stevie ran along the edge of the yard until he was at the northeast corner of the lot and then headed south. When he was parallel with the west side of the house, he crept up to the first window he came to. He cupped his hands around his face to see better, but the steam from his breath fogged the window. Backing away to wipe the window, he leaned forward and tried again. It was just as dark in the room as it was outside, so he couldn't see anything. He moved to the next window, but before getting there, he tripped on something, sending him head over heels to the ground. While going down he hit the side of the house hard, causing a loud thud.

"You idiot, get off your ass and get in there," the voice hissed at him. "She probably heard you and is calling for help. Get in there!"

Stevie groped around for something to break the window with and found a large clay flowerpot. He picked it up over his head and hurled it through the window. The sound of shattering glass filled the night.

Cathy was just starting to doze on the couch when she thought she heard something outside. She sat motionless for a moment, listening. Then the window exploded behind her. She let out a scream. Grabbing the children by their arms, she yelled for them to wake up as she pulled them toward the stairway. The children, half-running, half being dragged, finally realized the gravity of the situation and no longer needed assistance with the escape.

"What's happening, Aunt Cathy?" Michael screamed as they made their way to the top of the stairs.

"Someone is in the house!" Cathy didn't wait for any reply and pushed both children into the bathroom at the end of the hall. She closed the door behind them and turned the lock. Both children were crying, frightened by the sudden excitement. She turned around and faced Michael and Mara. "Shhhh," she whispered, holding her right index finger against her pursed lips. "You need to be quiet; there is a bad man in the house." She moved herself and the children to the back of the room, kneeling down in front of them. She wrapped her arms around the children and waited.

Clearing the last of the glass shards away from the window's edge, Stevie jumped up onto the sill and steadied himself. He then toppled headfirst into the room and scrambled to get on his feet.

"It's too dark. I can't see anything," Stevie complained.

"Get moving. They are hiding in the bathroom upstairs. You are the one, Stephen. You are the one. You are the one. You are the one," the voice repeated the phrase in Stevie's mind until he started repeating it aloud.

"I am the one… I am the one… I am the one," Stevie repeated as he found his way to the base of the steps. Taking two steps at a time, he made his way to the top. The hallway was dimly lit by a nightlight plugged into an outlet. He could see five doors, two on each side and one at the end.

"Go to the door at the end of the hallway. They are in there. Get them now. You do not have much time. Remember you are the one. You are my chosen one, Stephen."

"I am the one... I am the one... I am the one," Stevie chanted as he walked toward the closed door.

Cathy heard the intruder come up the stairs, and start down the hallway. As he came closer she could hear him say "I am the one" over and over. She could tell by the voice that the person was male, and he sounded young. The intruder kicked the door and it flew open with a loud bang, shattering the mirror that had been attached to the back. Cathy tried to shield the children from the explosion of glass by pulling them closer. The man entered the room and looked at them. He was still saying the words, "I am the one. I am the one. I am the one."

Stevie turned on the light and saw a woman kneeling down, hugging two children.

"Tell her you want the letters," the voice said in Stevie's mind.

Stevie stopped chanting his mantra, and took a deep breath. Staring blankly into the women's eyes, he said, "Give me the letters."

Cathy felt her skin crawl when she looked up at her attacker. His entire being was covered in dried blood. Legs spread wide, with tightly clenched fists at his side, he was breathing in loud rasps. His long greasy hair swung back and forth as he inhaled and exhaled. The children were crying and trying to climb farther into her housecoat. She couldn't believe that her attacker knew about the letters.

"Give me the damn letters!" he demanded again.

"I don't have them," Cathy whimpered. The man stood there for a minute and acted like he didn't know what to do. Staring at them blankly, he asked, "What do I do now?" He hesitated for a moment, and then it appeared that he heard something. He walked forward, grabbed Cathy by her hair, and dragged her a few feet away from the children, leaving her sitting on her knees. The children tried to follow, but he screamed for them to get back. Holding her by back of her head, he forced her to look up at him. He pulled a knife out of his pocket and ran it gently across her exposed neck.

"Tell me where they are, bitch," he growled.

"My husband has them and he's not here. Please, let us go," she begged.

He pulled Cathy aside by her long hair and then pinned her head against the wall with his knee. He leaned forward and peered into the faces of the children. Mara, looking up at him defiantly, tried to shield Michael from the blood-covered man.

"Get away from us!" Mara said.

Stevie just looked at the little girl and laughed. "Mommy, I think you're lying. I'm going to slice this little girl's throat open!" he said, pointing the knife at Mara. "That's what I'm going to do if you don't tell me where the letters are. I'm going to cut her fucking head off and let you hold it while I do the same thing to the little boy. Would you like that?"

Cathy, trying to come up with something to say to get him away from the children, finally said, "The letters are downstairs in the kitchen."

He let go of Cathy's head and she fell backwards. He took a step forward and picked up Mara like a rag doll. Holding the knife to her throat, he pushed Michael at Cathy. Then, with a growl, he said, "Get downstairs and find those letters, but don't try anything or I will cut up this little girl."

The four of them went downstairs. Cathy, with Michael by her side, started looking through kitchen drawers for the letters. The man waited by the stairway and held the knife to Mara's throat.

Jacob was close enough to the house that he could see the lights on in the kitchen. He thought it was strange for the lights to be on at this hour, instantly putting him on guard. As he cautiously pulled into the drive way, he noticed a strange car parked in the back of the church parking lot. He got out of his car, and walked quietly into the garage, dialing 911 on his cell phone. The operator answered. In a whisper Jacob told him his address and that someone was in his house. He gave a brief thought to the fact that there might not be, but at this point he was willing to risk it. He pushed the off button on his cell phone, then crept up to the kitchen door.

"Her husband is in the garage; grab him when he comes in. Do not hurt him until you get the letters," the voice said in Stevie's head. The woman was still fishing through drawers when Stevie yelled in a whisper, "Get over here, bitch, and bring the boy." Stevie motioned to them to stand where he was by the stairway. He put down the little girl and she took a few quick steps and moved next to the woman. He walked over to the door and waited behind it.

Cathy couldn't figure out what the man was doing until she saw the door knob start to turn. Wanting to warn whoever it was, she yelled, "LOOK OUT, HE'S BEHIND THE DOOR!" The door knob stopped turning and with a crash the door flew open, roughly pinning the intruder behind it. Pulling the children tightly to her, she saw it was Jacob. He rushed into the room, facing the man behind the door.

"I've called the police, they're on the way!" Jacob said firmly to the blood covered man.

Ignoring what Jacob told him, the intruder shoved the door out of his way and leaped at him. He grabbed Jacob by the collar, pushing him hard against the kitchen cabinet. They struggled back and forth trying to get one another off balance. Jacob got the upper hand, causing the intruder to go down hard. Jacob followed him down, landing on top of him. He threw an awkward punch to the face of the attacker, but it glanced off the side of his head, causing Jacob to lose his balance and fall next to the attacker. The two of them rolled around again, still trying to get the better of one another. The intruder ended up on top and savagely landed a punch to Jacob's jaw. Jacob went limp.

"Jacob!" Cathy screamed.

The man just sat there on top of Jacob with a blank look on his face. Cathy thought he looked like he was listening for something. Then the expression on his face changed.

"What?" he asked, as if someone had told him to do something ridiculous. Getting off Jacob he looked at Cathy and told her, "Get a pen and paper." He paused, cocking his head to left, then saying, "Write these words down. Bring the letters and meet me in hell if you ever want to see your family again."

Cathy wrote the words on the piece of paper and left it on the table. He didn't see her put the pen into her robe pocket.

The dirty man picked up Mara and then grabbed Michael by the back of his pajama shirt. He yelled, "Let's go!"

Cathy looked at Jacob as she was pushed by him on the way to the kitchen door. She saw him start to wake up and felt a sigh of relief to see that he was not dead. The man dragged the children through the yard and across the parking lot. He turned to Cathy and said, "You and the boy get in the back. I'll keep the girl with me."

Cathy helped Michael into the back seat, giving him a reassuring glance. Climbing in after him, she thought about trying to incapacitate the man with the pen she had taken from the kitchen, but if it didn't work she would put the children in more jeopardy. The man shoved Mara in through the driver's side door, and after taking a quick look around, slid in behind the wheel. He turned the key, bringing the motor to life. Yanking down on the gear shift, the car lurched forward.

"Shit, shit, shit," he mumbled as he left the parking lot of the church. As they drove west, Cathy twisted around to peer over the back seat. She could see the lights of two police cars coming from the east. Seeing them stop at the house, she let out a sigh of relief. She didn't know what was going to happen to her and the children, but at least Jacob would get help.

Chapter Twenty-One

Jacob woke up in a fog to find himself strapped to an ambulance gurney. An oxygen mask was strapped around his head and he fought to remove it. As his head cleared, he stopped struggling. He realized he couldn't move his head due to a brace wrapped around his neck to keep him immobilized. He recognized the ceiling of his own kitchen. The paramedic sitting with him saw that he had regained consciousness and pulled the oxygen mask off his face.

"How're you feeling, Mr. Litchfield?"

Still looking at the ceiling, Jacob answered, "I've felt better."

"I bet you have. You took quite a shot to the jaw, Mr. Litchfield," the paramedic said as he leaned over Jacob with an examination light, checking his pupils.

An officer walked into the kitchen from the living room and looked down at Jacob. Kneeling down near the gurney, he waited for the paramedic to finish the examination. Then he asked, "Mister, or should I say Pastor Litchfield, I'm Detective Harms from the Iroquois County Police. Pastor, where is your family?"

Like a lightning bolt hitting a transformer, everything came back to him. "Take off my restraints. I've got to go!" Jacob yelled, struggling against the straps that held him to the gurney.

"Settle down, Mr. Litchfield. You need to have a doctor look at you," the paramedic said, trying to calm Jacob down.

Detective Harms, trying to help, added, "Mr. Litchfield, please settle down. You need to see a doctor."

"I'm fine, let me get up!" Jacob demanded again. While the paramedic and the detective were trying to decide what to do, Jacob continued to struggle. Then he shouted at them, "Let me up, you idiots. You don't understand, that man took my family!"

"Who has your family, Pastor Litchfield?" the detective asked, amazed at the fact that the preacher called him an idiot. He motioned for the paramedic to take off Jacob's restraints. Once they were removed, Jacob stood up. Shaky at first, he walked over to the kitchen table and pulled out a chair. He sat in silence for a few moments with his head in his hands. The detective walked over to the table and sat down across from him. Giving Jacob a few seconds to regain his composure, he then asked him to explain the details of what had taken place earlier. Jacob told him everything that had happened. While Jacob and the detective were talking, a paramedic came in, asking Jacob to sign a release form. The atmosphere in the house was finally starting to settle down, except for two officers still walking through it looking for anything that might help in the investigation. Detective Harms continued with his questions.

"Pastor Litchfield, I found this on the kitchen table during my investigation," he said, handing Jacob a piece of paper. Jacob took it, read it, then gave it back to Detective Harms. The detective then asked, "Can you tell me what this letter means by, bring the letters and meet me in hell? Meet who in hell?"

Jacob didn't want to lie to the detective, but he didn't know how to explain it without sounding crazy. Trying not to visibly squirm through a boldfaced lie, he decided to play dumb. "I don't know what it means. I don't know if it means literal hell, or a place that reminds someone of hell."

"We'll talk more about it later," the detective said. "I talked to your wife earlier this evening at Ms. Vanderwall's. She said she was there because you had called asking her to check on Ms. Vanderwall. Why did she need to check on Ms. Vanderwall?"

Jacob had no idea how to answer that question. He shifted in his chair and remained silent.

Detective Harms noticed the shift in the pastor's posture, but decided to leave it alone. "Do you know a Stephen Jenkins of East Bradley Street in Champaign, Illinois?"

"No, I do not. Why?" Jacob asked weakly, still feeling the effects of the blow to his head.

"The car that was left at Millie Vanderwall's was registered to a Stephen Jenkins. Lifting a picture up for Jacob to see, he asked, "Is this the man who attacked you?"

Jacob, recognizing the man immediately, answered, "Yes, that's him."

"Why were you in Indianapolis this evening, Pastor Litchfield?"

Jacob didn't feel like answering any questions, but he knew the detective was just doing his job. Head still throbbing, Jacob answered. "My friend was attacked this afternoon and I went to see him in the hospital."

"You're talking about Jonathon Bailey, correct?"

"Yes, he died while I was at the hospital," Jacob answered, still holding his head in his hands.

"We think Mr. Jenkins is responsible for the deaths of Pastor Bailey and Ms. Vanderwall. He has a criminal history of various drug offenses, but never anything violent. His last arrest was for possession of crystal meth, and maybe through extended use of the drug, he just snapped."

"How do you know he was in Indianapolis?"

"We found a receipt in the car that was left at Mrs. Vanderwall's. It was from an Indianapolis Mc Donald's with yesterday's date and time that fits the timeline for Pastor Bailey's murder. Pastor Abrams gave us a description of Pastor Bailey's attacker that fits Stephen Jenkins to a T." Detective Harms paused for a moment and then continued. "The thing I'm having trouble with is why someone would drive from Champaign to Indy to kill a retired preacher, and then back to the little town of Cissna Park to kill an elderly woman, and then kidnap a third person's family?" Hesitating for a few more seconds, he asked, "Do you see what I'm getting at, Pastor?"

Jacob, looking at Detective Harms, could see the man was a no-nonsense type of guy. He was dressed in pressed khakis and a polo shirt and carried a long tan overcoat draped over his arm. Middle age was starting to creep in around the edges, a little gray around his temples, a few wrinkles around the eyes, and his shirt was just a little too snug around his midsection. It was evident that the detective never missed his bimonthly visit to the barber; his hair was combed neatly over to the left side of his head with every strand in place. Jacob saw him take reading glasses out of his coat when he looked at the note left by the attacker. It was then that Jacob noticed how tired his eyes looked. Even in a rural county like Iroquois, Jacob figured the man had seen things that would make a weaker man crumble.

"Pastor, do you see why I'm having problems sorting out this case?" the detective asked, interrupting Jacob's train of thought. "I'm having trouble understanding the connection between the two murders and the attack on your family. Can you help me with the connection?" Although he didn't say anything, the detective couldn't understand why the minister remained so calm. He sensed that the pastor was not telling him half of what he knew.

Finally answering the question, Jacob said, "You probably already know that Jonathon, or Pastor Bailey, and I worked together in Indianapolis. Pastor Bailey and I are, or were, close friends, and he was here last weekend to help me with a problem."

Interrupting before Jacob could continue, the detective asked, "This problem, did it have anything to do with Stephen Jenkins?"

"No, I've never seen or met the man before he attacked my family."

"I'm sorry for the interruption. Please continue," the detective said.

"Millie Vanderwall was my secretary, and along with my wife and Jonathon, we all met this weekend to discuss the problem," Jacob said while rubbing his temples in a circular motion. "I know. I know. You want to know what the problem was and that's the part that's hard to explain… Are you a religious man, Detective?" Jacob asked, noticing for the first time the expression on the man's face had changed.

"I…I don't know. I went to church with my mother when I was young, but I haven't gone since starting college. I guess I believe in a higher power," Detective Harms said, sitting up in his chair.

"Would you mind taking a walk with me?" Jacob asked the detective. He nodded in agreement, then followed Jacob out the door and over to Jacob's office in the church. Once there, the detective took a seat in a chair that Jacob offered him and Jacob took a seat behind his desk. Jacob opened the top drawer, pulled out the three envelopes, and handed them to the detective. The detective put on his reading glasses, opened the first letter, and read. Finishing the first letter, he then opened and read the second, then the third. When he finished reading all three letters, Jacob passed two more letters to him, saying, "Here are two letters that my sister wrote to me a few years ago. I think you'll find that the handwriting is the same." The detective compared the handwriting between the old and new letters. Jacob stood up and went over to the wall where a small decorative oval mirror was hanging. He took it down and then passed it to the detective and said, "Look at the reflection of the words written on the latest letters with the mirror."

The detective moved the letters and mirror around trying to see what Jacob meant. Finally, he realized he could see the paper but he couldn't see the writing. He even looked at himself in the mirror to make sure it wasn't some kind of trick mirror. "I don't get it!" he said. "Is it some kind of trick?" he asked.

Jacob then went to a kitchen drawer and took out a lighter. He went to the table, picked up one of the letters, and tried to light a corner on fire. Nothing happened, no fire, no blackened edge, nothing. Jacob stood the lighter up on the table, put the letter in the pile with the other letters, and then said, "They can't be copied or destroyed. I don't know why, other than the fact that something greater than me wanted it this way."

"My God!" the detective sighed while looking at the letters in disbelief.

Jacob then explained the events of the last week, the dreams, the visit from the angel, and what the four of them had discussed.

"So, you believe you can save your family by dreaming yourself back to hell?" Detective Harms asked, with an incredulous look.

"Let me ask you a question, Detective. What is worth more to a criminal than anonymity?"

"Nothing…why?" Detective Harms answered, wondering where the questions were going.

"Would a criminal kill to remain anonymous?"

"I imagine he would."

"Okay, if you believe in a higher power, do you believe that power to be a perfect good?" Jacob asked.

"Well, I never thought about it, but I guess it would be."

"If the higher power is good, then who causes the bad things?"

"I see where you're going with this. You're telling me that the devil causes all the bad things that happen. You're talking about the "Devil Made Me Do It Defense," aren't you?" Detective Harms said with a grimace.

"What would happen in the world if everyone believed that the devil was behind all the terrible things that happen?"

"It would make my job a lot easier, but I would say that most people in the world don't believe in anything good or evil. They just think they're here to live a miserable life until they die," the detective said.

"So what would it be worth to the devil to remain anonymous? Stop and think about the ramifications if the world were to realize that all evil happens because of his influence. Wouldn't the knowledge of the devil's existence drive more people toward a belief in God? Trust me, the thing he wants most is for the human race not to believe that he exists," Jacob said, once again rubbing his temples.

"You're saying that Stephen Jenkins killed Pastor Bailey, Millie Vanderwall, and kidnapped your family because of these three letters?" Detective Harms asked, holding up the letters in one hand.

"Yes, Jonathon told me right before he died that his attacker wanted the copies of the letters that he was taking to Pastor Abrams. What else makes any sense? Do you think that Jenkins just happened to wake up yesterday and decide to drive two hours to Indianapolis to kill one of the people who knew about the letters? Then, drive another two hours back into Illinois to kill the second person who knew about the letters, and then kidnap the third's family?"

"Well, if what you're saying is true, do you think I would keep my job if I put this in a report?" the detective challenged as he handed the three envelopes back to Jacob to put back in his desk drawer. Then he continued, "Look, this is what I'm going to do. I'm going to continue the search for your wife and children. I'm going to place an officer outside your house. If you find out anything, give me a call on my cell phone. Do not, I beg you, talk to anyone else about any of this. You talk only to me about this topic," he said as he passed his card to Jacob. The detective stood up and started for the door. Turning around, he looked at Jacob and asked, "Are you going to do what the note says?"

"I'm going to try, but I wouldn't mind if someone would come by the house in the morning to wake me up," Jacob said, giving Detective Harms a little smile.

The detective shook his head at Jacob, then walked out of the office. From the hallway, he called. "Pastor, I think, for the first time in years, I'm going to pray before I go to sleep tonight."

Chapter Twenty-Two

Jacob sat in his office and prayed for the strength to handle what he was about to experience. He decided to leave the letters in the church. If he lost them in his travels, he wouldn't have any leverage against whoever was doing this. He walked over to the house stopping for a moment to tell to the officer sitting in the patrol car to have a good night. The officer introduced himself as Officer Jorgenson and told him to have a good night.

He went to the garage to get a piece of thin clear plastic to cover the broken window in the living room, then picked up the big pieces of glass and ran the vacuum to pick up the smaller ones. When the window was covered, he went upstairs to take a shower. The gravity of the situation sank heavily into his mind when he saw the broken glass from the mirror. He tiptoed around the broken shards to start the shower, then went downstairs to get a broom and a dustpan. He swept up broken glass, set the broom and dustpan in the corner, and then stepped into the shower.

He breathed a sigh of relief as the hot water cascaded down his neck and shoulders. As the steam from the hot water covered the glass shower enclosure, he tried to imagine what it would be like to meet the devil, but figured it was futile. "I put it in your hands, Lord," he said aloud.

Finishing his shower, he dressed in comfortable sweatpants and a T-shirt, then went downstairs. He had a sandwich and a glass of milk. He watched television for a little bit, but there was one problem, he wasn't sleepy. His nerves were wound as tight as fiddle strings. He wanted to get this journey underway, but he didn't even feel like lying down, let alone sleeping. The more time he waited to become tired, the more frustrated he became. He went upstairs to see if there was anything in the medicine cabinet to help him fall asleep. He didn't know if Cathy ever took sleeping pills, but looking closer, he found an unopened box. Although he read the instruction, he took two times the normal dose for good measure. He went to the bedroom and climbed into bed, pulling the covers up around his neck. He missed the warmth of his wife. He wondered where Cathy and the children were and soon decided that he was never going to go to sleep if he didn't keep his mind clear of all stimulating thought. Rolling from side to side, he finally found a comfortable position and tried to focus on the day he met Cathy, saw her beautiful smile and heard her sweet voice…

Chapter Twenty-Three

Cathy sat in silence, watching the kidnapper as he drove the car along the dark country road. What could motivate someone to do this? He was definitely disturbed. He talked to himself or someone constantly. It was as if he was looking for someone. He kept saying, "Where are you, where are you." He twitched and jerked uncontrollably. With his burned-out appearance, Cathy figured him for a severe drug user, but still something else seemed to motivate him.

The lights from the dashboard illuminated the crystallized blood in his greasy hair like a set of demented red Christmas-tree lights. Cathy figured it was Millie's blood and the thought sent a shiver down her spine.

In the front seat, Mara had moved as far from the kidnapper as she could. Cathy admired the way the little girl stared straight ahead trying not to show fear, but the little quiver in her bottom lip gave her away. Michael laid his head against her arm and she could feel him shaking. Whether it was from the cold or fear she didn't know, but she could help him with the cold. She pulled him close and wrapped him inside her robe. The motion caused the ballpoint pen, she had taken back at the house, to fall out of the pocket and roll across the seat. She leaned over slowly to pick it up, careful not to draw attention to herself. Rolling the pen back and forth between her thumb and forefinger, she imagined ways it might be used as a weapon. Should she try to stop him? Could she stop him? She sighed. It didn't matter what she was going to do. She wasn't going to try anything in the car and take a chance on hurting the children in an accident. She stared out the window, deciding to wait.

Chapter Twenty-Four

Jacob didn't realize he was asleep until he found himself standing in a large mist-filled tunnel. The tunnel led upward at a slight angle and Jacob started walking. The ceiling and walls, appearing to consist of fog, were solid once he reached through the vapor. Behind the cloudy material was solid rock. The farther he went, the warmer it became. The smell he remembered from the earlier visits was not present, but what he did smell was the fragrance of flowers. When he came to a large wrought-iron and wooden gate, Jacob put his fist to it. The sound it made was like that of a large bass drum echoing from every angle. He repeated the action again. The gate opened with a groan and Jacob entered into a large courtyard. Once he was inside, the gate closed behind him. The beauty of the courtyard was breathtaking. The floor was a series of pathways made out of smooth flagstones. Flowers and plants of many different kinds grew everywhere and Jacob could smell the fragrance of the blossoms. Numerous kinds of fruit trees mingled with different flowering bushes throughout the garden. The fruit trees had both fruit and blossoms at the same time. He had never seen such a thing on earth. He could hear water falling somewhere ahead and walked toward the sound. He then entered an area surrounded by a white wooden trellis intertwined with leafy vines. Seated at a table, with its back to Jacob, was a winged creature of great size and stature. Jacob walked around the table made of white marble with golden metal legs, then faced the being. The stranger was dressed only in white linen that draped across its chest and tied at the waist. The beauty of the creature surprised him. As far as Jacob could tell, the being was male, not female, but he was beautiful.

"Hello, Jacob Litchfield. I have been expecting you," the being said, motioning for him to sit down.

The being's voice reverberated in Jacob's ear. Figuring he had nothing to lose, he spoke. "Are you Lucifer?"

"Yes, I am Lucifer, your devil." Lucifer's expression didn't change when he spoke, but his eyes blinked slowly, almost rhythmically every couple of seconds. His skin was smooth like fine white porcelain; his hair was jet black, falling to the middle of his waist. His gaze never left Jacob as he spoke. "Jacob Litchfield, you and your sister have become a great thorn in my side. I wanted to meet the human who, after all this time, has managed to do this to me." He stopped speaking for a moment to look even closer at Jacob. "You are not a powerful man by any means. You have no great wealth. You are not even physically strong compared to most humans. I cannot understand why the Creator always chooses the weakest of humans to carry out his little games. Do you know why that is?"

"I don't pretend to know the thoughts of God," Jacob said.

"So blind you are in your pitiful faith," Lucifer replied, shaking his head. "Are you not concerned about the wellbeing of your family?"

"My family is in the hands of God. I would be sad if they were harmed, but my life on earth is only the smallest fraction of time when compared to eternity as a whole," Jacob answered, looking directly into the eyes of the devil. He hoped that Lucifer didn't see the utter panic that was going on in his mind.

"Did you appreciate how I took the lives of your weak little friends?"

"They are in a better place. You did not know either of them," Jacob answered.

"I know them to be like any human…frail, weak, and easily frightened."

Jacob laughed at what Lucifer said, "Like I said, you didn't know either of them. Pastor Bailey was one of the strongest Christian men I ever met. Millie, I would guess, welcomed the end of her time on earth."

Lucifer, showing just the slightest hint of agitation, began to speak. "I think it is time to discuss the reason I brought you here. I will not let the knowledge contained in those letters get out in the world. I will not let the work I've accomplished in the past thousand years be spoiled by the writing of your eternally damned sister. I want those letters destroyed, and then, and only then, will your family be set free, unharmed of course. But don't take too much time,

Jacob Litchfield; the pathetic little human that is holding your family is a mite unstable."

"How do you figure the letters made it to me anyway?" Jacob asked.

Lucifer seemed entertained by the question. "The Creator has employed many little schemes like this throughout time. I have stopped them before and I will stop this one. I have no reason to lie to you, Jacob Litchfield. I am at war with the Creator and I will be victorious. Some humans seem to know the truth of our existence and I accept that, but this is a numbers game and right now I am winning." He paused for a second, then looking thoughtfully at Jacob, he stood up and placed his hands behind his back. He took a few steps away from Jacob and then swiftly turned around. With one eyebrow raised, he asked, "Do you realize how many human souls know the truth and just do not care?" He paused again to give Jacob time to think and then continued. "It is so much fun to watch them struggle through their pathetic lives trying to make enough money to have something just a little better than their neighbor. I always give them enough encouragement to want a little more. Take your sister for instance. A single whisper in her mind about how nice it would be to have the newest, most luxurious car on the market and she would work night and day to be able to afford it. The time she spent working so hard for the means to buy that car meant nothing to her, but it was time and I stole from her. Time she needed to realize what was important to the well-being of her soul, and, Jacob, we only have so much time. Keep raising the stakes a little at a time and soon a lifetime is wasted." Lucifer walked back over to his chair and took his seat. Placing both elbows on the table, he then folded his hands and raised them to his chin. He looked at Jacob, then smirked and said, "The thing I love the most is the surprise on their faces when they end up here. Poor and naked as the day they were born. It is so simple to distract a human with something shiny and new. Like a moth fluttering around a candle, you might say. I so enjoy doing it and I will continue to do it. The maker will not stop me from destroying as many human souls as I possibly can."

"What do you win in the end? Is it enough to take as many souls as you can from God? Is that the end of it, or is there more? Do you really think that your kingdom can defeat the kingdom of God?" Jacob asked.

Lucifer quickly stood up, causing Jacob to take a few steps backward. The devil smiled as he walked by. Jacob wondered if the angel that had visited him in the church had toned down his appearance.

"Follow me now. I have something I want to show you," Lucifer said as he led Jacob out of the garden. They walked for a while, not saying a word to one another. Jacob looked down at himself, curious about what he was wearing. He had on simple black pants, with a short-sleeved black pull-over shirt. Reaching down, he pinched the cloth of the pants between his fingers, surprised by the soft and supple feel of the material. The shirt he was wearing was made from the same material. His shoes were some kind of lace-less pull-on shoes. He had to admit that the clothes he was wearing were very comfortable.

As they walked, the plant life became thinner and finally became nonexistent. Jacob began to recognize the environment from his earlier visits. Darkness filled his vision, except for the firelight emitting from the three towers that stood ahead of them. He couldn't decide when exactly during their walk it became dark. Something was fuzzy in his thought process, and like the incompleteness of a dream, it felt as if time had suddenly skipped a cog.

"Where did we just come from?" Jacob asked.

"It is a neutral area between my kingdom and the Creator's. It is like the lobby of a large building, but there are only two ways that lead out of that garden."

Chapter Twenty-Five

They walked on an elevated rocky path that wound its way to the three towers, the same three towers Jacob had seen in the first dream. He looked over the edge of the walkway and saw nothing but blackness except for areas that glowed down below like ponds of liquid fire. The wind howled, blowing at a gale force, and it seemed to come from four directions at once. First it was hot, then it was cold. With the unpredictable winds, he was afraid to stand near the edge, and moved back to the middle of the path. Following Lucifer, Jacob had to admit to himself that he felt drawn to this being. The charisma that emitted from Lucifer was remarkable. He wondered if the human soul became so starved for spirituality that even an evil spirit was more alluring than no spirit at all. He made a mental note to remember that Lucifer was still an angel, even though he wasn't one of heaven's.

As they made their way farther down the path, the firelight from the castle turned everything different shades of red. With each step they took, the smell grew stronger. The path went up a steep grade, topping out on a large cliff that overlooked Lucifer's entire castle. They were close enough that Jacob could hear the screams and cries of the suffering humans.

"Just a little farther," Lucifer announced, continuing down the path. They arrived at a massive stone gate and a guard greeted Lucifer with a gracious bow, then opened the heavy door. Lucifer motioned for Jacob to enter the compound. What he saw was just as Sara had described in her letters and his first nightmare. Thousands upon thousands of hollow-eyed humans lined the walkways around the towers. The whole scene reminded Jacob of the pictures he had seen of the German concentration camps. Naked and dirty, the forlorn souls stared at Jacob until they saw who was walking behind him.

The guards in the compound were the first to drop to their knees, and then like a great wave, the multitude of humans followed. From the corner of his eye, Jacob saw a blur of motion. A poor soul failed to bow in time and something from the sky swooped down and carried it off. The beating of large leathery wings could be heard as the struggling human was taken to the shortest of the three towers. Jacob could hear the soul screaming as it was dropped through an opening in the roof. Lucifer smiled and motioned for everyone to rise.

"Someone is always last. I find it keeps them on their toes," Lucifer said as a smile spread across his chiseled face. They continued their walk through the crowd of damned humans. Everyone seemed to have the same blank look. Jacob stopped and really looked hard at the wandering horde around him. They were all naked. Some were catatonic and others who had come to realize that this was not a dream were starting to scream in horror. One man walked up to Jacob and asked, "Am I dead? Have you seen my wife, she died before me. This is not what I thought heaven would look like." The man lost interest in Jacob, his voice trailed off, and he walked up to others asking the same questions.

He noticed a woman curled up on the ground scraping her fingernails down the side of her face, etching bloody tracks into her graying skin. Her head was rolling back and forth as her eyes rolled back into her head. She was repeatedly yelling, "This ain't fucking real!" Jacob realized this was the case with everyone around him and he figured he could see the size of a crowd equal to that of a professional football stadium.

"It takes quite a while for the truth to set in. Especially the souls who thought they were Christians. They were not bad people, but they lacked faith. There are different levels of punishment in my kingdom. I think you will see that during your visit," Lucifer said.

Lucifer, motioning to Jacob, walked up to a beautiful woman. Jacob saw that she was trying to cover her nakedness with her arms. Lucifer lifted her chin, causing her to look directly into his eyes. At first, her eyes turned away from Lucifer's steel gaze, then her brow furrowed as if she was annoyed with his interruption. Lucifer smiled and said, "Welcome, my child. What is your name?"

At first, it seemed to Jacob that she did not understand the question; then a look of recollection slowly began to shine in her eyes and she said, "My name is Sandra…Sandra Harris."

"Do you know where you are, Sandra Harris?"

"This is a bad dream. I will wake up soon," she said in a monotone voice. Her face still held a blank gaze.

"You are mistaken, my child. You are in hell and you will be here for eternity," Lucifer said with a smile spreading across his angelic face.

She seemed to unravel at Lucifer's statement. Shaking her head furiously, she cried, "No, no! That is not right. I went to church. I gave money to charity. I was a good person."

"Did you ever, in all the time that you sat in your pitiful little church, stop to think whether you actually believed in your maker?" Lucifer asked.

Awareness suddenly shown across her dirty face and she dropped to her knees and began to loudly wail. "Noooo, noooo…I don't deserve this! I don't…I don't!"

Jacob watched in horror as Lucifer walked away laughing.

Jacob jogged a few steps to catch up. As he walked with Lucifer, he watched over his shoulder as two guards grabbed her by the arms and started to drag her away. Kicking and screaming, she aggravated one of the guards. He let go of her arm, kneeled down and grabbed her by the back of the head. The woman never stopped wailing, even though the guard screamed at her to shut up. Reaching back with his free hand, he violently punched her in the face. Her head jerked back and she went limp. Picking her up again, the guards continued their trek through the crowd of humans.

"What is going to happen to that woman?" Jacob asked.

"She will be processed and taken to her assigned level," Lucifer said flatly.

"How did you know what sins she committed in life?"

"I have that information. Let's just say it is all on record and I know every record," Lucifer said as he quickly walked toward the tallest tower.

"How long do they stay in this compound before they get their assignment?"

Lucifer took a couple of steps before answering. He stopped, turned, and looked down at Jacob impatiently. "What is the hurry, Preacher? Do we not have eternity?"

Jacob didn't say a word, but in his mind he realized that Lucifer did have a point.

Jacob had to hustle to keep up with Lucifer's long strides. They walked without speaking until they arrived at the tallest of the three towers. Lucifer opened the heavy wooden door and led him up numerous flights of stairs until finally coming to the top of the tower. Lucifer opened a door to a room.

"Welcome to my humble abode," Lucifer said with a hint of delight.

Jacob entered the room and could make out two large high-backed chairs facing a large stone fireplace.

Lucifer walked over to the fireplace, bent down, and started a fire. It was entertaining for Jacob to see the devil use a match to light a fire. Once the fire was roaring, he turned and motioned to the two chairs. "Let us sit down and talk awhile, Jacob Litchfield. Ask anything you desire."

When they were both seated, Jacob asked his first question. "Why did you rebel against God?"

"You really get right to the point," he said as his mouth widened into a smile. Then he became serious. "First of all, Jacob Litchfield, he might be your God, but he is not mine. Please refer to him as the Creator, if you must refer to him at all."

"That's fair enough," Jacob said.

"Now to answer your question, good sir. If you were to look at the extended timeline of creation, heaven and its inhabitants existed long before the earth. We watched with interest as the Creator did his little magic act of creating the earth and all its inhabitants. I might add that the book of Genesis is rather vague about the whole process. Then the Creator got around to the creation of the first human, Adam. He told us that it was going to be his greatest creation."

Jacob thought he picked up the smallest hint of sarcasm.

"A little time passed and the human male was lonely, so he created the first female, Eve. By the way, she had the stronger will of the two, a trait I exploited then and many times later. It was then that I, Lucifer, the most favored of heaven's populous, saw the flaw in his plan." Then he rolled his hand out in front of him like an English aristocrat. "I watched the weak little creatures walking around the beautiful garden, free to do whatever they desired. Meanwhile we, the original population of heaven, were supposed to rejoice and be glad for the weak little animals." Lucifer paused for a second, as if remembering something from when those events took place. He then started to speak darkly, as if angered by the memory.

"He turned his back on us is what he did. We were the greatest of his creation," Lucifer snarled. "We were supposed to be watchers, the caretakers of his creation. We were servants is all we were; slaves! It was not fair and I decided to do something about it."

Lucifer stood up and walked over to the fireplace. Grabbing the poker, he stabbed it into the stack of flaming logs. When he was satisfied with the results, he sat down and continued with the story. "I gathered the angels that I knew shared the same sentiment and we made our plans. First though, the general consensus was that I should try to talk to the maker about the situation; war was only to be a last resort. The Creator and I talked one day while walking in one of his flower-laden gardens." Lucifer went silent for a moment, as if suddenly lost in the ancient memory. He gave Jacob a quick smile, as if embarrassed by the extended pause. "I pled my case to him. I told him that I thought it was unfair that he had put the human creatures before his first created. He never got angry at me during our talk; he never raised his voice when answering my questions. He said, 'Lucifer, my child, it is not for you to say what I do, or why I do it. I love you, just as I love all my creations here, and on earth. Please remain patient, Lucifer, and you will see how all these things will unfold.' That is all he said. Then he walked me out of the garden. I think he could see that I was furious, and trust me, I was. I was boiling inside, but I did not say a word. What good would it have done anyway?" Lucifer leaned forward in his high-backed chair, folded his hands in front of him, and raised his brow. "He was not going to listen to me because his plan was set. I went back to the group and a great debate ensued. In the end, the plan for a rebellion was made. We thought we could destroy the Creator. Our plan was to surprise him in his fortress with a large number. We were close to a third of heaven's population. I should have raised that number before we attacked and we would have been successful. We had a member on the inside to help us sneak into his fortress and we made our way into his castle." Lucifer paused and shifted in his chair.

Jacob looked at the creature for a moment and then turned his gaze away. He could see genuine discomfort in the fallen angel and it surprised him. It was almost as if he reflected the human emotion of shame and defeat. Before Jacob could surmise anymore from Lucifer's body language, he spoke again.

Lucifer took a breath and said, "We thought we had surprise on our side, but we were met by his army of warrior angels. That is when I learned that the deck was always going to be stacked against us. Though a great battle it was, the sheer numbers were against us, and in the end we were defeated. Let me tell you something; a war between angels is not like anything you have ever seen. It is a different kind of warfare. It is a battle of light and energy. Of course, death is not a result of being wounded, but it definitely leaves a scar," Lucifer said as he pulled back the collar of his tunic, showing Jacob two scars, one located high on the left side of his massive chest and the other one in the center of his rippled abdomen. "After it was all said and done, we were all gathered together at heaven's gate, and the maker said, in his ever-mild manner, 'My children, you are no longer allowed in my kingdom. You will now become inhabitants of earth. I sentence you to the netherworld that lies far beneath the surface of the world that my human creation now walks.' The archangel Michael then escorted out us. Yes, yes." He chuckled lightly. "Just like in the paintings you've seen, in case you are wondering." Lucifer arose from his chair, raising his hands in two clinched fists. "Imagine the shame. We were not even allowed to walk upon his earth; we were cast into the bowels of the planet that had caused all the trouble to start with. Over time, we learned that we could walk upon the surface of earth by possessing the mortal bodies of humans or animals. Do not forget we still had the abilities of angels."

"When did you receive your physical body?" Jacob interrupted.

Turning to face Jacob, Lucifer's eyes narrowed and then he said, "It was at the time of judgment, and let me tell you, the humiliation of a physical body compares only to that of our journey out of heaven." Lucifer took his seat in the high-backed chair. Seeming to take a breath to clear his mental state, he continued. "You see, Jacob Litchfield, in this realm your judgment technically has already taken place. Your soul is already in heaven."

"So I'm something of a paradox."

"Yes, you could say that. Our timelines have crossed. Your future is my past, but we will all end up in the same present," Lucifer said with a smile.

"I apologize for interrupting you. Please continue."

Lucifer stood up and bowed to Jacob. "Thank you, Jacob Litchfield." Walking over to the fireplace, he placed both hands on the mantle and stared into the flames. "There was one question that I had with all that had happened. Why did the Creator not simply destroy us?" Lucifer turned around and looked at Jacob. "Was that against some ancient rule that even he could not break? I formed a council of what I considered to be the most enlightened of the fallen angels, and we discussed this question, along with many others. We discussed this fact, reasoning that if we could cause the human race to fall out of the Creator's favor, they would not be allowed through the gates of heaven. This, in turn, would cause him to rethink his position with us.

We studied our prey for some time. It did not take long to learn the ways of the human heart. We learned quickly that humans are creatures of habit and they always want what they cannot have. As you already know, the first humans were easily conquered. The Creator was furious. His human race was now tainted. A great celebration took place in our new kingdom when the first human soul entered our Shangri-La. Soon they would all end up here. The Creator was stubborn though, he never wavered from his original decision to banish us from his kingdom." Lucifer stood again. "I tell you the gloves were off now and can you blame us, really? As time went on, we learned more about the physical world and the rules that apply. Physical bodies could be duplicated, at least in appearance, and we were now free to roam the earth."

Lucifer crossed one leg over the other, then giving Jacob a smug look said, "The next part of the plan was to interbreed with the humans. If we all became one race, the Creator would surely have to take us back, or at least one would think he would. We waited centuries for the human population to increase in numbers. We watched and waited, and finally, it was time to make our move. Even I have to admit that there is nothing more desirable than the soft skin of a young human woman. So soft, so inviting, like the sweetest piece of fruit that is ready to be plucked. We drew straws to decide who would go, and the lucky ones went among the humans to take wives. We brought the humans technological advances. Nothing that made the Creator happy either; it moved the human race rather quickly along the technological timeline you might say. If you stop and really look at the changes we caused, they would have happened sooner or later anyhow." Lucifer moved away from the fireplace and walked back to his chair. He sat down and looked at Jacob. "This all went well. Our half-breed humans were becoming more numerous and let me tell you they were a vast improvement over the normal humans of that time, faster, stronger, and most of all, they were more intelligent."

"This is what Enoch wrote about, isn't it?" Jacob asked, interrupting Lucifer's tale.

"Yes, it was. The funny part about that is those writings did not even end up in your Christian Bible. Do you know why that is?" Lucifer asked.

"No, I don't," Jacob said with a shrug.

"Humans do not really want to know the truth," Lucifer said. "Let us get back to the history lesson. Do you know what happened next, Jacob Litchfield?"

"The flood?"

"Oh yes, the loving God, the father of mankind, wiped his beloved human race out. Can you believe it?"

"Yes, I can. You contaminated his creation. Think about it, he made the fact of your interbreeding a moot point. He started the human race over again," Jacob pointed out to his host.

"Yes, yes, he did," Lucifer said in a somber tone, and then his mood brightened. "Of course, there was a sudden explosion of population in my kingdom. You do realize that every human that perished in the flood entered through my gates? Government suddenly became a necessity to control the new populace and the first feudal government was created. The kingdom grew nicely. We built up our infrastructure. Our new purpose in life was to take every soul we could get from the Creator."

"What do you gain by taking souls?"

"I truly believe that if we take enough souls the Creator will have no choice but to bring us back into his fold."

"The flood wasn't enough to prove to you that this will never happen?" Jacob asked in a loud and unbelieving voice.

"Jacob Litchfield, do you really think the Creator would let two-thirds of his creation spend eternity in my kingdom?" Lucifer asked, answering Jacob's question with another question.

Jacob, no longer wanting to be involved in this debate, asked, "What happened when the Creator sent his Son?"

"Oh yes, you're talking about the ancient loophole. You know it is like playing blackjack with a dealer that knows what every card will be and the dealer never changes. Quite frustrating I might add, but we will still be successful in our plight, I assure you of that, Jacob Litchfield."

Jacob looked at Lucifer with dismay. He couldn't figure out how a being with the obvious intelligence that Lucifer possessed could be so stubborn. Maybe if one looked at all the different aliments that can inflict the human being, mental illness is simply one symptom that can be caught by being in close proximity to the devil. Maybe that's it; Lucifer is a masterful salesman of insanity. Of course, if one were to mix pride and insanity, it would be devastating to the human soul. Jacob snapped out of his self-induced trance and remembered where he was. He asked, "What happened to your kingdom when the Son was sacrificed?"

Lucifer, giving Jacob a dirty look, spoke loudly. "Yes, Jacob Litchfield, he descended into hell and on the third day arose from the dead, blah, blah, blah." Lucifer then laughed out loud. "He made his little tour through my kingdom. I no longer want to talk about the son," Lucifer said with a wave of his hand.

"Tell me more about your kingdom. Is it finished?" Jacob said.

"No, it is not finished. It is a work in progress. Soon though, it will be better than your world above." Lucifer continued before Jacob could ask another question. "The writers of the book made hell seem like such a horrid place. It is simply life on earth without the presence of the Creator. Even without the Creator's presence, everything is just simple science."

"Simple science?" Jacob interjected.

"Yes, simple science. We hit a few snags early on, but nothing that could not be fixed with a little more study. As you already know, food and water are not an issue here. Humans do not have to eat or drink to survive here. They just need order."

"How do you keep order in a place like this?"

"The first and most important thing is that we must achieve unity. None of this will work unless the entire kingdom is governed by one strong ruler." Turning, he looked at Jacob. "Look at the governments on your earth. Were they ever successful without a strong ruling king? A great king ensures everything runs like a well-oiled machine. To keep perfect order." The letter R rolled off his tongue when he pronounced the word *perfect*. "Look at Germany in your World War II. Think about what that little country achieved in such a small amount of time."

"Six million people were tortured and killed in that war. I wouldn't consider that a great victory. Hitler was a maniac," Jacob said.

Lucifer laughed out loud. "Humans always look at the bad side of everything. They never cherish the small accomplishments, the small victories. I always say, do not dwell on the failures. Everything that happens in life is a series of little successes or failures. Sometimes winning a few little battles is just as good as winning the war, if you know what I mean. Look at some of the greatest civilizations: Egypt, Rome, and the G.U."

"What is the G.U.?" Jacob asked.

"It was the last great civilization of your earth. The entire population of earth was controlled by one government. It was a beautiful thing."

"So you're talking about the new world order that the Book of Revelations talks about?" Jacob asked.

"Oh, I keep forgetting you are from an earlier time. That is very interesting, you being from an earlier time, I mean, I guess it will not hurt you to find out all this information about your future." He paused for a second. "You seem to be an intelligent human, and I am sure you are well-read in biblical matters. So technically, we are discussing subjects you already know, right?"

Jacob nodded at the statement. Lucifer was masterful at justifying his actions, Jacob thought to himself. Another question suddenly leaped into Jacob's mind. "You didn't mention the United States?"

"Oh, it was one of my greatest accomplishments," he said with a renewed excitement. "The modern Babylon, rotten to the core it was." His excited tone calmed a little. "I did not mention it because, on a timeline, the United States lasted only for a fraction of time compared to other great civilizations. I forget you are from the time before the implosion of that civilization. It was simply delicious to watch. We employed every trick in the book. Money, pornography, greed, drugs, lust, it was quite masterful. A whisper here and a little push there, and the whole thing folded like a house of cards. It was all in the name of democracy and freedom." Lucifer stopped, stroking his chin like a college professor about to unfurl some great truth to his students. "Democracy was not an effective government. Freedom causes humans to try to think for themselves; no rules means, no control. Besides you cannot control people when they have more power and money than their own government, it just will not work."

Lucifer paused and appeared to be remembering something. "I have listened many times to humans debate whether greed leads to lust or vice versa. The answer is, it does not matter." He chuckled to himself. "As long as you have one, you always have the other. Do you not agree, Pastor Litchfield?"

Jacob had to admit to himself, he did agree with Lucifer on this point, but all sin is bad. "Sin is sin. It does not matter which form it takes, it is all wrong," he answered.

Lucifer smiled at Jacob's answer and nodded to him. "You have been well trained, Preacher, brainwashed by his teachings, of course. I guess I would have been disappointed if you were not." Lucifer sprang from his chair and looked up to the ceiling of his chambers. "Let me ask you, if you want something, why not take it? If you see a beautiful woman, why not have her? What is wrong with wanting? Is it not the great motivator? What is wrong with going with one's desires? If we are not supposed to use them, why do we have them? Answer me, Preacher." Lucifer shouted loudly, turning his view from the ceiling back to Jacob.

"Everyone has the power to choose," Jacob said from his chair.

"Choose, make a choice. Free-fucking-will. Why should I have to? Why not do what I want, when I want?" Lucifer took a deep breath and appeared to relax. He sat down again and said calmly, "Well, we have covered enough about freewill." Lucifer looked at Jacob and asked, "Is there anything else you would like to know before we continue our tour?"

Jacob thought for a second. "Drugs, were they something you invented, or were they something that grew out of your advancement of man's knowledge of technology?"

"Ahh, yes, drugs, the modern tree of knowledge. Humans would come up with any excuse to dabble in the product. Just a little at first, then a little more. We would whisper in their ears, 'You can quit any time you want.' They would jump in head first, and then we had them. I believe they called it the expansion of their minds. However, to answer your question,

Jacob Litchfield, no, we did not create drugs. Humans distorted their use. Like most things on earth, something that serves the purpose of good can be turned around and used for evil. Like everything else, it was blamed on us."

"Why do you object to everyone blaming you for the evil that exists on earth? It seems to me that you would like the notoriety. I think you would revel in the fact that everything that is bad is entirely your doing," Jacob said.

Lucifer smiled broadly, then looked at Jacob. "You are probably right, Jacob Litchfield, but not everything that has gone wrong on the Creator's great green earth was our fault. I will tell you the most important thing we have learned about humans; if life is easy enough, they will forget about the Creator. I can tell you from experience that when a civilization turns its back on him, its time is short."

"What about time? When I was here earlier, it seemed like I was here for hours, and when I returned to earth I had only been gone for the time it takes to dream." Jacob realized he had just said something he shouldn't have. He watched for a change in Lucifer's expression, but he never saw one. Jacob was sure Lucifer heard the comment about being here before, but if he did, he never let on.

"It is simple; time is a form of energy not unlike electricity or nuclear fusion. Each realm, heaven and earth, have their own level of energy, two energies that move at different speeds," Lucifer stated simply.

"Explain further if you would," Jacob said.

"Okay, on earth, before we fell, angels could cross from one dimension to the other. Here on earth it is like crawling at a snail's pace. Heaven's dimension moves at the speed of thought. When we were cast out of heaven, we were locked into your physical world. We still had our abilities, but we could no longer travel between dimensions. It was very degrading, I might add," Lucifer explained with a distant stare.

"So you were locked into the underworld, and you could not travel on the surface without forming some kind of physical body." Jacob paused as he tried to digest this information. "Am I correct?" Jacob didn't wait for confirmation. "How is it then that the world thinks of demons as ugly and horrific creatures?"

"Well." Lucifer then chuckled lightly. "When I said we learned how to create physical bodies, I never said we stayed entirely in human form."

Jacob looked at Lucifer. "Basically, every roadblock the Creator set before you, you figured a way around it."

"You make it sound so dirty, Jacob Litchfield," Lucifer said with a smile. "Of course we did. What other choice did we have? As the Creator's newly created populace grew in numbers we appeared to them as great beings. We figured that confusing them about who the real God was would carry on through every generation to come." Lucifer turned to give Jacob a beaming smile. "I would hazard to guess we did a bang-up job, wouldn't you say?"

"Aren't you afraid of the final fallout of all your actions?" Jacob asked while shaking his head in disbelief.

"I will bet you are referring to the cryptic writings in your Book of Revelations? Well, I haven't lost any sleep yet," Lucifer answered without showing any concern.

"What about all the bodies that littered the outskirts of your kingdom?" Jacob asked.

"Do not worry, Jacob Litchfield. I know you have visited here before, three times to be exact. The bodies are from the final battle. It was so destructive that humans were forced to escape the surface of the earth. The surface became one huge firestorm. The last of the fighting took place here." Lucifer answered, lifting himself from the chair. "I grow tired of this. I want to show you something."

Chapter Twenty-Six

Cathy's mind snapped back to the matter at hand when the car started to slow down. Turning into the driveway of a deserted farm house, she couldn't believe that this was as far as he was going to take them. She was sure they hadn't traveled more than ten or twelve miles. She knew they were somewhere near Onarga, Illinois, a small town on the western edge of Iroquois county. It gave her a flash of hope; the authorities would surely find them quick, but it also showed the instability in the kidnapper's thought process. Maybe there wouldn't be anything for the authorities to find except corpses. She decided that she had to find a window of opportunity to disable the kidnapper and escape with the children.

He drove the car through the barn lot and into the alleyway of an old wooden corncrib. Shutting off the engine, he threw open the driver's door. "Get out," he growled as he pulled Mara out of the front seat by the arm.

"What are you going to do with us?" Mara asked, as she slid out of the front seat.

"Shut up, you little bitch," he scolded. He grabbed Mara by the back of her pajamas and jerked her toward him. Kneeling down, he wrapped his left arm around her chest, and with the other, he held the large knife to Mara's throat. In a shrill voice, he yelled to Cathy and Michael, "Get out of the car and walk to the house." Cathy and Michael quickly exited the car and started for the house.

She held tightly to Michael's hand as they crossed the yard. The owner of the farmstead paid to keep a security light kept on so the house yard was well lit. Cathy surveyed her surroundings as they approached the house. A corncrib, a garage that was missing part of its roof, and an enormous old barn that appeared to be in decent condition. The grass had been mowed recently with a tractor mower, leaving thick piles of grass. The house was a broken-down old Victorian, a grand old two-story structure with large gables on each side. A porch that split the massive structure could be accessed by a wide set of crumbling concrete steps. At one time, the entrance was a beautifully carved oak doorway, but time had left it weathered and rotted. The white paint, which once covered the house, had long since chipped away, leaving the gray cracked lumber underneath. Evergreens that had been a tasteful accent to the house's landscaping had now grown above most of the first-story windows.

They walked up the sidewalk, carefully stepping over the slabs of concrete heaved up from years of freezing and thawing. Beer cans from a recent party littered the steps and porch. It was clear to Cathy that this was probably a common meeting place for underage drinkers.

They walked up the stairs to the porch. "Open the door," the kidnapper commanded.

Cathy walked up to the door and turned the rusty knob. To her surprise, the heavy door swung open with a loud groan. The padlock and clasp that once secured the door had been broken off long ago. Numerous beer cans rattled at her feet as she walked through the threshold of the old house. She realized she was freezing and figured that the children had to be feeling the same. She prayed that there was something in the house to bundle them up with to keep warm.

"Get your asses upstairs," he said, as he picked up Mara.

Cathy was looking for a chance to disable the creepy man, but as long as he had Mara in his arms she couldn't take a chance. If he would just move away from Mara for a second she would make her move. Michael and Cathy walked toward the stairway. She held Michael's hand in her left and her right she slid into her robe pocket and grabbed the ink pen tightly. This might be her chance.

They started up the stairway, each step groaning from their body weight. Through the various windows and holes in the structure, enough light filtered in from the security light outdoors that they could see where they were stepping. At the top of the stairs he spoke. "Go in the last room down the hall," he said, as he indicated the direction they were to travel.

Cathy and Michael walked down the dark hallway. The musty smell of the abandoned house filled Cathy's nostrils. She could pick up the faint odor of something that had recently died. The dark walls seemed to radiate the cold like dirty blocks of ice. Arriving at a bedroom door, she turned to locate the kidnapper. Still holding Mara, he was at the other end of the hallway kicking through the garbage that littered the floor. What was he looking for?

Chapter Twenty-Seven

Lucifer led Jacob out of the room and down the stairs to a different door than before. They walked across an inner compound that connected the three towers. In the middle of the compound stood a stone arch with a stairway that led down below the towers. Setting in front of the stairway was a square stone, with a large crystal in the center. Jacob mentally compared it to the size of a large grandfather clock, and when he looked into it what he saw amazed him.

Lucifer, with his back to the crystal, said in a sarcastic manner. "Oh, yes, it is a gift from the Creator; a direct view into heaven, something to remind of us of what we are missing. He has a wicked sense of humor, does he not?" His voice trailed off for a second, and then he continued to speak. "I have tried to have it destroyed. I have tried to have it moved but to no avail. I guess it will just have to remain here for eternity. Do you not think it was a cruel thing to do?"

Jacob couldn't take his eyes off of the crystal. What he was seeing was beautiful and he realized why it was such a torment to Lucifer. Jacob finally turned away from the crystal and walked a few feet away. Looking across the compound at the humans, he felt a sudden flood of sorrow for Sara. He tried to conceal it, but Lucifer picked up on it immediately.

"Oh, yes, you're thinking about your sister Sara," Lucifer said with the tone of his voice suddenly changing. "Would you like to see her? She is here, of course. You did not think I would actually let her roam free to meet up with the other rebels, did you?" He now spoke as if he were enjoying the new topic of dialogue. "Like I said before, it would not be good government to not know what is going on behind one's back. Follow me, Jacob Litchfield."

Lucifer led Jacob to the stairway. The heat that hit Jacob's face as he looked down the stairway was almost unbearable; like a sauna turned up on high. The odor was sulfuric, just like the smell that had accompanied the letters. Gripping him gently by the arm, Lucifer walked him down into the stairway. Jacob realized that the structure on the surface was just the tip of the iceberg. Lucifer led him down a large corridor with numerous hallways. During the trek, Jacob heard the moans and screams of millions of humans.

"Why would you need to have a prison in a place like this? I don't think anyone is going to escape," Jacob asked.

"This is kind of like a reeducation camp. It is a place to keep troublemakers in check until they see the error of their ways," Lucifer said, never missing a stride or slowing his pace. He walked with his head up, chest jutted out, and both arms behind his back.

They arrived in a large octagon-shaped room illuminated by torches. The walls were lined with panels of highly polished silver and the floor was made of smooth white granite. In the middle of the room there was a large chair made of gold with red silk cushions. The chair was elevated on a platform that stood two feet higher than the rest of the floor. As Jacob looked around the room, he realized that when Lucifer sat on his throne he could see himself in each of the eight-mirrored panels. The workmanship was so flawless that with all the panels in place, Jacob couldn't find the door they had just entered.

Standing on each side of the chair was a creature that Jacob had never seen before, but he thought they were some form of seraphim. They each had six wings and reminded Jacob somewhat of a demonic dragonfly. Dressed in ornate armor, each carried a large lance and a broad sword at his side. They were impressive-looking creatures, not something you would want to tangle with.

"Welcome to my throne room," Lucifer said, and then he leaned to one of the guards and said something into his ear. The guard left quickly and soon returned with another chair. Placing it next to Lucifer's throne, but on the lower level, the guard grasped Jacob's shoulder roughly and sat him down in the chair. Jacob then heard another door open somewhere behind him and saw someone led into the room by two different guards. At first, he didn't recognize who it was, but then he recognized his sister Sara. Her hands were tied behind her back and she was being led into the room by a chain fastened to an iron collar that was placed tightly around her neck. She was naked, dirty, and she looked exhausted. She raised her head and looked at Lucifer defiantly.

"Sara!" Jacob shouted.

"Be quiet, Preacher!" Lucifer shouted. Standing up, he walked over to her, grabbed her by the chin and easily lifting her off the ground. She didn't try to resist and just hung from Lucifer's powerful grasp like a rag doll. "Such a clever little human, so pretty, so feminine, even in hell you drive the human males crazy with lust." Lucifer then closed his eyes and said the words "*pareo mihi.*"

Jacob understood enough Latin to know what Lucifer had just said, but nothing seemed to happen.

Lucifer repeated the words and still nothing happened. Jacob could see Lucifer's powerful body become tense with anger, but did not understand what he was trying to accomplish.

Lucifer turned toward Jacob and said, "Jacob Litchfield, your sister is going to pay. If you do not already know, pain is a little different here compared to pain on earth." Holding her off the ground, he lifted his free hand to where everyone in the room could see it then raised his index finger. A claw grew from the end of it. Turning back to Sara, he stabbed the sharp claw just below her breasts and ran it down her midriff to the top of her leggings. The skin of her stomach split open, blood ran down into her pubic area, flowing down onto her inner thighs, but then seemed to evaporate like steam before reaching the floor. She winced at the pain, but didn't make a sound. "Jacob Litchfield, you would not believe the amount of time I have to keep doing this to your sister. You might call it an eternity." Setting Sara down on her feet, he gave her a shove and she fell backwards, blood still oozing from the wound. He walked over to his throne and sat down. He leaned over, looked at Jacob, and asked, "Are you ready to talk now, Jacob Litchfield?"

Jacob looked back at Sara, who had managed, even with her hands tied behind her, to roll up onto her knees. She was rocking back and forth, as she had in the cave with the same blank look on her face. Jacob felt sympathy for his sister, but he knew there was nothing he could do for her. "No, my sister's future is already set and I don't believe anything I do now will change it."

Pointing at Sara, Lucifer said, "Take her away and put her back in the cell with Jenkins." Lucifer stood up and turned to Jacob.

Jacob wondered if it could possibly be the same Jenkins that had kidnapped Cathy and the children.

"Yes, Jacob Litchfield, it is the same person. Only now, Stevie Jenkins is not bound by any earthly rules. The concept of time is amazing," Lucifer said taking pride in the fact he knew what Jacob was thinking.

Jacob realized something at that point. It was easy for Lucifer to know what he was thinking if he always put the thought patterns into Jacob's mind. For instance, the mere mention of the name Jenkins was sure to make him think of the man who had kidnapped his wife and children. It was something that Jacob would have to remember.

"Well, Jacob Litchfield, I have tried to reason with you and I have tried to frighten you, but I guess that will not work, so I have to believe that the negotiations have only started," Lucifer said as he stepped down from the elevated perch. He walked a few steps away from his throne, with his back to Jacob he said. "Name your price, Jacob Litchfield. Something you want here, or on earth."

Jacob, trying to figure out where the devil's tactic was leading, said nothing. He knew he could not ask for anything—unless of course he could ask for something so horrid to Lucifer he could never agree to it.

"Everybody has their price. What is your price, Jacob Litchfield?" Lucifer said in a cajoling manner as he paced slowly back and forth. "I could let the claim I have on your sister's soul go," he suggested softly. "She could be in heaven with the simple agreement to destroy the letters. It is just as easy as burning three pieces of paper. That does not seem like such a large task to me. Does it to you, Jacob Litchfield?"

"Could you explain to me how this claim works?" Jacob asked, trying to buy a little time.

Giving Jacob an impatient look, Lucifer explained. "It is simple. The Creator and I have this agreement. The faithful are his to claim and the unfaithful are mine to claim. If I do not claim one, or release my claim to one, they are free to enter heaven."

"I did not know this," Jacob exclaimed. An alarm went off in Jacob's head. Jacob knew there was something wrong with Lucifer's statement. Why would God let someone who never loved Him into his kingdom? Jacob really doubted that Lucifer had any say in the division of human souls.

"So, it is that simple? I destroy the letters and you let my sister go to heaven?"

"What could be simpler?"

"First of all, those letters must be really important if you are willing to go through all this trouble. If God… excuse me," Jacob nodded to Lucifer, then continued. "If the Creator took the trouble to take the letters from here and then send them to me on earth, they must be of great importance. You mentioned a while ago that he has put these little schemes into action many times. What do you mean by other schemes?"

Lucifer was visibly beginning to tire of being nice, but decided to give Jacob an answer anyway. "I like to call them the fertilizers of faith—little miracles that are supposed to give you puny, little skin bags faith. Of course, the day of the big miracle was over long ago, because we could so easily discredit them with numerous scientific reasons as to how they happened. He then moved to the little personal miracles, for instance a child being born or one human saving the life of another; miracles that each human had to recognize or discover for themselves. You can imagine the increased workload those little gems caused us; there were so many of them to diffuse. Remember, Jacob Litchfield, the Israelites had bread falling from the sky and they still did not love the Creator. They saw an entire body of water split and walked upon the sea floor to escape the Egyptian army, and they still did not love the Creator. They had the Creator in their face and it did not matter. I can cloud the human mind to the point of blindness," Lucifer said in an arrogant rant.

"So, why are you so concerned about three pieces of paper? If you can so easily cloud the minds of humans, why would this be any different for you than manna falling from heaven? Actually, it seems to me that this situation would have little impact on the human conscience compared to the parting of the Red Sea," Jacob said. He wasn't sure if it was wise to push Lucifer, but he was beginning to believe that the letters were more important to Lucifer than he was willing to admit.

Lucifer looked perplexed for a second, then said, "It is the principle. I will not let the Creator get by with anything. I will always be the black to his white, the negative to his positive. The reason I can so easily cloud the mind of a human is that they are all looking for something, anything to give them meaning. They do not believe or fully understand that their pitiful existence on earth is simply the time they are allotted to find where they fit in the balance. In this allotted time, they do not understand that the choice they make will dictate where they will spend their eternity, a very unpleasant eternity for some."

"So, this kingdom of yours is unpleasant, I would have to agree with you," Jacob said.

"Now, Jacob Litchfield, making sport of someone's home is not a kind thing to do. Even though this place would not be my first choice of real estate, it is in fact, mine."

"If this place is yours, how did the letters that were written in your kingdom end up in my hands?" Jacob asked without thinking.

"GUARDS!" Lucifer screamed. "I grow tired of all this useless chatter! Put him in the cell with his sister." Lucifer walked back to his throne and sat down. "Jacob Litchfield, if you decide to take me up on my offer, just let one of the guards know, besides you need to see how your sister will spend the rest of her eternity. Oh, one last thing, Jacob Litchfield, you do realize that a lifetime in hell is equal to seconds on earth?"

"Yes, I've heard that," Jacob answered, wondering where this was leading.

"Jacob Litchfield, how many sleeping pills did you take before you went to sleep back on earth?" Lucifer asked as an evil smile spread across his porcelain-colored face. "Take this puny human away from me!" Lucifer shouted.

Lucifer's question sent a chill up Jacob's spine. One of the six-winged creatures walked over to Lucifer; then, after they spoke, the guard walked to Jacob and jerked him out of his chair.

Chapter Twenty-Eight

Cathy took Michael into a bedroom at the end of the upstairs hallway where they sat on what was left of a bed. A mouse, disrupted by the intruders, scurried from under the mildew-covered mattress. Cathy looked around the room. It was fifteen feet wide by ten feet long, with a closet near the entrance. There was a window positioned in the middle of the outside wall, with a view of the barn lot and driveway. The rotten mattress and the bed frame were the only pieces of furniture in the room. Smashed, dust-covered beer cans littered the hardwood floor, along with a pile of rotting curtains. Old floral-patterned wallpaper hung in tattered strips from the crumbling plaster walls with cobwebs filling numerous cracks and holes. The walls were streaked with brown stains from years of rain leaking through holes in the rotting roof. Eerie shadows danced across the walls, cast from a dead tree positioned between the house and the pole light.

The kidnapper and Mara entered the room. Cathy couldn't believe it, but the kidnapper was sipping a beer. He had found a can of beer somewhere in the house; in fact, he had found a whole six-pack. Another glimmer of hope shot through Cathy. If he would drink enough to dull his senses they might stand a chance of getting away. On the other hand, it might cause him to become violent or more irrational.

The man walked directly to the window to look out across the barn lot, never letting go of Mara. The little girl turned slightly to look at Cathy pleadingly. She was pale and looked cold. Cathy turned to look at Michael who appeared to be in the same condition. She had to do something. It dawned on Cathy at this moment that these were her children now… HER CHILDREN!

"Mister, may I look for something to wrap the children with? They're freezing." Cathy asked, as calm as her trembling body would allow.

"What?" he stammered.

"May I look for something to cover the children with?" she said, this time with more confidence.

He looked around the room and spotted the curtains lying on the floor. Letting go of Mara, he walked five or six steps to the pile of rotten linen and bent over to pick them up.

Cathy saw her chance. Sliding her hand into her robe pocket, she grabbed the ballpoint pen and ran toward the kidnapper with the pen held high above her head. She was almost on top of the kidnapper when he turned suddenly and swung a backhand at her head. The blow caught her squarely across the right eye and sent her sprawling backwards across the dirty floor.

"Stupid bitch," he mumbled as he stepped on her wrist and grabbed the pen out of her hand, and then he moved back to his place at the window.

Cathy did not move. Both children ran to where she was lying on the floor.

Mara, sitting on her knees, reached down to pat her softly on the cheek. "Aunt Cathy, are you okay?"

Cathy moaned.

"She's waking up," Michael whispered.

Cathy's eyes fluttered open. The man turned away from the window hollering in his shrill voice. "Get back on the bed, you little shits." He walked over to the curtains on the floor and rifled through the heap of material. Finding a thick cord, he moved behind Cathy and roughly lifted her into a sitting position. Then he tied her arms behind her back, stuffed a dirty piece of material into her mouth, and dragged her over to the bed. "Stay on the bed or I'll fucking kill you." He grabbed Mara and pulled her off the bed, and then took her back to the window. Taking off his coat, he wrapped her in it and sat on the floor putting her on his lap. He wrapped his arms around her and said, "Boy, get the curtains off the floor and cover yourselves up."

Chapter Twenty-Nine

The guard led Jacob out of the throne room and down another long hallway. He wondered if the number of sleeping pills would lengthen his stay in this place, and for how long.

He followed the guard until they came to another large room with a large circular twenty-foot-diameter hole in the middle of the floor. The light illumination from the hole lit the room up. As they got closer, Jacob could feel its intense heat, but before they got any closer, he was jerked away by the guard and pushed back into another corridor. The guard took a torch off the wall and continued down a narrow and dark rocky pathway. Jacob could hear someone screaming ahead of them. After another minute or two, the guard stopped, opened a large iron door, and told Jacob to get inside. Hearing the iron door slam shut behind him, Jacob froze, listening to the different noises that echoed through the jail cell. He closed his eyes in an attempt to stop the panic that was growing in his mind. The stench that filled his lungs caused him to start coughing violently. When he caught his breath, he was startled when a dirty faced human with long greasy hair jumped into his view.

"I know you, Preacher. Do you remember me, Preacher?" the strange human asked in a high-pitched voice.

Jacob did not recognize the man and he asked, "I don't know you. Who are you?"

The man circled Jacob, then pointed to himself with his thumb and answered, "I'm Stevie "Moonface" Jenkins. We met once. I knew your wife and children." He paused, "You know that you were the only one who ever tried to help me?"

"I'm sorry, I don't remember you," Jacob said with a confused look.

"What're you doing here, Preacher? You don't belong here, Preacher," Stevie said, then laughed in an insane little giggle.

"I don't really know. Is there anyone else in here with you?" Jacob whispered.

"Yeah, yeah, I've got two cellmates. Would you like to meet them?" Stevie left, returning in a flash, dragging a filth covered but beautiful female with him. Meet my future bride, Preacher. Master gave her to me. Hey, maybe you could perform the ceremony. Well maybe not. I better let the master do that."

Sara, jerking away from Stevie, rushed to her brother, grabbed him in a bear hug, and cried, "Jacob I knew that was you in the throne room. I can see you now." She held the embrace for a minute, and then, backing away from her brother, she asked, "What are you doing here?"

No longer unclothed, she was wearing the same leggings and combat boots she had worn during his last visit. Jacob noticed that the wound she had received from Lucifer had almost healed. Then, hearing something in the back of the cell, Jacob asked, "Who--or what--else is in here?"

"Some big creepy, but he's hurt bad," Stevie said from behind Sara, laughing with a shrill giggle. "He won't be getting up anytime soon."

Jacob walked over to where he heard the sound. The torches from the walkway outside the cell cast just enough light for him to see the fallen angel. Acubus was sprawled out flat on his back on the cell floor. The creature looked up at Jacob and then looked away quickly as if in shame. Jacob moved closer. Seeing numerous deep cuts that ran up and down his tattered body, Jacob's stomach turned. Acubus's arms and legs looked like raw meat, his midsection covered with deep cuts that crisscrossed over his entire torso and legs.

"Is there anything I can do for you?" Jacob asked.

Acubus tried to lift his head. Seeing the effort it was taking, Jacob tried to reach out to help him.

Shying away from the preacher's touch, he laid his weary head on the ground. "Preacher, they will be back soon to start the torture again. They could not get any information out of me last time, but they will try again," Acubus whispered weakly.

"They want to know about the rebels don't they?" Jacob asked. Acubus nodded his head in agreement. "We need to get you out of here before they come back."

"And go where, Preacher?" Acubus grumbled in a rasp, trying again to sit up.

"Do you know this place?" Jacob asked.

"Yes," Acubus said, starting to fall backwards. Jacob grabbed one of his powerful arms to help steady him. A look of surprise spread across the creature's face when he looked down at the arm that Jacob just touched. Jacob joined Acubus in surprise when he too saw that the wounds seemed to be healing over in all directions from the spot where Jacob had touched him. A powerful light wave ran across his body. The wounds closed and replaced with smooth healthy skin. Acubus looked up at Jacob in shock and said, "How did you do that, Preacher?"

"I…I don't know," Jacob answered in awe.

"Thank you, Preacher," Acubus said, as he looked down at his newly healed body.

Jacob took a few steps back and looked down at his two hands. God was with him even here, he thought to himself, but why was he given this gift? Was it just to heal Acubus now, or would it be a gift for later use? "He is here with us now, isn't he?" Jacob whispered out loud, looking around, trying to see something that could not be seen.

Acubus, without looking up said, "He is everywhere. That is the point that Lucifer cannot accept. Those of us who have realized this point have banded together to form the rebellion. We let Lucifer take us down; now it is his turn."

"Do you think there might be a chance for your salvation?" Jacob whispered.

"No…no, I do not. But he needs to pay for what he did," Acubus said as he raised his head and looked into Jacob's eyes.

Jacob remained silent, not knowing what to say. Finally, he said softly, "I am sorry."

Acubus smiled and said, "It was a choice that I made. You have no need to be sorry."

Sara walked over to Jacob and Acubus with Stevie right on her heels. Irritated by her new companion, she gave him a shove and yelled, "Get away from me, you son of a bitch!" To the amazement of Stevie and everyone else in the room, he flew ten feet through the air and landed hard against the jail cell wall. "How did I do that?" she asked with a confused look.

Acubus lifted himself from the rocky ground of their prison cell and stretched his powerful frame. Sara gasped. "How did you heal so fast?"

"The preacher here has been given a gift. I think you also have been given a gift," he said, motioning over to Jenkins who was moaning from the spot where he'd landed.

"We need to get out of here, and now, but how do we do it?" Jacob asked Acubus.

"The guards are the only ones who have the keys. Try to get one of them to come inside the cell and then overpower them," Acubus said, and then added, "Good luck!"

Jacob looked around the cell. Maybe there was something they could use to open the door.

"Wait, maybe we don't need a key, Preacher," Acubus said as he looked at Sara. "Sara, open the door."

Understanding immediately, Jacob chimed in, "Try it, Sara!"

She walked over to the large iron door. She reached up to the bars that formed a window in the door, taking a firm grasp, she started to pull. The muscles in her arms tightened and she clenched her teeth. At first a creaking noise could be heard, then with a loud crack the door splintered from the jam. Sara lifted the door and laid it against the wall of the prison cell as if it were made from cardboard.

Jacob walked over to Sara, patting her on the back said, "Unbelievable, sis." Acubus nodded approvingly. Stevie moaned from where he was still lying.

"We do not want you setting off any alarms," Acubus said. He walked over to Stevie and picked him up by the throat.

Jacob could hear the sound of bones cracking in Stevie's neck as he was lifted into the air by the powerful creature. Stevie's head was tilted oddly to one side, his face lost all expression. He just hung in the air shaking; a gurgling noise emitting from his throat. Acubus, looking pleased with his handiwork, dropped the quivering body to the floor.

"Is he… dead?" Jacob asked.

"No. No one dies here. I broke his neck. In a little while he will come around," Acubus said. "We need to exit this cell. They will be checking in on the preacher quite regularly. We will never make it out the way you came in, it's too close to the throne room and too well guarded. The main hall that leads from the stairway is not the only way out. I was one of the architects who designed this place. We need to work our way down to the bottom level. There is a way out where the river of fire flows. Only a small number of the fallen know about this, we found it one time while exploring the mountain." Acubus then dragged the listless body of Stevie Jenkins over to the wall, placing his wrists in a pair of empty shackles hanging from the wall. He then grabbed Stevie's left foot and violently twisted it, filling the room with what sounded like popcorn popping. "This will give us a little more time."

Jacob swallowed hard, looked at Acubus, smiled weakly and said, "You lead the way, big fellow."

Chapter Thirty

cubus took a torch off the walkway wall, then started down the rocky tunnel.

Jacob, following close behind Sara, asked, "How are you doing, sis?"

"I'm fine. Let's get going. We can talk on the way."

"Can we trust him, Sara?"

"I trust him. When the two of us were caught, he fought hard to protect me. They tortured him for information, but he never gave anything up. I'm glad I can see you now; Acubus told me that I couldn't see you before because humans can't see the astral body. So what is different about this time?"

"I don't know," he answered

Working hard to keep up with Acubus, Jacob told Sara about the events that led up to his arrival in hell. As he finished the tale, the three of them came to a large open cavern. Acubus motioned for them to keep quiet and squatted down to look out into the large cave. Jacob crawled up behind him to peer out across the open area. What he saw sickened him; rows and rows of sharpened stakes driven into the rocky ground with writhing humans impaled on them.

"What is this place, Acubus?"

"It is hell, Preacher," Acubus said with just a hint of a sarcastic smile. "This is one of the many punishment chambers."

"I mean this room, what is it?" Jacob asked, not believing what he was seeing. Sara moved up from behind Jacob.

"Oh, my God," Sara whispered as she looked out across the enormous cavern.

Acubus pushed the both of them back into the tunnel. "You two are going to have to be quiet." Acubus, pointing to the humans impaled on the stakes, said, "Do you want to end up like one of them? I don't know about you two, but I do not want to get caught again. What you see in this room is mild compared to other places in this castle. You two stay here. I will be right back." Acubus darted into the large room, crouched down, looked around, and spreading his enormous wings, lunged into the air. He hovered for a few seconds, then darted out of sight.

Jacob grabbed Sara's hand and pulled her back into the tunnel. "How did you get captured?"

"It wasn't long after your last visit. We were on the outskirts of the desert when suddenly the six-winged creatures attacked us. Acubus tried to fight them, but there were too many. I actually injured one, but there were just too many. We were brought back to the castle and placed in the cell. I was forced to watch them torture Acubus and then they put that disgusting human, Jenkins, with me. He tried to rape me, but he is a weak and pitiful fool. Soon after that, I was taken to Lucifer's throne room where I saw you. At first, I thought it was some kind of trick by Lucifer, but then you showed up in the cell and the rest, you know… I'm sorry about Cathy and the children," Sara said. Then, bowing her head, she said, "If I had known what trouble the letters were going to cause, I wouldn't have written them."

"It's not your fault. You just wrote them, you didn't send them. Someone else has plans for those letters, but I don't know what," Jacob said trying to comfort Sara. "Cathy and the children are in good hands and they will be taken care of. How is your wound feeling?"

Ignoring the last question, Sara asked, "What do you mean they will be taken care of?"

"Sara, you never did understand anything except how to make money and get the things you wanted on earth, did you?"

"What do you mean?"

"Do you not understand why it was that you ended up in this place? You tried to be your own God. You depended on yourself and your own ability to control life. It blinded you to everything that was important. Your husband, your children, your parents, and most of all, your Savior, everything that should have been important to you meant nothing and that's why you are here. Lucifer blinded you with the glitter and gold of the world and now it has consumed your soul."

Sara looked at him, then broke eye contact. Bowing her head, she sighed and confessed. "It was always in the back of my mind. Even when I was a child I knew better, but I could ignore it so easy."

The sound of beating wings interrupted their conversation as Acubus's large frame filled the entryway to the large cavern. "Come now. We will have to be careful, but if we hurry, we can get across without being noticed. Remember, we still have the element of surprise on our side, but when they find that we are no longer in the cell, an alarm will be sent out. Trust me when I tell you, if you are the keeper of that part of the prison, and you lose inmates as important as you two are, you would conduct a thorough search. You do not want to answer to the king of this world for failure. Now listen, there are two guards perched on each side of the cavern. Their job is to keep the humans on the stakes. I let four humans go free, so they will be busy for a while trying to catch them. We are going to go right through the middle of the tortured humans. Do not let them distract you," Acubus said, as he entered the cavern.

Jacob and Sara followed closely. When they got close enough to see the first few faces of the impaled humans, Jacob started to gag. Some were staked through the stomach, with the point exiting through the backs of their necks, others were laid horizontally with the shaft running through their midsections. The ones that caught Jacob's attention were the ones that were placed on the stake in the sitting position with the point coming out of their mouths. No matter what position the humans were in, they all squirmed in pain and agony. Jacob and Sara looked at each other as they passed these tortured souls. It was obvious to Jacob that she was thinking the same thing that he was. "Do not get caught." Noise was not going to be the factor that would give them away. The moans and cries were deafening. There were many humans who just seemed to be screaming purely out of insanity. Some of the faces didn't show pain, just a weird psychotic glow. Jacob tried not to look into the eyes of the victims, but he was having trouble not staring at the multitude of faces. Acubus motioned for them to halt. Crouching low, he pointed off to the right. Looking through the crowd of impaled humans, Jacob could see a guard preparing to place human escapees back on a stake. The stake was six feet tall with a stopper about two feet up from the bottom. Jacob knew the stop was in place to keep the victim from sliding to the ground. Huddled together, the three of them watched as the guard slid the wiggling human back onto the stake. The screams of the human were choked out as the sharpened pole exited through its throat. Jacob vomited.

"That is what happens to a human who escapes the pole. Pleasant, is it not?" Acubus said with a grin.

Jacob, still feeling queasy, noticed again that the blood didn't touch the ground. He could see the wounds made by the stakes, but that's where it stopped. He remembered the explanation of how pain works in hell, and realized the implication of this kind of torture. The longer it takes to wound a human, the longer it takes to heal. Jacob was trying to remember the time ratio of pain in Sara's letter. The time it takes to receive an injury multiplied by six hundred sixty-six. These humans were on these stakes for who knows how long. Hearing the cries and moans of the tortured soul, he couldn't imagine the pain they were experiencing. The sounds were unimaginable, not to mention the visual nightmare he was viewing.

Acubus stood up slowly and motioned for them to continue. Jacob tried to gauge how big this cavern was; but once he was to the middle of the large chamber, he realized he could no longer see either end. He guessed the number of the humans impaled on stakes was in the low millions. They traveled for what seemed like an eternity before Jacob could see the opposite end of the cavern. At this point, his thoughts turned to Sara. She walked without any expression on her face. He was wondering if the stark realization that she was going to be here for eternity had sunk in. She had always been so strong during her human life on earth, but how long would it be before she would finally break and go insane with despair and fear like everyone here seemed to do? He wondered if hunger and thirst was a factor here as it was on earth. Would hunger finally be such an irresistible urge that it would make a human go insane? Jacob stopped, turned to Sara, and whispered to Sara, "Are you hungry?"

"What?" Sara answered.

"Are you hungry or thirsty?" Jacob repeated.

"No," Sara said, giving him a funny look.

"Why not? You've been here a long time. Surely you must feel hungry, thirsty, or something," Jacob asked.

"Jacob, my brother, in this place humans only respond to pain and the thoughts that are put into their minds. When I first met Acubus, he told me about the power of suggestion. He also told me how they can use that power to put anything they want into the human mind. I won't feel anything until someone puts it into my mind, or I am injured," Sara explained. Noticing they were falling behind, they hurried to catch up with Acubus.

Near the last of the impaled humans, Acubus stopped, commanding them to halt. There was a span of fifty feet between them and the exit of the cavern. Crouching low, Acubus moved swiftly toward the opening. He was almost to the exit when a loud siren started to wail. Acubus waved to them, urging them to hurry. They both took off at a sprint. Sara easily passed Jacob in a few strides; reaching back, she grabbed his arm and pulled him with her toward the tunnel entrance. They had caught up to Acubus when suddenly he growled and sprung into the air, both Jacob and Sara feeling the blast of air from his powerful wings. Turning around, they watched as the first of two human guards approached them with swords drawn. Like a bolt of lightning Acubus dove in, easily dodging the attacker's first blow, he then grabbed the guard's free arm and swung him around in a circle, smashing him into the stonewall. The sound of flesh and rock meeting at that speed was grotesque and Jacob watched in horror as the guard's body slid down like a smashed grasshopper running down a car windshield.

"Sara, take his weapon and cut off his head," Acubus commanded as he prepared for the second attacker.

Sara rushed to pick up the wounded guard's fallen sword. Lifting it high above her head, she brought it down across the dazed guard's neck, separating his head from his body. With an arrogant look of satisfaction, she watched the body fall at her feet. Jacob ran out and pulled her back to the cave exit.

Acubus and the second guard had each other by the throat, moving in a tight circle. Acubus seemed to be working the guard toward them at the mouth of the tunnel.

"Give yourself up; the king cannot be defeated," the guard said.

Not saying a word, Acubus continued to back the guard toward the exit.

"There will be nothing but an eternity of pain for you, traitor. You know that," the guard threatened through clinched teeth.

Acubus remained silent, still working the guard in Jacob and Sara's direction. Acubus glanced at Sara, then yelled, "Now, Sara!"

With unbelievable speed, Sara flew into the battle, ramming the sword deep into the back of the second guard. She let go of the sword as he fell to the ground, thrashing back and forth, struggling to remove the sword from his back. Acubus moved in, grabbed the handle of the sword, and pulled it out. He then shoved it back in, twisting it back and forth, until it severed the human's spinal cord. With a look of astonishment, the guard stopped moving and shook uncontrollably. Acubus, with his talon-shaped foot, stepped down roughly on his head, causing his face to become grotesquely distorted under his great weight, and then pulled out the blade. He wiped it off with his tunic, then handed it back to Sara.

"Always sever the spine," Acubus said as simply as a father might tell his daughter to clean her room. "Let's get moving," he said as he stepped into the tunnel.

Chapter Thirty-One

Regaining consciousness, Cathy's eyes slowly began to focus. Her head throbbed with a dull pain and the vision in her right eye seemed clouded. She was lying on her side in a fetal position. Her fingers were numb from the rope that tightly held her arms behind her body. The kidnapper stared out the window, rocking back and forth. He kept repeating the words, "Where are you, where are you?" Four empty beer cans sat next to him. "Where are you, where are you?"

Michael was sitting on the end of the bed, wrapped in a moth-eaten linen curtain. He was staring blankly at the wall, his face showing no emotion. Where's Mara, she thought?

Chapter Thirty-Two

"Why are the preacher and his pitiful sister running free in my castle?" Lucifer asked the three guards standing in front of his throne. Lucifer calmly tapped his fingers on the arms of the royal throne. Standing up quickly and causing the guards to move back a step or two, he turned around and placed his hands behind his back. "Find them," he demanded.

"Sir, the fallen rebel is with them. They have incapacitated two guards in the impaling chamber. I think they are heading down to the lower parts of the castle to hide… Sir, there is talk among the fallen that she is the one…"

"Shut up!" Lucifer screamed. "Bring up the hunters! I want that preacher to watch his sister suffer in ways he cannot imagine. Go now and if you fail you will pay with your flesh." The guards rushed out of the room. Lucifer took his place back on the throne, and after a little while looked up and said, "I bet you are enjoying this, old man. We will see, in time, we will see."

Chapter Thirty-Three

"They will be coming in force now, so we must move fast," Acubus said as he marched down the slope of the tunnel.

"How far is the river?" Sara asked.

"The mountain is a series of tunnels and hollowed-out caverns. There are six levels. There is one vertical shaft with a lift that runs through the entire mountain. There are other stairways and ladders between various levels, but it would take a long time to work our way down by that means. If we get to the main shaft, it is a quick way to get to the bottom; and now that the alarm has been sounded, we do not have much time."

"What is on level six?" Sara asked.

"It would take too long to explain now. When we get out of here I will explain anything and everything, but right now, we have to find a way down to second level. Then we can make our way to the shaft. Preacher, have you ever used a weapon?" Acubus asked as they moved down the walkway.

"No, I've never handled a weapon," Jacob answered. "Why?"

Acubus had taken the sword from the second guard and now passed it to Jacob. "Do not injure yourself, Preacher… or the rest of us for that matter." Acubus smiled at the little joke he'd made, and then continued. "When we get into an altercation you two will need to watch each other's backs. Make each blow count. They will send the guards first. Even though they look otherwise, they are just well-trained humans, but if they send out hunters, that will be a different story. If you run across a hunter, you had better know what you are doing."

"What do you mean by hunters?" Sara asked.

"They are half-breeds, we crossed fallen angels with humans, and they are the result. The genetics in the experiment were very unstable and the results varied from case to case." Acubus paused for a moment, then, as an afterthought, he said, "They are angry, very angry."

"What do you mean by angry?" Jacob asked.

"In the eyes of the Creator they are an abomination, they never had a choice. They are very angry."

Sara and Jacob nodded with understanding. They came to a stairway leading down to the next level. "You two wait here until I call for you," Acubus said as he started down the dark stairway.

Jacob looked over at Sara seeing a look of determination that spread across her face. She was so beautiful, he thought. Even as children, Jacob thought she was beautiful. Now looking at her, her long black hair, though somewhat ratty in appearance, flowed gently down on her shoulders in a sort of simple elegance. Her facial features, hardened with a new determination, were still striking. Muscles rippled from beneath her tight clothing. Jacob thought her physique had strengthened in appearance from what he remembered seeing of her earlier. He might be mistaken, but he knew something had changed in her since his first trip here. Maybe it was simply that she was growing in confidence. The sad thing, Jacob thought, was she had never looked this alive during her time on earth. After a few minutes, Acubus called up to them. Jacob wrapped his hands around the hilt of the sword and started down. Sara did the same. When they reached the bottom, they could see down another long, narrow tunnel, dimly lit by a number of torches.

"What's on this level?" Sara asked.

"Research and the hall of temptation," Acubus answered as he continued down the tunnel.

Jacob, starting to laugh, said, "Did you say research?"

"Why do you laugh, Preacher? Do you realize how many souls we destroyed with the use of science? Where do you think the whole idea of evolution came from, or the whole idea of cloning the human body? Think about what the idea of man creating man did for our cause. We filled the minds of humans with so many ideas. Many times a new idea would contradict a previously proven fact and the argument would be on. For so many people, science became their god. Once again much of their time was wasted on stupidity."

Jacob looked at Acubus, shook his head in agreement, then said, "I guess I see your point. I apologize for laughing."

"Think nothing of it, preacher. There is not much laughter in this place and I enjoy hearing it—once in a while," he added. "We better move," Acubus said as he took a torch out of its holder on the wall. "Be quiet and keep your eyes open.

The king will not like it that someone has escaped. I'm sure they know we are heading deeper into the mountain, and most of them are wondering why. Lucifer will not know that there is a way out at the bottom, but there are four fallen angels that do. Two of them are rebels. The last one I have not seen in a long while. He is a tempter devil, so he might be busy with his duties."

They headed down the tunnel with Acubus leading the way. The tunnel curved back and forth and eventually came to a large iron door. The door was about seven feet tall with large iron hinges. It had an iron handle to unlatch the lock mechanism.

"Now what?" Sara asked.

"This is one of the research chambers. We have to go through this room. We have no choice if we hope to make it to the main shaft. We will have to deal with whoever is in here. Physical bodies here have one thing in common with earthly bodies, they still have a spinal column and the body cannot move if it is severed. It will repair itself quickly, unlike an earthly body, so strike fast and hard, make it count. Are you two ready for this?" Acubus asked.

Sara and Jacob nodded their heads in agreement. Acubus lifted the handle and the door squeaked as it opened. Putting out the torch, Acubus laid it down, then pointed to the structure in the middle. They saw that it was a building built inside of a large cave. Its walls were made of large flat stones with cut-out windows. The workmanship was flawless.

"Stay near the outer edges of the cave. We might be able to go around the laboratory without being seen," Acubus said.

"What kind of research do they do in there?" Sara asked.

"This is the animal-research station, genetics and breeding. The castle is filled with many different kinds of laboratories," Acubus whispered, hugging the outer cave wall as they started to move.

"Why would they do animal research now? There is no need for food," Jacob asked, trying to keep up with Acubus. Jacob looked behind him and gasped, "Where is Sara?"

Acubus turned around, looked for a second, then pointed toward the laboratory. "What is that damn woman doing?"

Jacob looked at Acubus, then back at Sara. Without hesitation, he ran after Sara. He looked back for Acubus, but he wasn't where he had been standing a moment ago. Hearing something overhead, he looked up to see Acubus high above him, near the roof of the cave. When Jacob reached Sara, she was looking into one of the windows of the laboratory.

"Sis, what are you doing?" Jacob scolded.

"Look, Jacob!" Sara said excitedly.

Jacob looked into the window, "What kind of animals are those?"

"I don't know. They look like some kind of lizard or dinosaur, don't they?" "Let's get out of here before somebody sees us," Jacob urged.

"I want to get a better look, Jacob."

Jacob looked for Acubus who was keeping watch from his elevated vantage point. Jacob waved for him to come down. Reluctantly, he landed next to them. "What are you two soft-brained humans doing?" Acubus asked.

Sara, still looking in the window of the laboratory, backed away and looked to the left and the right. "How do you get in?" she asked.

"What are you doing, woman? We have to get out of here," Acubus said with anger in his voice.

"You two do what you want, but I'm going in. I heard something in there and I want to see what it is," Sara said.

Acubus was angry and Jacob knew it. Trying to play the middle man, he asked, "What did you hear?"

"Something was calling my name."

"There is nothing in there that would know your name, let alone call it," Acubus warned, trying to hold his temper.

"I heard something and I'm going to find out what it was," Sara said, edging her way along the outside wall of the laboratory.

Jacob and Acubus followed her until she reached a doorway. She stepped inside and was greeted by rows of cages with different kinds of infant animals. She walked right over to one particular cage.

"Look at this. What kind of animal is this?" Sara asked as she opened the cage door.

"Careful, sis! You don't know what you're messing with," Jacob said.

"It looks like some kind of lizard with wings," Sara said, as she pulled the creature out of its cage.

"Sara, put it back! We need to get out of here!" Jacob pleaded.

The creature was making a queer crying sound as Sara stroked its leathery head.

"Can't you hear it saying my name, Jacob?"

Acubus walked over to look at what Sara was holding. "Be careful with that thing woman. That is a crezden. They're partial to human flesh. I do not know why it has not yet chewed off your fingers.

"What is it?" Jacob asked.

"Humans referred to them as dragons. We set a few loose in early times, but it was something that caused humans to pray to the Creator. Besides, humans kill anything they do not understand, and after they were all killed, we gave up on the plan. It was an early hybrid of a pterodactyl crossed with an allosaurus. They are now used to hunt human runaways. They are attracted to the human scent and are normally ferocious when in the vicinity of a human," Acubus explained.

"I'm taking it with me," Sara said.

"It will slow us down and we need to get moving. Besides, it makes too much noise and will give away our position," Acubus argued.

The animal snuggled to Sara, no longer making any noise, except for a quiet purring sound.

"It seems to like her," Jacob added with a smile, and after a few moments asked, "What other hybrids have been crossed here?"

"Let's get moving. Let her take the creature, but do not say a word if it tries to eat her," Acubus said as he walked out the door of the laboratory.

Acubus was only gone for a split second before he returned, slowly backing through the door. Grabbing the two humans, he pulled them farther into the laboratory and told them to get down. "There is a hunting squad coming right toward us." Looking at Sara, he said, "Damn you, woman, and your curiosity. Let me tell you what happens to runaways when they are caught. You think the impaling chamber looked grotesque, you have not seen anything yet!"

"Leave her alone," Jacob said, "How many are out there?"

"They hunt in parties of three, one hunter with two guards. We are going to have to go through the other side of the laboratory to get out." Acubus stayed low and started moving deeper into the lab. When he saw both of them lagging behind, he gave them an angry look and whispered harshly, "Now!"

Jacob and Sara both jumped at Acubus's stern command. Sara, holding the crezden, took off after Acubus. Jacob followed Sara, looking around as they walked through the lab. What he saw was all manner of creatures. Some were alive and in cages, and some were experiments that had gone ghastly wrong. Grisly carcasses in variously sized jars lined the walls. Acubus came to a door and opened it slowly. Hunched low, he moved through it with Sara and Jacob following closely. Suddenly the crezden started making a hissing sound. Acubus quickly stood up and took two steps forward. He grabbed a human dressed in a dirty lab coat, and before Jacob and Sara realized what was going on, he snapped its neck. Acubus quietly laid the quivering body on the floor and motioned for the two of them to follow him. Acubus moved so quickly between the different lab tables that

Jacob and Sara had to run to keep up. They entered another room, and again the crezden started hissing. This time Jacob immediately saw why. The room was a maze of large cages filled with different species of hybrid animals. It appeared to Jacob that the lab workers had attempted to cross everything from mice to horses. Everything in the room seemed to come to life with an array of strange animal sounds. The crezden, adding to the ruckus, was straining to attack the animals in the cages. Sara pulled it back and held on to her new pet, stroking its head and telling it to be calm.

Jacob could not figure out how this research served Lucifer and the fallen. Maybe it had something to do with gaining knowledge that would be leaked to the humans on earth. Jacob chilled at the thought of how powerful a weapon that knowledge could be. The power of genetics had given Jacob the willies back on earth, but until now, he never stopped to think about what a mess God's creation would be if this power were ever unleashed on earth. Of course, the new power would begin with good intentions, and then, as with everything on earth, greed and power would distort and twist it until it became a weapon in the quest of world domination. A genetically engineered super race of humans could rise up, acquire power through their shear strength, and rule the world with unstoppable power while the weaker masses would be at their mercy.

"Snap out of it, Preacher!" Acubus said.

"He always was a daydreamer," Sara whispered loud enough for her two companions to hear.

"Stay alert, I will be right back," Acubus said as he headed off and disappeared from sight. Jacob looked for Sara and saw that she had placed the crezden on the ground behind her and had grabbed her sword. Jacob did likewise and they both moved forward.

"Sara, stay away from the cages. I don't want anything grabbing you," Jacob said. Jacob couldn't believe the crezden was following Sara like a little puppy.

Sara's new pet was about the size of a large house cat, but including its tail it was over three feet long. It was covered in thick-looking scales that were bluish-green in color. Its head was serpentine in shape with brilliant green reptilian eyes. It used its five-foot leathery wingspan to steady itself as it awkwardly chased after Sara on its two talon-garnished legs. Jacob wondered if Sara had ever enjoyed the company of a pet back on earth.

They heard a commotion coming from somewhere ahead. Then Jacob, hearing something coming toward them, hunkered down and gripped his sword tightly. Looking over to make sure Sara wouldn't be caught off guard; he noticed she was already poised for action. Expecting the worst, they were both surprised to see Acubus appear from around the corner of the cages in front of them.

"I found the way out. Follow me!" Acubus said in a rush.

Jacob, this time not hesitating, stayed on Acubus's heels. Turning around to make sure Sara was following, Jacob saw that she had picked up her new pet and was right behind him. They turned left around the last of the cages and ran into a long corridor that ended with a large iron door. Jacob saw Acubus step over the quivering bodies of two lab workers he must have disabled a few moments earlier.

Acubus pointed to a tunnel opening across a wide-open span of rock and then said, "Make your way to that tunnel. I will give you cover."

Acubus shot through the door and sprang into the air as Jacob and Sara made their way through the door. The crezden started hissing. Behind them, a hunter and two guards were coming down the corridor, stepping over the bodies of the disabled lab workers. Running into the large open area between the laboratory and their exit tunnel, they both dashed for the illuminated opening in the rock. Sara passed Jacob; even with the added weight of the hissing crezden, she was much faster than he was. From beneath Sara's right arm, the creature was looking back at the laboratory, hissing loudly. Jacob, hearing the sound of the door crash open, looked back in time to see the hunter spring gracefully into the air as the two guards continue coming toward them on foot. Jacob looked up ahead and saw that there were still seventy yards between them and the opening in the rock wall. Panic shot through his body at the stark realization that they would never make it before their pursuers would overtake them.

Jacob heard the sound of beating wings closing in on them from above. They still had fifty yards to go before they made it to the exit. Suddenly the hunter landed twenty yards in front of them, with a sick look of pleasure upon his face. Then, out of nowhere, Acubus set down in front of him.

"You take care of the guards and I will take care of this one," Acubus shouted as he and the hunter readied to do battle.

Putting down the crezden, Sara pulled out her sword and turned around to face the attackers. Jacob moved alongside his sister and made ready for battle.

The two guards pulled swords from the scabbards that were attached to crude leather belts wrapped around their immense waists. Separating, they moved in, one to each side of Sara and Jacob. Slowly at first, then leaping in unison, they made their attack. Jacob swung at his attacker from overhead, straight down like someone swinging an axe. The guard easily deflected the awkward blow and Jacob's sword clanked off the rocky ground. The guard, seeing that Jacob was off balance, moved in and attacked swiftly, but Jacob saw it coming and jumped back in time to evade the blow. Backpedaling like an awkward crab, Jacob continued to escape the vicious blows that rained down on him.

Meanwhile, the other guard moved in on Sara, but was not quick enough to dodge her first blow and was sliced deeply across its bicep. A look of surprise spread across its face as it reached around to feel the opened flesh on its arm. Then the guard made its next mistake, it took a split second to glance down at its wound. Sara, seeing the opportunity, spun around in a blur and sank her blade deeply into the stomach of her attacker. A scream filled the cave as her attacker went down. She then removed the guard's head with an effortless swing of her sword. Seeing that Jacob was in trouble, she leaped in between Jacob and his attacker.

Jacob, thrilled to see his sister come to his aid, shouted, "Thank you, God!"

He stepped back to make room for Sara and what he saw next stunned him. Sara was wielding her sword with a sudden expertise that caused a sense of confusion to fill his questioning mind. Expertly delivering blow after blow, attack and counterattack, she and her attacker were dancing back and forth like two lovers on a dance floor. Then suddenly leaping high into the air, much too high for a human, she did a forward flip with a twist, and landed behind the stunned creature. Then, with a sweeping horizontal arch of her blade, she separated the creature's head from its body.

Jacob went to his knees dumbfounded with what he had just witnessed. He turned to see if Acubus had seen it, but saw that he was busy with the hunter. Listening to the conversation that passed between the two warriors, Jacob moved around to the opposite side of where Acubus was standing.

"I remember you, Acubus."

"And I remember you, Syerus. Still taking orders, I see," Acubus said trying to work a better angle on his opponent.

Jacob noticed how massive the hunter was. Huge bat-like wings sprang from its muscular back. Large black expressionless eyes reflected the torchlight that flickered from the edges of the cavern. The hunter had more characteristics of a human being than it did of one of the fallen. The shape of its feet appeared to look human, though they were covered with tall laced-up boots. Its hands seemed to have ten fingers, but with all the movement, Jacob was unable to tell for sure. It looked every bit human, except every attribute of this creature was huge. Not fat, not disproportioned, but just a lot bigger than a normal human, and of course, it had wings. Even for its size, Jacob thought it moved like a large feline. He wondered about the heritage of the giants from the fairy tales he read as a child. Maybe there was something to the Book of Enoch.

Drawn out of his thoughts, Jacob could hear more of the conversation that passed between the two large creatures.

"You are a fool, Acubus. You and your rebels really think that this is the human spoken of in the prophecy?"

"I will let you be the judge of that, Syerus," Acubus said, and at that moment the blade from Sara's sword exploded through the chest of Syerus. The creature lunged forward and looked down at the blade. Sara jerked down on the hilt, causing the blade to sever the being's spinal column, dropping him like a sack of wet cement.

Jacob looked back to where the two guards lay quivering on the rocky floor. The heads of the guards that Sara had removed had somehow reattached themselves. He then looked back at his sister, who stood motionless with a look of satisfaction on her face.

What was it he heard about a prophecy? He would have to ask Acubus what was meant by that statement. "I can't believe it, sis," Jacob said as he walked up to her, putting his arm around her shoulders. He felt something pushing against his leg and looked down to see the crezden working itself between him and Sara.

"Yes, good job, woman. I never thought I would see the time when a human could dispatch a hunter that easily," Acubus said with an approving look.

Looking modest, but with a new sense of confidence Sara said, "Let's get moving." She walked over to where a torch was perched in its holder and removed it. Without saying a word, she strode off down the rocky tunnel with the crezden close behind.

Acubus started to follow, but Jacob stopped him and asked, "What did the hunter say about a prophecy?"

Acubus looked at Jacob for a moment, and then said, "It is from the tablet that was given to Lucifer at the time of our fall. A human, a woman, would be sent by the Creator to torment the tormentor for eternity. It is his punishment for the temptation and destruction of Eve. Ironic, is it not?"

"What tablet?" Jacob asked with spiked interest.

"When we, the fallen, were cast out of heaven and sent to earth, the Creator set the rules and they were literally set in stone. It is all written on four stone tablets that are kept in Lucifer's private chamber."

"Have you ever seen them?" Jacob asked.

"I have seen them from a distance."

"Do you think Sara is the woman?"

Acubus seemed to ignore the question and said, "We better catch up."

Jacob led the way down the tunnel with Acubus bringing up the rear.

Chapter Thirty-Four

The boardroom was close to the size of a basketball court. Its smoothly chiseled stonewalls held rows of flaming torches that gave off an uneven light that bounced off the faces of the creatures milling around the room. Scattered throughout the room, they were collected in little groups like children on a playground. The members of Lucifer's head council were called together for an emergency meeting. Suddenly a hush went through the room and everyone took their seats. Once all the members were seated, Lucifer entered the room carrying four large stone tablets. Everyone stood immediately upon his entrance. Setting down the tablets, Lucifer took his seat and everyone in the room followed his lead.

"I called you all here to discuss a problem that has come to my attention. Some of you know about the situation and others of you do not. I believe you all know the prophecy about a human woman rising to power. I will not bore you by reading it again." He sat quietly for a few seconds. He seemed to wait for everyone in the room to relax, and then, jumping out of his chair, Lucifer screamed, "This will not happen!" Making a fist and then slamming it on the large wooden table, he continued with his tirade, "How could a puny human woman ever gain dominion over me? Once we were the mightiest angels of the heavens above and now the greatest beings of this kingdom." Pausing for a second, he then continued with a quieter voice. "Why have we not caught these humans yet? If we capture this woman, we can stop the prophecy. If we catch her brother, we will have all the leverage we need to control her. We will put this woman in chains, tie them to heavy stones, then cast the whole mess into the river of fire and I will make her brother watch the whole thing."

Tianasus, sitting just to the right of Lucifer, asked," Master, what about the rebel? He is not going to be easily captured."

Lucifer's brow furrowed sharply. Looking across the room at his council, he said gruffly, "We will capture him and make him an example for the rest of the kingdom to see." Lucifer moved around to the back of his chair, stood with his hands on his hips, and asked, "Have we managed to locate the rebel camp yet?"

No one in the room said a word. Lucifer looked at his twelve council members. Everyone, trying to avoid the menacing glare of the master, kept his head down. Lucifer's anger was beginning to boil again and the council members knew it. The rebels were something new to the kingdom. There had always been dissention among the fallen angels, but until recently, no one was ever courageous enough to do anything about it. That is, until Acubus put together his little group of miscreants. Lucifer couldn't believe that anyone doubted his leadership. Who was it after all that had led the revolt against the Creator? Who had set up the government here and ensured that everything ran smoothly? Lucifer took his seat again and placed his folded hands onto the table. Looking at his council members he said, "Somebody speak."

Tianasus was the first to speak. "Sir, two guards and a hunter were taken out in the laboratory cavern and a crezden is missing. Sir, we think they are headed for the main shaft which means they have to go through the hall of temptation to get there."

"They have a crezden? Those things are bred to hate humans. Why would they take one of those?" Lucifer asked, amused by the news.

This time Cassinitus, the head of genetic research, spoke. "Sir, I do not know what happened. I could hazard a guess that the Creator has put his influence on the crezden and this is all part of the prophecy."

"This damned prophecy. You do realize that this cannot come to pass. The Creator does not have the power down here, I do. I will not allow it. How do we stop it? Speak to me," Lucifer said leaning back in his chair.

Nargal, the head of security, spoke up. "We know they are still in the castle. We have covered all the exits. They are trapped."

"So far your tactics have not impressed me, Nargal. How did the rebels manage to put together a force under your watchful eye?" Lucifer asked with an accusing tone.

Nargal bowed his head in shame and did not say a word.

"Is there anyone here who knows what is going on?" Lucifer screamed as he jumped out of his chair and looked around the room. After a few tense moments he calmed down, smiled, and took his seat. "I have an idea. Let me ask some questions that should have been asked some time ago. Why have we not closed down every level? For some reason they are moving down inside the castle. Does anyone know why they would be moving in that direction?" No one answered so he continued, "I want the shaft closed off. I do not care if you have to destroy it, we can rebuild it later, and then I want the army brought up. Get moving! Now!"

The council broke and left the room. Lucifer sat quietly, placed his head in his hands, and let out a deep sigh.

Chapter Thirty-Five

Officer Nathan Owens had one hour left on his twelve-hour shift. He was tired, and he was pissed off that his shift would end halfway across the county. He was looking for some drugged-out junkie who had murdered two people and then kidnapped a preacher's wife and children. "A preacher's wife, why in the name of hell would anyone kidnap a preacher's wife," he muttered to himself.

He was on Road 300 W, a couple miles northwest of the town of Onarga. He really doubted that the kidnapper would only run fifteen miles from the scene of the crime, but hell, he was a junky. Officer Owen slowed down in front of the old Anderson place and switched on the patrol car spotlight. He scanned across the abandoned farm lot. A reflection appeared from inside the corncrib. Probably nothing, but he'd better check it out. He drove slowly up the driveway and across the farm lot. Parking by the corncrib, he exited the patrol car and switched on his flashlight. He walked over to the entrance of the corncrib and was surprised to see a blue sedan parked in the alleyway. The hood was still warm.

Chapter Thirty-Six

Jacob and Acubus caught up with Sara and the crezden. The trio moved down the dark stone tunnel. Every twenty feet a torch was fastened to the wall to illuminate the walkway. With all the commotion earlier, Jacob had not noticed the extreme heat, but now he felt as if he were walking into a furnace.

"How much longer before we get to the shaft?" Sara asked.

"We have yet to go through the hall of temptation. We are close now," Acubus answered.

They walked another two hundred yards before coming within twenty yards of a doorway that led to a cavern. Two guards, dressed in full body armor and carrying long spears, stood with their backs to the opening. When the crezden saw them, it started to hiss. The hackles on its back were rising until Sara reached down and stroked its leathery head.

"The king has increased security. I am going to guess we are going to run into soldiers before long," Acubus said as he looked toward the two guards that blocked the opening to the cave.

Sara moved up behind Acubus. "Acubus, I will take out the two guards. As soon as I clear the doorway, you get through and get above us. You are going to be our eyes in this place." Turning around, she then spoke to Jacob. "You stay right behind me. Your job is to let me know if anything is coming at us from behind. Keep up with me, Jacob; I am not going to wait. Do you understand?"

Jacob nodded his head. Sara pulled her sword, then took off at a dead run. She whistled for the crezden to follow. The two guards, hearing a commotion from behind, turned around, and found themselves in a firestorm of flashing metal. Sara cleared the doorway and felt Acubus spring into the air right behind her. She turned around to make sure that Jacob was behind her. "Let's go, little brother!" She yelled, then took off at a run with Jacob and the crezden right behind her.

As they ran, Jacob could see rows of stone cubicles off to their right. Seated in each was a fallen angel with a large rectangular shaped crystal placed in front of them. Tubes running from the sides of the crystal ran to the ears and temples of each creature. The more Jacob looked the more details he noticed. The creatures appeared to be a permanent fixture seated in front of each crystal. They did not move. They did not make a sound. Jacob could see that whatever they were seeing in the crystals held their attention, because they seemed oblivious to the intruders running through the cave. As he got closer to the cubicles, he could see what they were looking at and stopped running. With no thought of the consequence, Jacob moved over to the closest cubicle and watched over the shoulder of one of the fallen that was seated in front of a crystal. The being did not notice his presence. Jacob and the fallen angel were watching the life of a human through its own mental pictures and thoughts. From the tubes that led from the crystal to something that looked like a megaphone, Jacob could hear a voice. Leaning in close, he realized he could overhear the voice of this human's conscience, just as if its inner thoughts were being broadcast over a complex radio system. The voice spoke about being bored, wishing that three-thirty would get here quickly. The voice also wondered what mom was making for supper. Jacob was so enthralled by what he was hearing that the seriousness of the situation no longer mattered. He then looked at the crystal and realized that he was seeing through the eyes of a human. In a trancelike state, the angel sat with its hands placed on another set of crystals lying flat on the table in front of it. The fallen angel's hands fit perfectly on the crystal and Jacob figured it was some type of control system for the eavesdropping mechanism. The more Jacob looked at the spectacle, the more he realized that the hands of the fallen angel and the crystal appeared to have become one. Jacob could hear the fallen angel say something in a language that he could not understand. Jacob deduced that the human who was being watched was a small male child sitting in a classroom, surrounded by other students. Jacob could see a little blond girl getting ready to take her seat in front of the watched child. The fallen one whispered something and Jacob saw the hand of the boy reach up and place a thumbtack on the seat of the little blonde girl. Jacob saw the little girl sit down and immediately jump up screaming. Jacob thought he could hear the little boy laughing through the tube running from the crystal. The fallen angel's head rolled back and its eyes closed. The vision on the crystal changed and just like a television being switched, Jacob watched another life come into focus somewhere on earth.

Jacob's attention was drawn back to the present situation when he heard Sara yell his name. He noticed that she was almost three hundred yards ahead. Jacob heard a noise from behind him and turned. He could see twenty or so armored guards entering the cavern with weapons drawn. Jacob wondered why they didn't use firearms here. Maybe it was the fact that a sword or blade does more damage than a bullet. Gunpowder might not work here. That might explain the lack of electricity here. Surely, with all the scientific knowledge they had here, they could produce some kind of power. Jacob remembered even in the laboratory everything was handwritten. He figured that computers would be used here, but with no power that was not possible. But on the other hand, look what the fallen had accomplished up to the twentieth century, before the invention of computers. Jacob suddenly became aware that Sara was surrounded by guards and hunters. A battle was soon to begin. Jacob took off in a dead run to help Sara.

"Preacher, can you see the shaft from where you are?" Acubus yelled as he swooped down from above.

Jacob looked ahead, but could not see anything except a group of hunters flying in from the right of Acubus. Jacob pointed to where they were coming from to warn him. Acubus veered off toward the hunters.

Jacob was getting close to where Sara had already begun to battle the attackers. He could see that four of the hunters were down and that Sara was still battling with the remaining group. Jacob pulled his sword and attempted to join into the battle. He took a clumsy swing at the closest guard, but once again, his skill was subpar. The hunter easily deflected the blow and spun around, landing a kick into Jacob's chest. Jacob landed hard on his back. The hunter was closing in on Jacob when its attention was drawn back to Sara. She had another three hunters down and was after the hunter approaching Jacob.

Acubus, trying to lead the flying hunters away from Jacob and Sara, flew in a wide circle. He didn't figure he could manage the number of hunters that were following him, but if he could separate a few away from the pack at a time, he could handle a smaller number. He dove and spun until he lured the leader away from the rest. Pulling his sword, Acubus quickly spun and cut the closest hunter in two. The other hunter stopped in mid-flight, surprised to see a fellow hunter cut down so quickly. Taking advantage of the moment of distraction, Acubus flew in and slashed the next closest hunter. The wounded hunter spiraled down like a dead leaf and Acubus shot away. Acubus could see light emitting from the vertical shaft that led down to the bottom level. Looking to find Sara and Jacob, he yelled to get their attention. Pointing to the direction of the shaft, Jacob signaled that he understood. Acubus, in his flight to escape his attackers, turned to see that the opening in the cave that they had come through earlier was now filled with soldier-class fallen angels.

Two to three hundred archers, dressed in full battle gear, were forming ranks. Lucifer had decided to get serious about capturing them.

Swooping down toward Sara and Jacob, Acubus picked up both of them, then flew in the direction of the vertical shaft. The hunters were staying right behind him and he dived and swooped in an attempt to evade their attack. The extra weight of the two humans was slowing him down greatly. There was only two hundred yards to go before they would reach the shaft, but they would be lucky to make it.

"Look out, there are archers lining up behind us!" Sara yelled.

Glancing around, Acubus yelled, "I know!"

Jacob, wrapped tightly in one of Acubus's arms, struggled to see what was going on, and he too could see the large number of soldiers filling in the opening behind them. What he could not figure out was why the soldiers were not moving toward them. They had formed ranks, but were holding their position. The question was answered the second he looked toward the shaft. What he saw reminded him of angry hornets flying out of a nest. Hundreds of flying soldiers were streaming up out of the shaft in front of them, blocking their exit. Jacob realized then that the soldiers to the rear were nothing more than a gate that was closed behind them.

Acubus realized they were never going to make it to the shaft. Landing short of their escape, the three of them spread out and prepared for battle. A squawking sound grabbed the attention of the three fugitives. The crezden, half running, half flying, was heading straight for Sara. Dropping her sword, she caught the creature up in her arms.

"Sara, put that thing down!" Jacob yelled.

"What difference does it make anyway? If you haven't figured out yet, we're screwed."

Jacob grimaced and said, "Yeah, yeah, you're right."

The soldiers from the rear were starting to march in their direction and the soldiers that came up through the vertical shaft had landed and were now closing rank in front of them.

Acubus, shaking his head said, "I'm afraid this will not be pleasant."

The three of them stood and watched as the soldiers closed in. When the soldiers from both sides marched up to their location, they halted. Walking through the ranks of soldiers, Lucifer appeared, dressed in a long, flowing red robe. Flanked by two of the six-winged guards, Lucifer motioned for them to be disarmed. The crezden in Sara's arms would not let them get close enough to take her sword. Seeing no reason to fight, she handed her weapon to them.

Lucifer walked up to Acubus and said in a cheery tone, "Acubus, my old friend. I hear you have made new friends." Lucifer, with hands behind his back, was now slowly pacing back and forth in front of Acubus. "You have been a pain in my ass since the time of our fall. You must have believed in me at one point though. You trusted my judgment enough to rebel in the first place. Do you remember the role you played in the rebellion? Maybe your new friends would like to know the key role you played." Turning toward Sara and

Jacob, Lucifer continued with his monologue. "You see, your friend Acubus was one of the Creator's chosen. Being one of the highest ranking archangels in heaven, along with me and a few others, he had certain privileges, or should I say, he was the gate keeper. I guess what I am trying to say is that Acubus was the one who held the back door open to the fortress for us. Imagine how the Creator felt when he figured out that one of his highest ranking angels stabbed him right in the back!" Lucifer, turning on his heel, faced Acubus. "What did he say to you after it was all finished? Probably something to the effect of, 'Acubus you really let me down, or, I am so disappointed.' He probably shook his finger at you like an accusing father. Am I correct?"

Acubus, with his head lowered in shame, said nothing. Lucifer walked over and stood in front of Sara. Squirming to get at Lucifer, the crezden hissed insanely, and Sara stroked its head, trying to keep it calm.

"Do you realize, Sara Bennington, that if you showed that much attention to your husband and children you might not have been given the privilege of visiting us?" Lucifer laughed at his little joke and then the expression on his face got serious. "So you think you are the chosen one, eh?"

A quizzical look appeared on Sara's face.

"You do not know what I'm talking about, do you? Well, let me explain it to you.

At the time of the angelic migration to earth, there came about a prophecy. In a nutshell it explains how a human woman will come to have some kind of power in this kingdom and cause the ruler great agitation. That would, of course, be me, and of course I will not have it." Turning around to face the entire population, he spoke softly and then ended his statement with a shout. "Do you all hear what I am saying? It is over!"

Lucifer quickly regained his composure and walked over to Jacob. "Last but not least, Jacob Litchfield, the preacher. You did not seem to appreciate my hospitality much. I tried to be polite. I answered your questions honestly. I showed you my kingdom and what did I get in return?" Raising his mighty arms to the ceiling, "I received belligerent manners from a man who is a spokesman of the Creator. Ah, Christians, you are all the same!" Lucifer, stroking his chin with his right hand, asked one more question. "I wonder what your wife and the children are doing right now. I am going to imagine that Mr. Jenkins is keeping them well entertained." Lucifer signaled for the three of them to be taken into custody.

The guards secured the hands of Jacob and Acubus with irons, but when they got close to Sara the crezden went berserk. The guards looked to Lucifer to see what to do and Lucifer spat. "Let her keep the damn thing. When it figures out that she is human, it will eat her alive." As they began to leave, Lucifer added one last comment. "Preacher, I think you will enjoy the show."

Chapter Thirty-Seven

Cathy was watching the longhaired man when he suddenly went rigid. He lifted the little girl from his lap. "Get on the bed with your mom."

He watched out of the window for a few seconds and then turned around. Holding his head in his hands, he looked at the ceiling and shouted angrily, "What the hell do I do now? Where the fuck are you?" He paced for a few seconds and went back over to the window. "Shit, shit, shit!"

Chapter Thirty-Eight

The three rebels were put into three separate cells, all in view of each other. Jacob was the first to speak. "So, what happens now?"

"I am guessing torture or some other form of delightful degradation," Acubus answered.

"Oh, wonderful," Jacob quipped. A noise caught their attention and they both looked over to Sara's cell. She was sitting on the floor, legs crossed, with the crezden facing her. They were playing together like a small child with a little puppy. Jacob noticed that the creature seemed to have grown since Sara got him from the laboratory. "Tell me more about the crezden. How fast will that thing grow?" Jacob asked.

"It will be deadly in no time. It was bred in this time dimension so it will mature quicker than an animal would on earth."

"How big will it get?" Jacob asked.

"It will be big enough that one of the hunters would be able to ride it. So it will be quite large."

"You said that they usually go crazy at the smell of humans. If that is true, how is it that that thing likes her so much?"

"If she is the chosen one, the rules will not apply. You do realize that Lucifer will fight this to the end. It will not be pleasant for your sister," Acubus said.

"I know. If I may ask, how large is your rebellion?"

"Be careful, preacher. You do not want to know any information they might be able to get out of you. I will tell you though it is a large force and I think your sister will play an important part."

"What does Sara have to do with all this?" Jacob asked with a confused tone.

"I'm not sure yet, but I believe she has an integral part to play. Maybe she is the one to finally pull the rebellion together."

The sound of the crezden going into a rage stopped their conversation short. Someone was coming down the walkway and the crezden did not like whoever it was.

Two guards appeared in front of Sara's cell. They entered one at a time. The first guard entered carrying a five-foot pole with a loop at the end. He cornered the crezden and fought to place the loop around its neck. Sara was going into frenzy, attacking the guard who was trying to capture her new friend. Jumping on his back, she put him in a sleeper hold. The guard being attacked dropped the pole to fight off Sara, and when the crezden saw its chance, it joined in the battle. Growling ferociously, it sank its teeth into the leg of the guard that had Sara on its back. The three of them turned into a spinning mess of growls and shrieks. The second guard, trying to figure out how to help his comrade, kept trying to jump into the ruckus. Finally grabbing Sara, he tore her off the back of his comrade. The second guard held Sara in a bear hug while the first guard pried the crezden off his leg. Jacob didn't notice it right away, but Acubus was laughing so hard he was doubled over, holding his midsection. Seeing Acubus laughing so hard was infectious and soon Jacob was laughing also. The first guard had the crezden cornered and every time he would try to get a hold of it, it would snap at him, causing the guard to jump like a frightened child. This happened numerous times causing Acubus to laugh even harder. Even the second guard holding Sara snickered once or twice. Finally giving up, the first guard motioned to the second guard to let Sara go.

As the guards left the cell, they heard Jacob and Acubus's laughter. The wounded guard hissed, "Shut up!"

Their shadows dancing along the wall was the last thing they saw of the guards as they disappeared down the tunnel. Sara sat down to pet the crezden, cooing at it like a mother would with her baby.

Chapter Thirty-Nine

Officer Owens radioed the dispatcher with the license-plate number and the number came back as stolen. He was told backup was on its way and to sit tight until it arrived.

The second unit was there in ten minutes. Officer Owens had been watching the house and thought he had detected motion in one of the upstairs windows. Officers Hoffmann and Robbins exited their squad car to walk over to where Owens was sitting in the car.

"What do you have, Nathan?" Hoffmann asked.

From inside the cruiser, Owens answered, "Someone is in the house. I'm sure I saw movement in one of the upstairs windows," and pointed toward the house.

Chapter Forty

"She had two beautiful children, Michael and Mara," Jacob said, as Acubus and he watched her play with the crezden in her cell that was located fifty feet from their cell.

"I know nothing about such things," Acubus said.

"Her son, Michael is having trouble getting over her death. It seems weird to see her sitting here and yet when I get back I'll have to watch her children suffer."

"Why are you telling me this, Preacher? Do you think that any of that matters to me?" Acubus asked with impatience.

"What if it does? What if the fact that she's remorseful for her earthly life is the reason she is the chosen one?"

"We do not know for sure that she is the chosen one. What if she is just a skilled warrior? The human being has many skill sets that are never used due to one's position on the evolutionary timeline."

"Explain that one to me, big boy," Jacob said with a smile.

"For instance, how many times have you heard the words 'that person is a natural'?"

"Quite often," Jacob answered.

"Some physical trait or attribute sets a human being apart from the general populace."

A light suddenly switched on in Jacob's mind. "I get it! It's the explanation why one man can throw a ninety-mile-per-hour fastball and the next person cannot."

Giving Jacob a strange look, Acubus asked, "What is a fastball?"

"You surely know about baseball. Remember steroids? You folks down here probably had something to do with all that too," Jacob said.

"You do realize that not everything that has gone wrong on earth has been directly due to our influence," Acubus argued.

"You're wrong about that. God never intended for anything to go wrong until you tempted man into sin," Jacob shot back.

"Free will, preacher. I do not see where it is completely our fault that man sinned. It was always still a choice."

Jacob was about to continue the argument when Acubus motioned for him to be quiet. The shadows of the returning guards were visible before they could actually be seen by the captives. This time there were four guards and one of the fallen. They walked right by Sara's cell and came to where Jacob and Acubus were being held. Opening the cell door, the large fallen angel walked in and called out to Sara. "Woman, are you going to allow us to take you out of here, or do I have hurt your brother?"

Sara looked up from stroking the crezden and answered. "Leave him alone, I will go."

"Sara, don't!" Jacob yelled, but the fallen angel quickly swung his arm, sending Jacob headlong into the wall of his cell.

The large creature walked over to where Jacob was lying and bent down. Rolling Jacob over, he said, "You be quiet, preacher man."

The fallen angel remained with Jacob, while the four guards entered Sara's cell.

"Stay! Be quiet!" she told the crezden as she stood up. To the surprise of the guards, it obeyed. Sara walked toward the guards, turned around, then placed her hands behind her back, allowing herself to be put in irons. Three of the guards led her out of the cell while one remained. Walking up to the crezden, he kicked it violently, causing it to land in a heap in the corner of Sara's cell. The crezden never made a sound as Sara had commanded.

Seeing what the guard had done, Sara went into a rage. "NO!" she screamed. She threw herself into the closest guard, sending him reeling, but because she was in irons the other two easily kept her under control. "You bastards are going to pay for that," she yelled as the guards dragged her down the walkway.

The fallen angel in Jacob's cell gave him a look and said, "I am ordered not to hurt you. Why, I will never know. You will remain here until someone comes to get you. I think you will enjoy the entertainment planned for you, though." He ordered the remaining guard to take Acubus. Acubus did not struggle, but allowed himself to be put into irons. Shutting Jacob's cell, the fallen angel led Acubus and the guard down the walkway, and out of Jacob's sight.

Chapter Forty-One

Jacob sat on the floor of his cell, resting his head in his hands. A million thoughts were spinning through his mind. His first thought was of his wife and the children. He had no idea how long he had been here and wondered what that amount of time equaled in his time. Then his thought turned to Lucifer; was he really that concerned about the three letters or was it the prophecy that he was trying to stop? With Lucifer's arrogance, he was sure to find out.

Something stirred from inside Sara's cell. Jacob could see that the crezden had lifted its head. Unsteady at first, then, gathering its strength, it stood up and shook its head. It looked around searching for Sara. When it did not see her, it let out a blood-curdling scream that echoed throughout the castle.

Sara, still being led by her three captors, smiled to herself when she heard the cry of the crezden.

Jacob sat quietly in his cell, listening to the crezden whimper. For how long, it was hard to guess, with the concept of time being what it was here. Eventually he heard footsteps coming down the prison walkway and a large figure walked up to his cell. The crezden hissed loudly. Jacob recognized Lucifer and stood up to greet him.

Lucifer walked up to the cell door. "Well, Preacher, how are you doing by now? Did you enjoy the tour of my castle?" he asked as he unlocked the door to Jacob's cell.

"I'll have to say that it was interesting. I'm very impressed with your science department," Jacob said, pointing in the direction of the crezden. "How do you suppose that happened, anyway?"

"I am sure that it is just an anomaly and is nothing you need to concern yourself with," Lucifer said with a dismissive gesture. "Are you ready to watch the spectacle I have planned for you?"

"I really doubt I have a choice."

"You do learn quickly, Preacher," Lucifer said as he bowed, and swung his left arm in a sweeping motioned toward the open cell door. "After you, my good man."

"I do have a question for you though," Jacob said over his shoulder, as he walked through the cell door.

"Have I not been an open book to you, Jacob Litchfield?"

Stopping, he turned toward Lucifer and asked, "Sara explained to me about the fallen's power to control the human mind. How come you didn't use it when you could have put an end to all this a long time ago?"

At first Lucifer bristled at the question, and then he smiled. "It would not work on her."

"She is the one, isn't she?" Jacob exclaimed, turning to continue down the walkway.

"Not for long, Preacher. Not for long," Lucifer replied, following Jacob out of the cell.

The statement sent a shiver down Jacob's spine. "Where are we going?" Jacob asked, not really wanting to know the answer.

"Well, I am going to personally escort you to the lower level of my castle. I believe it is where you were heading earlier. Am I correct?"

"I think Acubus might have mentioned something about the sixth level," Jacob said.

"Have you ever seen a river of fire? I am going to guess the closest thing to it on earth would be the flow of one of your volcanoes. The river is very delightful to see. It is a spectacle that will certainly take your breath away," Lucifer said as he ushered Jacob past the door of Sara's cell.

Jacob pointing at the crezden, asked, "What are you going to do with that thing?"

"Sometimes research can be very frustrating, but for now I will just leave it where it is. I am sure it can be cured with the proper application of science."

The two of them walked through a series of tunnel walkways, passing numerous prison cells and other rooms of captivity. A wide variety of tortured souls in each cell made Jacob wonder what each human being had done to deserve these different punishments. "Who dictates what punishment is given to each human?"

"If you really must know, I am only allowed to punish a human in accordance with his or her earthly life. I believe you have witnessed the impaling chamber. It is reserved for pedophiles. I think it is a most fitting exercise of torture. What do you think?" Lucifer asked gleefully.

"I do not like to see anyone hurt, no matter what crime they committed," Jacob said as they continued to walk down the torch-lit hallway.

"Are you telling me, Preacher, that if a murderer of children is convicted and sentenced to die, it would not make your heart leap with excitement?"

"Think of all the lives that are affected when something like this happens," Jacob responded. "Think of the mother and father who have to watch their son die."

"He deserves to be punished for murdering children," Lucifer said.

"You're the one that introduced murder into the world. What do you deserve?" Jacob countered.

"Now, Jacob Litchfield, I can only lead a horse to water, I cannot make it drink. Think of it this way: we just give humans a full scope of their options," Lucifer said as they entered a large room that contained the shaft that Acubus had told them about earlier. The hole spanned about twenty feet. It had a large pole that ran vertically in the middle with a series of cables and pulleys. As they approached, Jacob could feel the heat emanating from the opening. He had to shield his eyes from the intense light, until a circular platform made of stone appeared from below, blocking the light. Two guards, using the cables, were raising the lift. Once the platform was level with the floor, the two beings secured the cables and moved to the back. Lucifer led Jacob onto the platform while the two guards returned to their positions and began to lower the crude elevator back down the shaft. Jacob had counted five floors before the stone structure jerked to a stop. What Jacob saw and heard stunned him. Millions of humans were immersed in the river of fire that ran before his eyes. Screaming and wailing filled his ears. Numerous grotesque creatures carrying long poles walked the banks, pushing anyone who tried to escape back into the fiery liquid. He could see that the fire was not consuming the bodies of the humans, but their skin was black and blistered. There was no doubt that they were in unbelievable agony. The river filled with thrashing bodies spanned left and right as far as his vision would allow him to see. Looking out across the river, Jacob figured the distance to be over a thousand feet. The bright light that emitted from the molten lava hurt his eyes, causing him to look away from it. Looking to his right, he could see a line of humans, about a hundred abreast, on a cliff that jutted out twenty feet over the river. Jacob watched them fight to remain on the edge, but the sheer numbers being herded down to that point forced one after another to fall off the ledge. Following the line back to its origin, he saw that it was formed by humans falling from an opening in the roof of the cave.

"What do you think, Preacher?" Lucifer asked with pride.

"It's horrible," Jacob answered, unable to take his eyes off the falling humans.

"Walk with me now. I have something else I want to show you."

Jacob followed Lucifer along the river. Having trouble believing what he was experiencing, he fought to keep his mind from melting down.

"We are in the lowest level of my kingdom. If you have not figured it out yet, each level is a degree or two more sadistic. After judgment, each soul immediately enters their place in eternity. This…"

Interrupting Lucifer, Jacob asked, "What have these souls done to deserve this kind of punishment?"

"Let us call them my black shepherds. My pied pipers you might say. You understand what I mean, do you not?" Lucifer asked.

"Yes. These are the people who've led others away from God. So, what's your punishment going to be, Lucifer? Will you end up there?" Jacob asked pointing toward the river.

Lucifer ignored the question and continued walking. As they came around an outcropping of rock, Jacob saw a crowd gathered by a large structure. A long metal framework jutted out over the river at a forty-five degree angle. Jacob gasped when he saw Sara hanging by a crude chain that had been wound numerous times around her waist. She was wrapped from head to toe with rope, and a piece of material had been shoved in her mouth. Spinning slowly, she struggled to see what was going on around below her, her eyes alive with fear.

"Where is Acubus?" Jacob asked.

"You will see him soon enough," Lucifer answered smugly.

They walked over to the base of the large structure, and then two guards escorted Jacob a short distance away to a large stone bench, forcing him to sit down. Jacob watched as the crowd of hellish beings formed a circle around him. Lucifer walked into the middle of the group, carrying a large stone tablet. There was some kind of writing on it, but he could not make out the language.

Lucifer raised his hand for everyone's attention, and then read from the stone tablet. "*And behold, there will come a time in the kingdom of suffering that a great tribulation will arise. A woman, once human, will rise up from the populace and cause a great chaos to this kingdom's ruler. The blood of the righteous will be in her veins, but she will fall short of the mark to enter heaven. Upon her soul's arrival in the kingdom of suffering, she will recognize her sins and repent. Through the power of My will, she will communicate through written word with the sibling that shares her day of birth. The strength and abilities of all the fallen will be mirrored in this woman. This woman will have dominion over the fallen and will lead a great rebellion against the ruler of the kingdom. No peace will ever settle on this kingdom. This is retribution for the destruction of Eve. It shall be so.*"

Lucifer laid the tablet gently on the stony ground. With his hands folded gently behind his back, he turned and calmly looked at the council of the fallen angels around him.

"Preacher, I would like to introduce the twelve members of my high council. Yes, these are the highest ranking of the great rebellion. We…" He faced Jacob with outstretched arms. "We were all there. Of course there were others, but we were the leaders, the generals of the great war in heaven above,"

Lucifer said as he stood inside the circle. "Bring in Acubus," Lucifer shouted.

Two guards wheeled Acubus in on something that resembled a set of refrigerator trucks. He was bound from head to toe with the same kind of rope that Sara was wrapped in; he also had chains wrapped around his waist. The guards stood Acubus up near the edge of the platform and removed the cart. It was at that point that Jacob noticed that Acubus's mighty wings had been cut from his body. Two ragged stumps were all that remained.

"Secure the stones," Lucifer commanded. Two guards, each carrying large stones with metal eyelets entered and secured them to chains attached to Acubus. Finished, the guards moved away and disappeared around the corner. Lucifer walked up and whispered something into Acubus's ear, then moved back.

"Acubus, my friend, do you have anything to say before your sentence for the crime of treason is carried out?" Lucifer asked.

Turning to look directly into Lucifer's eyes, Acubus smiled and then said, loud enough for everyone to hear, "Kiss my ass, Satan!"

Lucifer leaped at Acubus and, using his foot, shoved him into the river. The stones attached to Acubus's chains were the last thing to slide off the platform and disappear beneath the fiery surface. Jacob watched in horror as his new friend disappeared.

"Preacher, I think you probably know what is coming next. Are you ready to negotiate now?" Lucifer asked.

Jacob didn't know what to say. He did not want to see his sister suffer, but he knew there was nothing he could do for her. Her fate had been set at the time of her judgment and nothing could change that. With his family being held hostage back on earth, Lucifer seemed to be holding all the cards.

"Preacher, all you have to do is destroy the letters when you get back home. Once that is accomplished, everything in your life will go back to normal. There seems to be only one choice," Lucifer said in an all-too-soothing voice.

Jacob suddenly realized that Lucifer thought he could put a stop to the prophecy if the letters could be destroyed. That's what this whole mess was about; everything that had taken place since the first letter arrived was because the devil wanted to stop the prophecy. There was no stopping it as far as Jacob could see. Lucifer was desperate and would try anything. Jacob didn't know what to do; then he remembered his Sunday school days when one of the teachers said, "In a time of utter despair, prayer is the only way to turn." Jacob dropped to his knees and then bowed his head. "Heavenly Father, help me!"

Looking at Jacob in total astonishment, Lucifer could not believe what the preacher had just done. He screamed, "Guards, drop that bitch!" The guards came running from around the corner. The closest pulled the release lever, and Jacob watched her fall.

A loud hum suddenly filled the air and all motion stopped. Jacob looked in Sara's direction and what he saw mystified him. She was suspended in midair; a bright and beautiful winged creature held her in its arms.

Lucifer screamed, "NO!"

From out of thin air, a man, surrounded by glowing white lights, appeared in the middle of the crowd. Jacob felt a wave of peace wash over him, not unlike the time back in his office, but much stronger. He knew immediately who this being was, and fell to the ground, afraid to look at his face.

"Arise, Jacob," the voice commanded. "Do not be afraid."

Jacob stood, looking directly into the eyes of the man, feeling what can only be described as a spiritual orgasm. The man embraced him, saying, "My child, all you had to do was ask and I would have arrived much sooner." The man smiled to Jacob, then said, "Wait here, I have something I need to attend to." He moved to where Sara was now lying on the rocky ground; he touched the rope that was wrapped around her and it fell to her feet in a pile of dust. Looking down at her, he spoke. "My child, I'm sorry that I have never met you before, because I wish that I had, but my child, you are the chosen one. You are the first and only human to repent in this kingdom, and by doing so you have fulfilled the prophecy." He helped her to her feet, then continued to speak. "You know you can never enter my kingdom, and for that I am greatly saddened. Because of these truths, I have three gifts to give you now, Sara." The man raised his arm and one of the floating white lights separated itself from the rest and moved toward Sara, materializing into a beautiful angel. It laid a broad sword and shield at her feet, then returned to its earlier form, rejoining the other floating lights.

"The second item I have for you is an old friend of yours," he said. A deep roar filled the room, and then from behind a large rock formation the crezden appeared, lifting itself a little higher with each downward motion of its wings. It was now fully grown, a beautiful creature with a wingspan of thirty-five to forty feet. It had lost its baby fuzz, which was now replaced with a coat of steely blue metallic-looking scales. Its large crystal-green eyes had a look of intelligence, unlike any other beasts of this kingdom. It flew over to where Sara was standing, gently landed next to her, then began to nuzzle her with its serpentine nose. She reached up, and stroked its leathery head, and smiled, saying, "Thank you, my Lord."

"The third and last gift I have for you is the power to heal. I must warn you, though: it will weaken you for a time after you use it."

Again Sara bowed, saying, "Thank you."

The man then pointed to Lucifer and said, "Don't give that one a moment of peace."

"Yes, my Lord," Sara said, giving Lucifer a slight smile.

The man walked over to Lucifer and placed his right hand on the devil's left shoulder. They stood in silence, just looking at each other, until the man spoke. "Lucifer, my old friend, do you really think that you could change the will of my father? Will you ever learn?"

"Why can you not just leave us alone?" Lucifer scorned.

"Rules, my friend, there are always rules. One last thing," the man said.

Suddenly the sound of bubbling liquid arose from the river's edge and Acubus lifted from the fiery river, screaming in agony. The chain and stones that had weighted down his body still hung in their place. The poor creature's flesh was black and blistered; the fire had destroyed his hair, leaving him completely bald. He set foot on the ground in front of the man, immediately falling backwards into a violent convulsion. Shaking, he gasped for breath. The man reached down and touched Acubus on the forehead with his right index finger. A bright light shone from the point where he was touched, then spread out across his blistered body. Blistered flesh was magically replaced with new skin. Wings grew from the butchered stubs, restored to their original splendor. Acubus stood up with legs spread to shoulder width and let out a loud cry. Leaning back, with arms curled tightly at his sides, Acubus unfolded his mighty wings. He now stood in front of the man, completely healed. He dropped to one knee and bowed.

"Thank you, my Lord. I do not deserve such grace."

"You have helped, Jacob, and I am pleased with your actions."

"Thank you, my Lord."

"Acubus, you know I cannot forgive you for your actions, but I do know that you are truly sorry for what you did." The man turned away from Acubus, then came back to Jacob. "Come over here, Sara Bennington."

"You two need to say your farewells. Jacob, you will not see your sister, Sara, again." With that said, the man turned and walked away.

Jacob moved to Sara and wrapped her in his arms. "Sara, I'm sorry there is nothing I can do for you, don't forget to write to Michael and Mara."

Looking up at her brother, she replied, "I won't forget. Thank you, Jacob… I love you. I love Michael and Mara. Take care of them and please don't let them end up here. Make them believe. Make sure they know the truth." Tears streamed down her cheeks as she hugged her brother for the last time. When they had separated, she walked over to stand next to Acubus.

The man walked back over to Jacob, saying, "I have two special people here to escort you home. Goodbye, Jacob Litchfield. I look forward to your arrival in my kingdom."

Two beings quietly walked up from behind. The taller one spoke first. "Hello, old friend. Are you ready to go home?"

At once, Jacob recognized the voice. "Jonathon Bailey, is that you?" He then looked at the person with Jonathon. "Is that Millie with you?"

"Yes, the Creator thought it would be a nice surprise if we took you home."

"Hello, Millie," Jacob said while giving her a big hug. "I must say you two look so young. What is it like?"

"I cannot wait until you can experience it, Jacob," she said as she locked arms with Jacob. A sudden commotion from downriver drew their attention. Looking over, they saw a large number of sword-wielding angels closing in from above.

With a smile, the man said with a shout, "Sara, meet your army." The fallen angels landed, then stood at attention. Acubus helped Sara up onto the crezden, and with a mighty roar, it flapped its wings, lifting off the ground. With each surge it went higher and higher.

The man yelled from below, "Leave this place now and take your new queen!"

Her new subjects lifted from the ground, then followed her downriver.

Before leaving, Acubus, with a challenging grin spread across his face, shouted to Lucifer, "You might want to see about how they entered your castle so easily."

Shaking with fury, Lucifer replied, "You will pay for this, Acubus. You will all pay for this!"

Acubus lifted upwards, then followed the others downriver.

The air grew thick with the same mist that Jacob recognized from when he arrived. He opened his eyes and was back in the garden where he first met Lucifer.

"We can go no farther, Jacob," Jonathon said. "You will go on from here alone."

Millie moved in against Jonathon, then waved goodbye. Jonathon put his arm around Millie, then waved also.

"I will miss you two so much," Jacob said.

"You will be with us in no time, Jacob. It is definitely worth waiting for," Jonathon said with a smile.

"See you soon, Jacob," Millie said, still waving.

Jacob turned and started walking back up the tunnel. He turned to say one last thing, but they were no longer there.

Turning back, he continued walking. The mist grew thick, almost to the point that he could no longer see.

Chapter Forty-Two

The kidnapper quickly turned away from the bedroom window. He walked over and pulled Mara off the bed. "If you two make a sound or try to leave this room, I'll slit her throat." He left the room leading Mara by her arm. They went down the stairs and from the front door window, he watched the three police officers move toward the house. One split off and moved around to the back, as the other two climbed the front steps.

"What do I do now," he whispered to himself. "Think, damn it!"

"Why don't you let us go," Mara whispered.

The kidnapper looked down at her, surprised that she had spoken. "Shut up," he replied coldly. The voice would surely come back and tell him what to do; all he had to do was hold the police off until it did.

Opening the door a couple of inches, he yelled in a high-pitched voice, "If you come any closer, I'll kill the little girl I've with me." The cops froze. Then, as an afterthought, he added, "I want to talk to the preacher and only the preacher."

The two officers moved back off the porch. Owens keyed his handheld, "Robbins, meet us back at the patrol car. We're going to have to call in a negotiator." As he secured the radio to its position, he could hear sirens in the distance. "Here comes the cavalry, Hoffmann," he said as they started back for the police cars.

Chapter Forty-Three

He heard a voice telling him to wake up. Opening his eyes, Jacob recognized the officer who had been sitting out in front of his house the night before standing over him.

"Pastor Litchfield, they've found your family."

Jacob looked over at the clock and only seventeen minutes had passed since he last remembered looking at the time. Jacob sprung out of bed and quickly got dressed. His brain was like a thick fog. The sleeping pills he took were messing him up. He followed the officer out to the squad car and climbed into the front seat.

"Jenkins drove to an old farmhouse about fifteen miles west of here. He has your wife and children up on the second floor. No one has talked to him yet."

"Are they okay?" he asked while rubbing his heavy eyes.

"As far as we know, they're all okay," Officer Jorgenson replied; then after a few moments he asked, "Pastor, what would possess a guy to act this way?"

"You wouldn't believe me if I told you," Jacob replied.

The officer gave Jacob a strange look and continued to drive as he called Detective Harms, letting him know they were in route.

They soon arrived at the abandoned farmhouse, which was surrounded by numerous squad cars with flashing lights. The officer brought the car around to where a group of men was standing. Detective Harms opened the car door for Jacob.

"Long time, no see. Did you take care of that other business?" he asked, shutting the car door.

"Yes…it is finished," Jacob replied. Jacob noticed he was starting to wake up. He guessed it was the adrenaline flow from the situation that was doing the trick.

Giving Jacob an unbelieving look, he said, "You'll definitely have to tell me about that later, Pastor.

"What do you want me to do, Detective?"

"Nothing right now, just sit tight. We're still waiting for the state negotiator to arrive, but in the meantime, I'm going to go in to try and talk some sense into this kid," he said as he put on a bulletproof vest. Removing his gun belt, he folded it carefully and passed it to the officer standing next to him. "I'll be back in a minute," he said with a weak smile, then started for the house. He walked to the front porch, then climbed the stairs. Reaching the entryway, he slowly opened the door and yelled, "My name is Detective Harms. I'm with the Iroquois County Police Department. I am not carrying a weapon. I want to come in and talk to you. Is that okay?" There was a reply, but only the detective could hear it. He turned to signal that he was going in, and then walked through door.

Jacob looked around his surroundings, he observed two snipers, each aiming rifles with large scopes toward the house. He counted nine officers in all, or at least the ones he could see, figuring there were others that were spread out around the house. An ambulance and its crew waited farther back in the lot behind the squad cars. Jacob wondered what was going through Cathy's mind right now. Knowing her the way he did, her first concern would be the children. She was becoming a wonderful mother to Michael and Mara and that was something he would tell her when he saw her. He hadn't realized until that point how much he wanted to see her again. Jacob leaned back against a squad car and watched to see if he could detect any motion in the windows. He thought he saw movement in the window of the front door and then the door swung open and Detective Harms walked out of the house, going directly to Jacob. "Are they okay?" Jacob asked.

"They're fine for now, but that Jenkins kid is a mess," the detective answered.

Growing impatient Jacob asked, "When is the negotiator going to get here?"

"Pastor, they're on the way, but the county doesn't have its own, we have to use the state's."

"The state's, where's that?" Jacob asked.

"It doesn't matter anyway; he says he won't talk to anyone but you," the detective said, clearly frustrated.

"What?" Jacob asked.

The detective took a few steps away from the group of officers that had gathered, then, with his back toward the group, said, "It's up to you, Pastor Litchfield. It's against every protocol, but the state man has to come all the way from Springfield and I don't think Jenkins can hold it together much longer. I can go in with you, but he said no farther than the front door."

Jacob took a deep breath and said, "I'll go." How bad could it be compared to what he had already gone through tonight?

With Detective Harms by his side, Jacob walked up to the house. He climbed the steps to the front porch and slowly opened the front door. Harms stepped through first and yelled, "Jenkins, I've brought the minister. He's going to come up now, is that okay?"

From upstairs a strained reply could be heard. "You come alone, Preacher, or I'll hurt the little girl. I mean it, I will hurt her."

"I'm alone, Stephen. I am going to come upstairs now." Jacob started up the stairway. His weight on each step caused the old wood to groan loudly. At the top Jacob looked around when to his left a door opened at the end of the hallway and Jacob heard Michael's voice.

"In here, Uncle Jacob."

Jacob hurried over to Michael, asking, "Are you okay, Michael?"

"I'm scared."

"I know, Michael. So am I, but we have friends who are closer than you could ever imagine."

Michael looked blankly at Jacob and said, "I'm supposed to tell you to come in and keep your hands where he can see them."

Jacob put Michael behind him, then carefully opened the door to the musty-smelling bedroom. He first saw Cathy lying on the bed. She was tied up and had a dirty rag stuffed into her mouth. He couldn't tell whether she was dead or alive. Jacob looked around to find Mara in the arms of Jenkins. They were huddled together near the window. A beam of light cast by the police lights from outside caught him horizontally across his ratty, hair-shrouded face. Jacob could make out his panicked expression and said, "Stephen, are you doing okay?"

"What do you care, Preacher? You are just like everybody else," Stevie said gruffly.

"I do care, Stephen. Are you still hearing the voice or has it stopped now?"

"How… How do you know about the voice?"

"That voice will do nothing but hurt you, Stephen. It only cares about its own agenda."

"It's my friend. It's been helping me. Nobody else has ever tried to help me," Stevie said as he tightened his grip on Mara.

Jacob could see the reflection of light from the long knife that he held at Mara's throat. "It will be okay, Mara, just hang on."

"Shut up, Preacher!" Stevie spat.

"I saw the two people you killed today. They are in a much better place now. They told me to tell you that they forgive you."

Taking a few steps away from the window, Stevie laughed with a high-pitched giggle. "You're crazier than I am, Preacher." Motioning toward the bed with his head, he said, "Get over on the bed with your wife."

Jacob walked over to the bed and sat down. Michael followed him and Jacob pointed to the opposite side of the bed. Looking at Cathy, Jacob could see she was still breathing. "What do you want, Stephen?"

Appearing more agitated by the moment, Stevie answered, "I…I don't know."

Looking up at the ceiling, he screamed, "What now? Where the hell are you?"

"He is gone, Stephen. He no longer needs you and now you're on your own."

"How the fuck do you know that, Preacher?" Stevie screamed.

"I just do. Please, let the little girl come over to me, Stephen. You don't want to hurt her. Do you, Stephen?" Jacob said with a quiet voice.

Stevie hesitated for a moment, and then pushed the little girl in Jacob's direction. "No…I guess not."

"There are people who can help you, Stephen, if you let them," Jacob said. Cathy started to stir. Looking at her, Jacob saw her eyes flutter open. He noticed that her right eye was nearly swelled shut. "It's okay, Cathy, I'm here now," he whispered.

"It's not okay!" Stevie screamed.

"Stephen, you have me now, let the lady and children go."

"Fuck no, Preacher!" Stevie said.

"Trust me, Stephen. The voice only wants the letters. It doesn't care about you or the woman and children."

Still looking around the room trying to hear the voice he so desperately needed, Stevie said, "It told me that I was the one."

"It is a liar, Stephen," Jacob said in a quiet voice.

"It's not," Stevie said. "It helped me do things. It told me things."

"It used you for its own purpose, Stephen. Now it is finished with you. Please, I beg you, let the woman and children go. They have done nothing to you."

"I don't know, Preacher."

"How long has it been since you have heard the voice?"

Stevie was shaking his head as he murmured, "Where are you? You were my friend. I need you now…now. I've never had a friend like you." He was visibly trembling and tears were welling up in his blood-shot eyes. He then dropped the knife and both hands went up to his head. He then dropped to his knees and began to cry.

Jacob moved in quick and grabbed Mara. "Take your brother and get out of here. Aunt Cathy will be down in a minute," he whispered sternly in the little girl's ear. She took Michael's hand and started for the door. Before exiting, she looked back for one more look and Jacob waved her on.

Jacob untied Cathy and pulled the dirty rag out of her mouth. She sat up on the bed and began rubbing her wrists. Jacob leaned in to her and whispered, "Tell Detective Harms not to do anything rash. I think I can convince him to give up."

She nodded and gave Jacob a weak smile. He kissed her on the forehead and then she left. He then stood up and walked toward Stevie. "Let me walk you out of here, Stephen. No one will hurt you."

"They will put me in jail forever," he said, trying to stop crying.

"Stephen, believe it or not, that is not as long as you might think."

"What do you mean by that, Preacher?" Stevie began looking around thinking that Jacob was up to something.

Realizing his mistake, Jacob tried to explain further. "No, Stephen, don't panic. What I meant was that I know our time on earth is just a blink of an eye when you compare it to the eternity that follows. Yes, you will have to pay for your crimes here on earth, but if you asked for forgiveness from the Lord, eternity will be a wonderful place."

Taking a deep breath, Stevie looked at Jacob in a strange manner and asked, "Are you telling me that God and all that stuff really exists?"

"Yes, they do. The ultimate price has been paid, so you and I do not have to pay for all our sins." Jacob noticed the man standing before him was a picture of human wreckage. Stevie's body was waving back and forth as he fought for balance with eyes half shut.

"I've killed people, Preacher. How could anyone forgive me?" Stevie said despairingly.

"To the Lord one sin is no greater than another. Thinking about killing someone is the same as actually doing it. Imagine how many people in this world are guilty of murder in God's eyes."

Stevie laughing weakly, said, "I guess I'm no worse than anyone else. Am I, Preacher?"

"No, Stephen, you are not. You still broke man's law and you will have to do your time. You do understand that?" Jacob asked, his heartbeat starting to calm just a little.

"Yes…yes, I guess I understand," Stevie said as he went over to the bed to sit down. "I'm so tired, preacher. I just want to sleep."

"It's okay, Stephen. It's all over now. You can finally rest," Jacob said in a soothing tone. He continued to talk to the man for nearly thirty minutes. He watched Stephen's eyes grow heavy and soon he could hear the rhythmic breathing of someone passing into sleep.

Jacob watched him for a little while, then quietly left the room to get the police. Opening the front door, Jacob calmly walked out and went over to Detective Harms.

"He's upstairs. He's sound asleep."

"What?" Harms asked.

Jacob started to explain further when one of the police officers yelled and pointed to the house. Jacob turned to see Stephen's face in the window.

"Oh no!" Jacob said as he ran back toward the house.

Chapter Forty-Four

Stevie opened his eyes, unaware of his surroundings. Then he heard the voice. "Get up, my warrior. It is time for you to come home."

"What do you mean?" Stevie asked, looking around the room. "I knew you would come back!"

"Take the knife and run it across your throat. There will be just a little pain and then you will just go to sleep. You will then come home to the ones who really care about and love you." The voice said soothingly.

"But the preacher said that everything was okay and that I was forgiven."

"You fool. Do you know what they are going to do to you in prison? Some big fellow is going to have his way with you. Is that what you want? If it is, I will leave now."

"No, no, just wait," Stevie said. He was trying to weigh all this information in his drugged-out, tired mind. "Why did you leave me, I thought you were my friend."

"I am your friend, Stephen, come with me now and all your pain will be over."

Stevie saw the knife lying on the bed. He didn't remember leaving it there. He picked it up, then walked to the window. He could see all the police standing around outside. In the *crowd he saw the preacher talking with a man in a long coat. He watched them all turn and look up at him. He looked at the preacher and shook his head, as if to say he was sorry. He then lifted his chin and swiftly ran the knife across his throat. Blood sprayed across the window, blotting out his view of the people outside. Dropping the knife, he put his hands up to his throat, feeling the deep cut. The last thing he saw was the preacher running into the room, and then a mysterious mist started to fill the room around him.*

Jacob made it to the room in time to try to stop the blood rushing out of his lacerated neck with one of the curtains lying on the floor. Stephen looked up at him, or maybe through, then tried to say something. No sound came out but a gurgling noise, but Jacob understood the words. "Sorry." Then he was gone. Jacob remembered all the lost souls in hell and he cried.

Chapter Forty-Five

Things at the Litchfield house had finally started to get back to normal. Between the police and the reporters, the whole family was glad it was over. Some other gruesome event had taken the attention away from the Litchfield family and placed it in someone else's life. Jonathon and Millie's funerals were over. For Jacob, it was surreal seeing his two friends lying in their caskets when he had just seen them in their new bodies. He tried to remember though, that the ceremony was not for the deceased but for the living that remained.

He was sitting in his recliner watching television with the children. They seemed to be recovering well. Maybe with all the heartbreak from the death of their parents, this whole mess was just an off-handed distraction. He remembered Sara's last words to him concerning the children and vowed to himself not to let her down. He would eventually tell them the entire story of his adventures, but for now, they were too young.

Hearing Cathy's car pull into the garage, he went to greet her at the back door. The black eye she had received from Stevie Jenkins had lost most of its color; all that remained was the varied spectrum of yellows and blues. He opened the door for his wife and she entered the kitchen. She was sorting the day's mail, when he saw a look of horror spread across her face. In her hand was a strange-looking letter. Yellow and stained, it emitted the familiar sulfuric odor. Jacob took it from her, quickly reading the envelope to see to whom it was addressed and then slid it into his shirt pocket. "It's the children's letter from their mother." He hesitated, then added," I told you about that."

"I know, but the thought of where that letter comes from still freaks me out," Cathy said.

"You're not kidding," Jacob said as he slid on a jacket. "I'm going out to the office. I'm going to call the district president about the letters."

"What do you think they will say?"

"I have no idea. The consensus with the Lutheran faith is that miracles happen on a daily basis. We just need to look around us to see them," Jacob said as he moved toward Cathy. She met him and they hugged.

With her head on Jacob's shoulder, she stared out the kitchen window with a furrowed brow. "I don't know if this whole mess is a miracle or a curse?"

Jacob laughed weakly, then said, "Remember, dear, everything happens for a reason."

"That's what scares me," Cathy said as their embrace broke.

Chapter Forty-Six

Jacob was a few steps out of the house when he heard the door behind him open. "Hey, honey, would you put this in the mailbox. You know the electric company has no sense of humor about being late with their money," Cathy said, leaning out of the back door reaching toward Jacob with the envelope.

Jacob laughed and took the letter from his wife and headed for the mailbox. He went over what he was going to tell his district president about the recent occurrences. Would they just think he was a lunatic? Sadly, the death of Pastor Jonathon would give some merit to his story. Jacob also wondered what would be Lucifer's next move. To think all this was over would be foolish. What should he do with the letters? He had them locked away in the church safe now, but was that enough? He was reasonably sure that the letters could not be destroyed, so theft would be the only action that made sense, or the elimination of all knowledgeable parties. What actions would Lucifer take to stop the news about the letters from getting out? A cold shiver ran up his spine as he crossed the tar and chipped country road to put the letter in the mailbox. He was so deep in thought that he did not hear the old red Ford pickup truck racing toward him.

Harold Ehnen was a mean and angry old man. He climbed into his old pickup and jammed the key into the ignition, twisted the key mechanism, and punched the gas. The old machine exploded to life and roared its mighty roar. Harold jammed the gear-shift lever into drive and tore out of the driveway, spitting gravel into the tall grass that lined the pathway. His wife just loved to piss him off. You would think that after forty-three years of marriage that she would know not to spend "his" money on those damn religious television shows, but he had found another cancelled check in the bank statement this morning. Hell, maybe she did it just to piss him off. Hell, maybe she was just dumb. He knew the whole thing was a money-making scam for those big-toothed smiling preachers that held their pedicured hands out for donations. Why couldn't she see it? It didn't matter, a few Busch Lights would cure all that ailed him.

Harold stomped the gas pedal and the old Red pickup lurched forward. The motor roared, and with the old exhaust system it made a nice rumble. Harold, when not in such an exasperated state, would have admired the noise, but this morning he did not notice. Harold looked up ahead and saw the church his wife attended every Sunday morning. "That's where the other half of my fucking money goes!" he yelled as he approached the church lot.

Ring…Ring…Ring… His cell phone sang out its high pitch from the front pocket of his bib overalls. He glanced at the road quickly and pulled it out. He quickly glanced up again to scan the road and then looked down to read the caller ID. "Shit, that woman can't leave me alone for five minutes," he said.

Jacob slammed the mailbox door shut and lifted the red metal flag. He turned around and took two steps into the road when his self-induced thought coma was suddenly broken. Fifty yards from where he was standing was a pickup baring down on him at a high rate of speed. The driver was looking down at something and Jacob recognized him to be Harold Ehnen, the husband of Suzy Ehnen. Jacob, without a thought, ran for the other side of the road.

Harold hit the decline button on his phone and was about to slide it back into his front pocket when he glanced up and saw the man running across the road. "Oh shit!" he yelled as he slammed the brake pedal to the floor. The cell phone fumbled out of his hand and bounced off the steering wheel and then to the floor. The rear tires locked up, causing the high-pitched shriek that happens when rubber slides across roadway. The vehicle started to fishtail and Harold turned into the direction of the slide. The rear tires moved onto the edge of the road where loose gravel had accumulated over the years of tar and chipping.

Jacob made it to the other side of the road as the truck slid by. Gravel, mud and grass pelted him as he jumped into the grass of the church lot. The truck came to a stop seventy yards down the road. Stopping half on the road and half in the shallow ditch. The driver shut the motor off and then there was a second of eerie silence. The world snapped back to life as the driver's window opened and he leaned out to view the situation.

Harold, afraid to see the result of what just happened, lowered his window and turned in his seat to look back. Expecting to see a mutilated body lying in the ditch, he instead saw a very angry Lutheran minister waving his hands in his direction.

Jacob's anger exploded! "What the heck is wrong with you?" he yelled while waving his arms in the truck's direction.

Cathy, upon hearing the commotion, ran out of the house to find her husband waving his arms like a football referee signaling a successful field goal. She hurried across the yard and saw the old red Ford angled across the road with the driver staring at them through the opened window. "Are you okay?" she asked Jacob as she approached.

"I think so," he muttered. He was visibly shaken. Little beads of sweat had formed on his forehead.

"Is that Harold Ehnen?" she asked. She moved close to Jacob and helped him clean up. Then hugged him.

"Yes, in all his glory," Jacob exclaimed as he held Cathy. He moved away a step and then began brushing the dust and grime off his pants. The truck's engine started and the driver's window began its climb upward. They both looked toward the red truck.

Harold saw the minister's wife arrive on the scene and decided everybody was okay and realized he didn't really want any part of the conversation that was sure to ensue. He turned the ignition and closed the window. He put the transmission in reverse and corrected the truck's angle to the road and then put it in drive. He punched the gas and roared off down the road. He really needed a beer now.

"That SOB just drove off!" Cathy exclaimed. "What the hell is wrong with people?"

"Cathy!" Jacob said shaking his head with a smile. "I'm going to my office and make that phone call to the district. You might as well listen in."

"You are not going to do anything about what just happened?" she asked.

"What good would it do? It would just cause more trouble for Suzy Ehnen and that poor woman doesn't need any more reasons to fight with that husband of hers."

"I guess you are right," she said, still watching the truck move down the road.

"You going or not?" Jacob asked, beginning to move toward the side entrance of the church.

"Yeah," she said, still staring after the truck. "That was way too close."

"I know. We are going to really have to be careful. I believe our new insight into the other world might have made us targets," Jacob said as he fished the keys out of his pants pocket.

"I wish you never got those damn letters," Cathy stated matter-of-factly.

"Oh no!" Jacob said.

Cathy saw what he was referring to immediately. The side door had been kicked in and was still open about six inches. "Jacob, wait!" she yelled, but he pushed the door open and entered the building. She ran in after him.

They entered his office and saw that it had been ransacked. Drawers pulled out and dumped. Papers scattered everywhere. The desk lamp was tipped over and the bulb was shattered across his desk. Jacob hurried over to the closet and opened the door. He flipped on the closet light and peered down into the little room. "Oh no!" he said as he fell to his knees. "They took the entire safe."

"What?" Cathy asked, moving up next to him.

"They took the entire safe. The letters were in the safe!" he said. He bowed his head and closed his eyes. He then pinched the bridge of his nose shook his head slowly. "I should have known better," he said softly.

"How could you have known?" Cathy said, beginning to move around the room, picking things up.

"Oh, think about it. Look at the things that have happened in the last two weeks," Jacob said. He arose and moved behind his desk and brushed the broken glass shards off his chair. He sat down and leaned back. "We've seen everything there is to see on the other side. I saw heaven and I visited hell. I spoke with the devil! What made me think that we were going to get out of this easily?" he muttered to himself. "What made me think that I was going to be able to use those letters to prove that God was real?"

Cathy, still gathering loose papers, asked, "Are you going to call the sheriff?"

Jacob leaned forward with a look of shock and said, "Let's get out of the office. There might be some evidence that would find our thief." He stood up and led her out of the room.

Chapter Forty-Seven

Jacob made the phone call to the police and sat at the kitchen table contemplating the whole matter. Cathy had made him coffee and was now in the living room trying to answer the questions the children had about the phone call to the police. Jacob couldn't help but feel sorry for them. They didn't need any more stress added to their lives. What scars did they carry from their life experiences already? What would the result of those scars be by time they reached adulthood? "Only time will tell," he whispered to himself.

The thought of the letters settled back across his mind. They were the only proof he had that the whole experience had even happened and now they were not in his possession. He could feel the tendrils of anger starting to grow through his mind. Why would God put them in his possession and then let them be snatched away? Why would God put his family through everything they had gone through just to let it all end up meaning nothing? There was no story he could tell without the letters other than that a psychopath killed Jonathon and Millie, then kidnapped his family. No reasons as to why, as to what motivation the killer had to do what he did other than mental illness. "Ha." Jacob chuckled to himself, because he now knew that mental illness was nothing more than a doorway to let other influences take control of one's thoughts and actions. He didn't doubt that everything happened for a reason and that God was in total control of every second. He just wished he could see the endgame, but of course, he knew better than to think that he would see that in his lifetime. Maybe… "Wait a minute," he said, and then with growing excitement felt his front shirt pocket. He stood up and pulled out the letter he had just received from Sara.